THE MYSTERY OF THE PEACOCK'S EYE

BRIAN FLYNN was born in 1885 in Leyton, Essex. He won a scholarship to the City Of London School, and from there went into the civil service. In World War I he served as Special Constable on the Home Front, also teaching "Accountancy, Languages, Maths and Elocution to men, women, boys and girls" in the evenings, and acting in his spare time.

It was a seaside family holiday that inspired Brian Flynn to turn his hand to writing in the mid-twenties. Finding most mystery novels of the time "mediocre in the extreme", he decided to compose his own. Edith, the author's wife, encouraged its completion, and after a protracted period finding a publisher, it was eventually released in 1927 by John Hamilton in the UK and Macrae Smith in the U.S. as *The Billiard-Room Mystery*.

The author died in 1958. In all, he wrote and published 57 mysteries, the vast majority featuring the super-sleuth Antony Bathurst.

BRIAN FLYNN

THE MYSTERY OF THE PEACOCK'S EYE

With an introduction by
Steve Barge

DEAN STREET PRESS

Published by Dean Street Press 2019

Copyright © 1928 Brian Flynn

Introduction © 2019 Steve Barge

All Rights Reserved

The right of Brian Flynn to be identified as the Author of the Work has been asserted by his estate in accordance with the Copyright, Designs and Patents Act 1988.

First published in 1928 by John Hamilton

Cover by DSP

ISBN 978 1 913054 39 7

www.deanstreetpress.co.uk

INTRODUCTION

"I believe that the primary function of the mystery story is to entertain; to stimulate the imagination and even, at times, to supply humour. But it pleases the connoisseur most when it presents – and reveals – genuine mystery. To reach its full height, it has to offer an intellectual problem for the reader to consider, measure and solve."

THUS WROTE Brian Flynn in the *Crime Book Magazine* in 1948, setting out his ethos on writing detective fiction. At that point in his career, Flynn had published thirty-six mystery novels, beginning with *The Billiard-Room Mystery* in 1927 – he went on, before his death in 1958, to write twenty-one more, three under the pseudonym Charles Wogan. So how is it that the general reading populace – indeed, even some of the most ardent collectors of mystery fiction – were until recently unaware of his existence? The reputation of writers such as John Rhode survived their work being out of print, so what made Flynn and his books vanish so completely?

There are many factors that could have contributed to Flynn's disappearance. For reasons unknown, he was not a member of either The Detection Club or the Crime Writers' Association, two of the best ways for a writer to network with others. As such, his work never appeared in the various collaborations that those groups published. The occasional short story in such a collection can be a way of maintaining awareness of an author's name, but it seems that Brian Flynn wrote no short stories at all, something rare amongst crime writers.

There are a few mentions of him in various studies of the genre over the years. Sutherland Scott, in *Blood in Their Ink* (1953), states that Flynn, who was still writing at the time, "has long been popular". He goes on to praise *The Mystery of the Peacock's Eye* (1928) as containing "one of the ablest pieces of misdirection one could wish to meet". Anyone reading that particular review who feels like picking up the novel – out now from Dean Street Press – should stop reading at that point, as later in the book, Scott proceeds to casually spoil the ending, although as if he assumes that everyone will have read the novel already.

It is a later review, though, that may have done much to end – temporarily, I hope – Flynn's popularity.

> "Straight tripe and savorless. It is doubtful, on the evidence, if any of his others would be different."

Thus wrote Jacques Barzun and Wendell Hertig Taylor in their celebrated work, *A Catalog of Crime* (1971). The book was an ambitious attempt to collate and review every crime fiction author, past and present. They presented brief reviews of some titles, a bibliography of some authors and a short biography of others. It is by no means complete – E & M.A. Radford had written thirty-six novels at this point in time but garner no mention – but it might have helped Flynn's reputation if he too had been overlooked. Instead one of the contributors picked up *Conspiracy at Angel* (1947), the thirty-second Anthony Bathurst title. I believe that title has a number of things to enjoy about it, but as a mystery, it doesn't match the quality of the majority of Flynn's output. Dismissing a writer's entire work on the basis of a single volume is questionable, but with the amount of crime writers they were trying to catalogue, one can, just about, understand the decision. But that decision meant that they missed out on a large number of truly entertaining mysteries that fully embrace the spirit of the Golden Age of Detection, and, moreover, many readers using the book as a reference work may have missed out as well.

So who was Brian Flynn? Born in 1885 in Leyton, Essex, Flynn won a scholarship to the City Of London School, and while he went into the civil service (ranking fourth in the whole country on the entrance examination) rather than go to university, the classical education that he received there clearly stayed with him. Protracted bouts of rheumatic fever prevented him fighting in the Great War, but instead he served as a Special Constable on the Home Front – one particular job involved warning the populace about Zeppelin raids armed only with a bicycle, a whistle and a placard reading "TAKE COVER". Flynn worked for the local government while teaching "Accountancy, Languages, Maths and Elocution to men, women, boys and girls" in the evening, and acting as part of the Trevalyan Players in his spare time.

It was a seaside family holiday that inspired him to turn his hand to writing. He asked his librarian to supply him a collection of mystery novels for "deck-chair reading" only to find himself disappointed. In his own words, they were "mediocre in the extreme." There is no record of what those books were, unfortunately, but on arriving home, the following conversation, again in Brian's own words, occurred:

> "ME (unpacking the books): If I couldn't write better stuff than any of these, I'd eat my own hat.
>
> Mrs ME (after the manner of women and particularly after the manner of wives): It's a great pity you don't do a bit more and talk a bit less.
>
> The shaft struck home. I accepted the challenge, laboured like the mountain and produced *The Billiard-Room Mystery*."

"Mrs ME", or Edith as most people referred to her, deserves our gratitude. While there were some delays with that first book, including Edith finding the neglected half-finished manuscript in a drawer where it had been "resting" for six months, and a protracted period finding a publisher, it was eventually released in 1927 by John Hamilton in the UK and Macrae Smith in the U.S. According to Flynn, John Hamilton asked for five more, but in fact they only published five in total, all as part of the Sundial Mystery Library imprint. Starting with *The Five Red Fingers* (1929), Flynn was published by John Long, who would go on to publish all of his remaining novels, bar his single non-series title, *Tragedy At Trinket* (1934). About ten of his early books were reprinted in the US before the war, either by Macrae Smith, Grosset & Dunlap or Mill, and a few titles also appeared in France, Denmark, Germany and Sweden, but the majority of his output only saw print in the United Kingdom. Some titles were reprinted during his lifetime – the John Long Four-Square Thrillers paperback range featured some Flynn titles, for example – but John Long's primary focus was the library market, and some titles had relatively low print runs. Currently, the majority of Flynn's work, in particular that only published in the U.K., is extremely rare – not just expensive, but seemingly non-existent even in the second-hand book market.

In the aforementioned article, Flynn states that the tales of Sherlock Holmes were a primary inspiration for his writing, having read them at a young age. A conversation in *The Billiard-Room Mystery* hints at other influences on his writing style. A character, presumably voicing Flynn's own thoughts, states that he is a fan of "the pre-war Holmes". When pushed further, he states that:

> "Mason's M. Hanaud, Bentley's Trent, Milne's Mr Gillingham and to a lesser extent, Agatha Christie's M. Poirot are all excellent in their way, but oh! – the many dozens that aren't."

He goes on to acknowledge the strengths of Bernard Capes' "Baron" from *The Mystery of The Skeleton Key* and H.C. Bailey's Reggie Fortune, but refuses to accept Chesterton's Father Brown.

> "He's entirely too Chestertonian. He deduces that the dustman was the murderer because of the shape of the piece that had been cut from the apple-pie."

Perhaps this might be the reason that the invitation to join the Detection Club never arrived . . .

Flynn created a sleuth that shared a number of traits with Holmes, but was hardly a carbon-copy. Enter Anthony Bathurst, a polymath and gentleman sleuth, a man of contradictions whose background is never made clear to the reader. He clearly has money, as he has his own rooms in London with a pair of servants on call and went to public school (Uppingham) and university (Oxford). He is a follower of all things that fall under the banner of sport, in particular horse racing and cricket, the latter being a sport that he could, allegedly, have represented England at. He is also a bit of a show-off, littering his speech (at times) with classical quotes, the obscurer the better, provided by the copies of the *Oxford Dictionary of Quotations* and *Brewer's Dictionary of Phrase & Fable* that Flynn kept by his writing desk, although Bathurst generally restrains himself to only doing this with people who would appreciate it or to annoy the local constabulary. He is fond of amateur dramatics (as was Flynn, a well-regarded amateur thespian who appeared in at least one self-penned play, *Blue Murder*), having been a member of OUDS, the Oxford University Dramatic Society. Like Holmes, Bathurst isn't averse to the occasional disguise, and as with Watson and Holmes, sometimes even his close allies don't recognise him. General information about his background is light on the ground. His parents were Irish, but he doesn't have an accent – see *The Spiked Lion* (1933) – and his eyes are grey. We learn in *The Orange Axe* that he doesn't pursue romantic relationships due to a bad experience in his first romance. That doesn't remain the case throughout the series – he falls head over heels in love in *Fear and Trembling*, for example – but in this opening tranche of titles, we don't see Anthony distracted by the fairer sex, not even one who will only entertain gentlemen who can beat her at golf!

Unlike a number of the Holmes' stories, Flynn's Bathurst tales are all fairly clued mysteries, perhaps a nod to his admiration of Christie, but first and foremost, Flynn was out to entertain the reader. The problems posed to Bathurst have a flair about them – the simultaneous murders, miles apart, in *The Case of the Black Twenty-Two* (1928) for example, or the scheme to draw lots to commit masked murder in *The Orange Axe* – and there is a momentum to the narrative. Some mystery writers have trouble with the pace slowing between the reveal of the problem and the reveal of the murderer, but Flynn's books sidestep that, with Bathurst's investigations never seeming to sag. He writes with a wit and intellect that can make even the most prosaic of interviews with suspects enjoyable to read about, and usually provides an action-packed finale before the murderer is finally revealed. Some of those revelations, I think it is fair to say, are surprises that can rank with some of the best in crime fiction.

We are fortunate that we can finally reintroduce Brian Flynn and Anthony Lotherington Bathurst to the many fans of classic crime fiction out there.

The Mystery of the Peacock's Eye (1928)

"What happened exactly at the Hunt Ball at Westhampton a year ago last February?"

THE DENTIST'S chair, despite the terror it can induce in the reader, is an uncommon setting for a murder mystery. The most memorable Golden Age examples are *Death In The Dentist's Chair* by Molly Thynne (1932) and Agatha Christie's *One, Two, Buckle My Shoe* (1940) but this, from 1928, seems to be the earliest example. Admittedly here Flynn uses it as just one of the many threads that form this tale, rather than the central theme, but the notion of death during one of the most unpleasant necessities of life is a chilling one.

Brian Flynn never hid his admiration for Sir Arthur Conan Doyle and Sherlock Holmes, but perhaps never more so than in *The Mystery of the Peacock's Eye*. A person desperate to keep their identity secret, only to be quickly revealed as European aristocracy, approaches the great detective to help them prevent a blackmail attempt that threatens his forthcoming marriage. While this describes the Grand-Duke of Cassel-Felstein in the first Holmes short story, "A Scandal in Bohemia", it also matches the Crown Prince of Clorania in *The Mystery Of The Peacock's Eye*, the third outing for Anthony Lotherington Bathurst. But while Flynn may have taken his inspiration for the opening from his hero, he rapidly sets out to tell his own story, as the blackmail attempt becomes linked to a murder and the mysterious Peacock's Eye.

Bathurst finds himself investigating the crime alongside Chief Detective-Inspector Richard "Dandy Dick" Bannister, one of the "Big Six" from Scotland Yard, who is on an interrupted holiday in Seabourne where the murder is committed. In reality, Scotland Yard really only had a "Big Five", consisting of the Detective Chief Superintendents in charge of the four London districts in the Met, along with their colleague in charge of H.Q. C.I.D., but presumably Flynn chose not to step on the toes of the real police officers. Bannister is the third police ally of Bathurst in three books, and Flynn continues to rotate this role for a while before eventually settling on Inspector Andrew Macmorran, who makes his rather brief debut in this book. Taking a slightly more substantial role is Commissioner of Police Sir Austin Kemble, who will go on to involve Bathurst directly in many more of his cases, quickly getting to the point where his first reaction when presented with anything that looks remotely complicated is to ask Anthony for help, rather than relying on his own officers!

Sutherland Scott, in his work on the genre, *Blood In Their Ink*, describes the book as containing "one of the ablest pieces of misdirection one could wish to meet" and it's a statement that is hard to argue with (although Scott does then go on to spoil the ending for his readers). Reviews at the time were full of praise for the book, published in the UK as part of the Sundial Mystery Library imprint by John Hamilton and reprinted in the US by MacRae Smith, and it certainly stands one of Flynn's finest works. It was the book that introduced me to Brian Flynn and Anthony Bathurst and started something of an obsession that I hope to be able to pass on to my fellow fans of the Golden Age mystery – it is a true long-lost classic of the genre, now back in print after ninety years. Enjoy!

Steve Barge

Chapter I
THE HUNT BALL AT WESTHAMPTON

The foot-fascinating strains of the Red Ruritanian Band died gently away—to commence again after a short interval just as exquisitely. The Hunt Ball at Westhampton was the outstanding event of the season and this year it had exceeded all past successes and even present anticipations. It was actually honoured, so it was whispered, with the presence of Royalty—which interesting fact although not announced publicly or even hinted at in the Press—was nevertheless an open secret to at least half-a-dozen of the most influential people present. Life in the Midlands is a very different proposition from life in London or in the residential neighbourhoods that are within that great city's reasonable range. Social distinctions mean very much more—there is the sharply-definite cleavage of class—determined very often by "County" prejudice—a line of division against which there is little or no chance of struggling with any degree of success.

The Westhampton Hunt Ball represented all that was select, some of what was superior, and most of what was supercilious in the county of Westhamptonshire. There had been fears, and recent fears at that, that this year's Ball might possibly be held under a shadow. But happily for the peace of mind of Westhampton, this shadow had been partially lifted from the town. The affair of the "Mutual Bank" frauds that had at one time seriously threatened to involve more than one of the most exclusive County families in an upheaval that would have resulted in their financial ruin, had been brilliantly handled by those in charge of the case and the final crash triumphantly averted—with the sensational arrest of Sir Felix Warburton, one of the Bank's most important directors. Whereat the more distinguished portion of Westhampton—albeit shocked and startled—breathed freely again and welcomed its Annual Ball with all its accustomed avidity.

On the February evening in question the Red Ruritanian Band was in its most scintillating form, and beautiful women piloted by bronzed men—sun-tanned and wind-tanned and released for the time-being from the accustomed lilt of the galloping feet of horses—swept round what was unanimously acclaimed as a perfect floor, on twinkling toes and endeavoured with the assurance of the expert dancer, to do it the strictest justice.

Sir Matthew Fullgarney, Lord Lieutenant of the County made his way bustlingly from the refreshment-room specially reserved for the more distinguished guests, and brushed his perfectly-trimmed white moustache with a gesture that betokened complacent satisfaction. Then he courteously waved his hand to the smaller of two men who were at that moment passing him.

"Good evening, Major! Wonderfully fine show this evening—what?"

The man addressed smiled a reply as he walked by with his companion.

"Who's that Carruthers is trotting round with him to-night, Pauline?" asked Sir Matthew, turning to his charming young wife—"can't seem to place him at all!"

Lady Fullgarney turned interestedly, and threw a quick glance at the two retreating figures. "I don't think I know," she answered—with a slow shake of the head—"the man's a perfect stranger to me—I feel certain."

Sir Matthew growled unintelligibly—he always liked a satisfactory reply to any question that it pleased him in his wisdom to ask. He felt that any failure to supply this satisfaction savoured of disrespect to him.

But on this occasion he suffered Lady Fullgarney to lead him back again to the ballroom—to be flattering himself very soon that he was cutting as fine a figure as any man present despite the annoying fact that his question remained unanswered. Meanwhile, the Chief Constable—Major Carruthers—was entertaining the subject of Sir Matthew's curiosity in the refreshment-room that the Lord Lieutenant had so recently, and it must be admitted—regretfully—left. Sir Matthew had a discerning taste in more than one direction.

"Your health, Major Carruthers!" said the tall man—raising his glass. Carruthers bowed and looked across at him with a certain measure of criticism, perhaps—but nevertheless approvingly. "Glad you came to-night?" he questioned.

The man addressed emptied the glass deliberately and took his time before replying. No doubt he was accustomed to have people wait upon his words.

"Yes—and no," he answered. "These things, of course, make some sort of an appeal—it would be idle to pretend otherwise—yet I can't help feeling that they are what I may term counterfeit. They represent the shadow rather than the substance of Life. They lie far apart, for instance, from my own destiny and work." He put down his glass.

Carruthers smiled. "I think I know what you mean. Like you, I am primarily, I suppose, a man of action. The open spaces are to me the places that count most. Yet I find time to appreciate this sort of thing intensely. There is a joyousness about it all that sets something in me going in vivid response—perhaps you don't experience it."

His companion shook his head. "Only to a degree," he admitted.

The Major laughed at the cautiousness of the reply. "I suspect that's all you feel inclined to admit—your somewhat peculiar position with regard to Society has given you what I'll call a bias—a warp perhaps would be a better description." He half turned impetuously in his chair—then gave a sudden exclamation. "Pardon me a moment," he said, and rising quickly walked to a table that stood some distance away on the other side of the room.

The tall man turned and watched him a little lazily perhaps, as he made his way across. A girl rose to greet him—her hand outstretched impulsively. Then she turned and indicated her escort shyly—yet prettily. The man who had been left behind discarded his indolent mood and saw Major Carruthers bow with an almost studied dignity. Then his eyes—keen and alert by now—swept back to the girl who had first engaged the Chief Constable's attention. It did not take him long to appreciate her beauty—of a type as unusual as it was outstanding. Wonderful auburn hair—the true Burne-Jones tint—crowned a dainty head that was superbly poised on a pair of trim shoulders. She had also the perfect complexion that almost invariably accompanies that particular shade of hair. The man that was watching her was seated too far away to see the colour of her eyes but he was satisfied that her carriage was charmingly assured and her limbs curvingly supple with the grace and glory of youth. Major Carruthers bowed gallantly over her finger-tips—whispered something that caused her to blush exquisitely—and sauntered back. His companion greeted him immediately.

"Almost am I in a mind now to qualify my last remark." He flicked the ash from his cigarette. "Who's the lady?" His eyes eagerly awaited Carruthers' reply.

"I perceive," said the Major, "that among your other gifts you include an eye for beauty. That's Sheila Delaney—and by way of being a very great favourite of mine, I may say! You see I have a taste in that respect too."

"Tell me about her—I'm interested."

"There's not a great deal to tell," rejoined Carruthers, "she's the only child of the late Colonel Delaney of the Westhampton Regiment. Her father died in 1917—he was drowned—poor chap, while home on leave from Gallipoli. When her mother died three years later she was left entirely alone in the world—except for an old nurse-companion who had lived with the Delaneys since Sheila's birth. She lives a few miles out of Westhampton—at a charming little old-world place called Tranfield. Colonel Delaney left them pretty comfortably off in more ways than one. She's always been rare 'pals' with me—I'm very flattered to think so—I regard it as a very fine type of compliment." He puffed at his cigar.

"She's certainly a very beautiful girl, Major! I'm glad now that I came, without any reservations—the beauty of the world always helps me to forget so much of the ugliness."

Carruthers looked over his companion's shoulder. "You don't ask me about her dancing partner," he ventured. The other man raised his eyes, turned deliberately and looked across to the other table—his eyes seeking the man who was in Sheila Delaney's company. Apparently he saw little that he found of interest. "Seems to be quite an ordinary young fellow," he murmured, "what am I expected to find about him that is extraordinary?"

Carruthers shifted in his chair, leaned across the table and spoke in an undertone. "I fancied his name might interest you—that was all." He paused.

"His name?"

"Yes—that young fellow is Alan Warburton—nephew of Sir Felix Warburton."

The tall man whistled softly. "Really now—and he's here to-night, so soon after the scandal—I take it he must have a special interest in Miss Delaney?"

"I haven't noticed it before," replied Carruthers—"but of course, it wouldn't surprise me—Sheila, as you may well imagine has hosts of admirers—so that one more won't make a lot of difference. I fancy she relies on the safety that comes with numbers. As to his being here to-night—well—the young soon forget—you know." He smiled across at the tall man.

"And forgive?" questioned the latter.

Before Carruthers could find time to frame a reply, a warning movement from his companion served to check him. The two young people that had been forming the subject of the discussion were on their way and already almost abreast of the Major's table. Carruthers smiled a greeting which Sheila Delaney was quick to return. As she did so, her eyes caught the frankly admiring glance of the Major's companion. For a brief space their glances held each other and for the man concerned the world seemed suddenly to stand still. Then the girl's eyes dropped demurely to her fan and she passed on—her hand on Alan Warburton's arm and her cheeks aflame with an exquisitely entrancing blush. The tall man turned to the Chief Constable of Westhamptonshire.

"Do me a favour, Major," he exclaimed with sudden impulse. "Please! As I said I withdraw those early remarks of mine, absolutely and unreservedly. Introduce me to Miss Delaney!"

Major Carruthers appeared to hesitate for a moment then he looked up at the man that had made the request. "As—" he waited interrogatively for his companion to intervene.

"As Mr. X," came the reply—immediately. "I prefer to retain my incognito—you know that."

Carruthers caressed his cheek with his fingers. "I didn't bargain for this when I brought you along—you know. And Sheia's a thoroughbred—I shouldn't like anything—"

His companion squared his shoulders with an unmistakable dignity. "There is more than one attribute of aristocracy, Major," he murmured quietly. "I—of all people—"

Carruthers rose from his chair. "I know the truth of that," he declared. "I've knocked about too much not to realize that. Come along—let's find Sheila—time's getting on."

The other rose after him—debonair and distinguished—and followed him through the thronging press of the dancers congregated in the vestibule of the ballroom. He looked at his watch. It showed a few minutes past ten.

"She's dancing," said the Major.

"Superbly too," said the other.

The two men waited for the dance to finish. "Come," said Carruthers, touching the other's sleeve, "it's now or never."

Sheila Delaney saw them coming and did not wait for them to complete the distance of their approach. Instead she made her apologies to her young partner and came forward herself to meet them. Thus it was that the encounter materialized in the middle of the room.

"Sheila," exclaimed Carruthers, "my friend here is something more than anxious to make your acquaintance. But for important reasons of his own, which must be nameless—he desires you to know him as Mr. X. Strictly speaking you see, he is not supposed to be here at all—therefore I submit to this whim of his." He effected the introduction. "Talk to him for a few moments, Sheila," he added, "you will find him as intriguing and as mysterious as the name under which he is temporarily cloaking his identity. I'll return when I think you've been sufficiently entertained." He waved his hand and slithered away across the dance-floor. Sheila Delaney looked at the man who had sought her out. He indicated two of the lounge seats that were arranged at the side of the ballroom.

"Well!" she said.

"Well!" he replied.

She leaned over and tapped him on the arm with her fan. "You hold a distinct initial advantage over me, you know, Mr. X. Anonymity is such a terribly strong position in which to entrench one's self. To you I am Sheila Delaney—to me you are—an unknown quantity."

He smiled appreciatively. "Yet one usually concludes by finding the value of X—shall we say."

"If one is successful," she replied, "you have to be successful, you know, to discover the *true* value."

He smiled again.

"I think I am going to like you," she went on very frankly and disarmingly, "there is something about you that attracts me—you have a—what shall I call it—a *je ne sais quoi*—"

He fingered her fan with a kind of mocking assurance playing round the line of his lips. She lifted her left hand as he did so. "Hark!" she exclaimed, "those violins—I love violins—they *croon*—don't they? They've got something in their music that no other instrument has—'silky susurrus of petticoats ravishing—violins crooning above—drowsy exotics their essences lavishing—whispers of Scandal and Love'—I'm afraid I've misquoted," she continued breathlessly, "but a perfectly topping dance always makes me think of that."

"You like dancing?" he asked simply.

"I adore it," she answered just as simply—then relapsed into a contemplative silence. Suddenly she looked up at him with mischievous eyes. "Do you dance?" she inquired.

"Very seldom—but I'm sorely tempted to dance to-night." His eyes held a depth of meaning.

"That's very charming of you," she remarked, "and if you're anything like me—and I'm sure you are in some things—you delight in yielding to temptation." Her eyes caught his and challenged them. They were—he concluded—in a quite breathless summing up—rather extraordinary eyes. Quickly changing colour, at this precise moment they seemed to be flecked with strange shades of light green. They were challenging his now with an allurement of demure and dainty invitation. She rose and placed her finger-tips on his broad shoulder. "I'm convinced you dance beautifully," she murmured as they stepped off to the rhythm of the Red Ruritanians, "so don't attempt to deny it."

It did not take Sheila Delaney long to realize that her conviction was right. Her companion proved a worthy partner for her. She looked at him provocatively. "Why have you no business to be here, Mr. X?" she queried softly.

He shook his head. Then the Spirit of Audacity and Adventure caught him and held him securely captive. "One day—perhaps, I'll tell you," he declared, "till then, you must possess your soul in patience."

"Supposing I don't choose to wait?" She summoned all her resources of disdain to her aid and let it tinge her question. Her partner merely shrugged his ample shoulders. "If you continue to surround yourself with this dreadfully mysterious atmosphere," she went on, "I shall begin to think that I'm dancing with the guest of the evening—His Royal Highness, The Crown Prince of Clorania—one never quite knows." She looked at him with arch invitation—so much so that Alan Warburton from the end of the room felt suddenly murderous as he watched her laughing face and the broad back of her partner. But her curiosity was to remain unsatisfied. Mr. X was apparently in no mood for the exchange of confidences. He looked at her with a smile that conveyed a mysterious much, yet confessed a negligible nothing. Carruthers threw her silk shawl across her shoulders when she returned to her seat—the dance over; then he turned to the other man a little critically.

"You didn't tell me you intended to dance," he exclaimed. "That wasn't part—"

"Blame Miss Delaney," came the unruffled reply, before he could complete his sentence. "Actually I had no intention of doing so myself—but Miss Delaney in the role of the temptress, I found deucedly hard to resist."

Carruthers was about to demur when Sheila laid her hand upon his wrist. "I have to thank you, Major, for a most delightful experience. Mr. X"—the green eyes glinted mischievously—"dances beautifully—I should like to carry him around with me as my dancing partner."

The person complimented bowed his thanks as the Chief Constable turned towards him. "I think I had better be going, Major," he said gravely. Carruthers looked at his watch—then deliberately at the speaker. "So do I," he agreed; "we must also make our departure very shortly, Sheila."

The sweeping eyelashes covered eyes that flickered and themselves quivered dangerously as she gave the two men her hand. Carruthers gave it an affectionate clasp, but his companion bent over it with a studied gallantry. "Good-bye," she said with some deliberation in her voice-tone. "Good-bye—Mr. X." He looked at her with frank admiration in his gaze—then spoke very quietly—yet with infinite meaning, "Au 'voir—Miss Sheila." He turned on his heels smartly—then followed the Chief Constable down the room—and out.

When Carruthers returned half an hour later, he found that the number of dancers had thinned considerably and that the ballroom was a far more comfortable place than it had been before. Sheila Delaney was one of those that had remained. Her nature was such that it was a physical impossibility for her to be dull for very long, yet Major Carruthers was definitely conscious that a fit of depression had overcome her. He rallied her with cynical generosity. "Give me," he exclaimed teasingly, "and every time at that—the girl who is content with her lot—who doesn't sit sighing for what she has not—" he paused and was somewhat startled at something he seemed to see in the expression on her face.

"I'm not sighing, Major," she spoke with a certain wistfulness, "I'm very far from sighing if you only knew." She rose and faced him confidently. He caught her by the shoulder with an air of parental proprietorship—looked at her intently—then said abruptly, "Where's young Warburton?"

"I haven't the least idea," came the reply—touched with unexpected frigidity, "gone—I expect."

"Dance this with me, then," said Carruthers, "before we go."

"I don't want to dance a bit," she responded, "but I will—for *you*, Major."

As their finger-tips met he noticed how cold she seemed. "You worry me when you're down in the dumps, Sheila Delaney," he remonstrated, "you're quite cold."

"If you want to know," she laughed, making a spirited attempt to throw off her mood, "when you came along just now, I was shivering."

He swung her adroitly round a vacillating couple who appeared likely to impede their smooth progress. "What's been happening since I left you?" he inquired. "May an old friend inquire without appearing too inquisitive?"

"Nothing of any consequence," she rejoined. "I just feel *disturbed*—that's the best word I can think of."

"Telling me that tends to disturb *me*," he replied with quiet sympathy, "and I refuse to allow that to happen. Come—dance your very best."

When it had finished, he thanked her and piloted her back to her seat.

"Daphne has been looking very beautiful to-night," she said. "Aren't you proud of your niece?"

He looked at her curiously. "She has an extra special reason to look nice to-night." Then he changed the subject. "If you come now, I'll motor you home; being a bachelor has some advantages—there's nobody else here to-night about whom I need worry."

"I should love it, Major,"—she accepted his offer of service with genuine enthusiasm—"Pinkie will be waiting up for me."

"How is Pinkie these days—hale and hearty?"

"Wonderful—for her age—she's over sixty, you know—nobody could look after me like Pinkie does."

He drove her home. As they turned the corner of the High Street—where the Grand Hotel stood—the newsboys were calling an extra-special edition—late though the hour was.

"What is it?" she said, clutching at his arm; "it must be something frightfully important."

He checked the car and listened. Then he turned back to her as the shouts became intelligible to his ears. "Bank Frauds' Sensation—suicide of Sir Felix Warburton—in his cell." He accelerated immediately. "Pretty rotten business that," he declared with anxiety, "and the Chief Constable glad-ragging it at the Hunt Ball. I shall be in the soup properly if I'm not careful."

But Sheila Delaney's sympathy was not entirely for him. "Suicide," she whispered, half to herself, "how awful."

They drove home quietly—neither saying much. As she ran down the garden path of her bungalow, Carruthers called out to her. "I'll come round before Easter, Sheila—and take you for a spin—may I—are you on?"

"Of course," she sang back. "Good night." But she never rode with him again. On a wet night during the following month of March, Major Carruthers was motoring home, when his car skidded badly and overturned . . . when that happened Sheila Delaney lost a good friend and the public service a very gallant gentleman.

Chapter II
MR. BATHURST RECEIVES A DISTINGUISHED VISITOR

Anthony Bathurst propped the letter against the side of the matutinal coffee-pot and read it carefully for the fourth time since he had received it less than half an hour before. As he finished it he grimaced deliberately and removed the brown top of his second egg somewhat absent-mindedly. The letter and envelope were of heavy cream-laid notepaper—extremely strong and stiff. The heading was "Hotel Florizel, W." The letter read as follows: "There will call upon you to-day—between 11:30 and 12 o'clock—a gentleman who desires to lay before you a matter of urgent and peculiar importance. Besides this importance it possesses an exceedingly delicate significance which will entail your strictest discretion. This gentleman, who is also the writer of this letter, is aware—upon unimpeachable authority—that in this last respect you may be thoroughly relied upon inasmuch as your unique ability is matched by your tact and integrity. Your services in any circumstances will be handsomely rewarded—particularly so in the event of your bringing the affair in question to a successful conclusion. The writer thoroughly understands that it is not your practice to undertake work of this kind professionally—yet hopes to awaken your interest in his case sufficiently intensely for you to render him the assistance he requires."

"H'm," grunted Anthony. "He does, does he?" He pushed his plate on one side, pulled at his top lip and lit a cigarette. "I wonder who's been singing my praises to this gentleman who writes so enigmatically? I can hardly suppose that he has had any immediate connection with Scotland Yard that has caused him to run across Detective-Inspector Goodall—and I haven't heard that Baddeley has reached the Metropolis yet—still—after all—it's a small world and sometimes people link up quite unexpectedly." He looked at his watch. It showed the time at half-past nine. "Two hours before my unknown caller arrives." He walked to the bookcase and took down what he always described as his "Encyclopaedia of London." Turning to the section dealing with hotels—he found the "Florizel" and rapidly read through the particulars given. The tariff was extremely high—in every particular—and it quickly became obvious to him that the hotel concerned could only be within the range of the comparatively wealthy. He took the letter from the table again—and gave it yet another close inspection. The paper was not the hotel note-paper, the address "Hotel Florizel, W." having been written at the top by the writer of the letter. He held the notepaper up to the light—without tangible reward. The writing was firm and bold—somewhat florid in style and letter-formation—yet withal—the writing of an educated man. If it had any special feature it lay in the somewhat ornate formation of the capital letters. The three "T's," the "B," and the "Y"—looked un-English somehow. There was an ornamentation about them that gave Anthony much food for consideration. "'German,' is my opinion," he murmured to himself after a moment or two, "possibly a German professor who has mislaid his science notebook containing the recipe for diamond-making. That would account for the heavy demands to be made upon my powers of discretion! Still—I'm making a mistake theorizing with precious little data to build upon. I'll go for a stroll till the time comes for me to receive my mysterious client." He put on his hat and went out. He was a firm believer in as much walking exercise as was humanly possible, as a sure means to physical fitness. In his case physical fitness coincided completely with mental fitness; he was a splendid example of the *"Mens Sana"* doctrine.

At twenty minutes to twelve—or to be absolutely accurate—at eleven-thirty-eight, Bathurst heard a car draw up outside his flat. He quickly walked to the window that commanded the street and looked down. "Rolls-Royce, eh," he said to himself, "I'm moving in more illustrious circles than ever." A minute or two later there came a rather peremptory tap upon the door of his room.

"Come in," he called. His visitor entered at the invitation.

"Have I the pleasure to address Mr. Anthony Bathurst?" he interrogated.

"You have," replied that gentleman—indicating the armchair with a graceful gesture—"won't you sit down?"

The visitor hesitated for a moment—then accepted the proffered seat. Mr. Bathurst waited imperturbably for him to continue the proceedings. This was a habit of Mr. Bathurst—he generally found it profitable. After a second or two that seemed to suggest a certain amount of uneasiness the caller looked across at Anthony and proceeded.

"Before I state my case, Mr. Bathurst," he remarked with an air that may be best described as one of dignified arrogance—"I should like to preface it with the information that it is my intention to conceal from you my real identity—it will make no appreciable difference as far as I can see, to your handling of the case—and it will be a precaution that will serve to protect many highly-influential interests. To you, I should prefer to be known as Mr. Lucius," he paused as he uttered the name, as though to divine if possible the effect of his announcement upon the man who listened. Save for a slight suspicion of the guttural, his English was as faultless as his dress. The lounge-suit he wore, unmistakably betokened the craft of Savile Row—while his shoes, socks, tie and collar were in complete harmony and equally irreproachable taste. Mr. Bathurst smiled.

"In that case then," he said softly, walking again to the window, "I shall be in a position to continue—almost immediately—a most interesting little brochure that I have here, upon the habits of that particular Nematoid worm believed to be the cause of Trichiniasis."

A bright colour flooded the cheeks of the visitor and the strong line of his jaw set even more strongly and rigidly. He half-rose to his feet from the luxurious depths of Mr. Bathurst's armchair, and a wave of anger took possession of his features. Only momentarily—however. He sat down again; then with a strong effort succeeded in controlling himself. "I am to understand, then," he declared with considerable hauteur, "that you decline to accept my case?"

"Under those conditions," replied Mr. Bathurst in honeyed tones, "most certainly!"

"Nothing, I presume, that I could offer you in the shape of an inducement would persuade you to take a different view of the matter?" The suggestion came with an undoubted amount of eagerness.

"I am quite unable to contradict you," responded Mr. Bathurst.

His visitor allowed an exclamation of impatience to escape his lips—then rose again from his chair and paced the room nervously. For a brief period there was silence.

"You will see, I am sure," continued Anthony, "that it would be worse than useless for me to undertake a case—with any hope of bringing it to a successful conclusion—if the identity of my principal were to be a secret from me. It is tantamount to asking me to fight somebody with one hand tied behind my back."

His visitor paused in his pacing—abruptly; then wheeled round upon Anthony with a vehement gesture.

"You are right," he declared impulsively. "I ask your pardon; it was wrong of me to consider, even, such a possibility. Wrong—and equally foolish! I quite understand that in dealing with a case of this kind—complete confidence must exist between principal and agent." He thought for a moment—then went on. "After all, I have done nothing of which I need be ashamed." Anthony waved him to the armchair again and pulled up the chair opposite for himself.

"You are aware, I know," he said quietly, "that I am not a professional inquiry agent. Your letter this morning told me as much. At the same time I shall be pleased to hear your story, and if at all possible, to help you in the matter. Consider me at your service."

His companion inclined his head—then raised it again and looked Bathurst directly in the eyes. "It may interest you to know, Mr. Bathurst," he commenced, "that you have been addressing The Crown Prince of Clorania."

Anthony accepted the intimation with becoming reserve. "I am honoured," he murmured. His Royal Highness went on quickly:

"I am not sure whether you are a close student of European history. That fact, perhaps, is somewhat beside the point. Let it be sufficient for the moment for me to tell you that in December next I am marrying the Princess Imogena of Natalia. This union, it is confidently believed by all who are competent to judge, will bind Clorania and Natalia, in an irrevocable alliance. It is also, I may inform you, a love-match." He coughed, looked at his hearer, then continued—without stopping to hear any comments that were tolerably certain in his own opinion to be superfluous and beside the point. "The Princess is as charming as she is beautiful and I may tell you that she is considered by many excellent judges to be one of the six most beautiful girls in Europe. In other words she is worthy of me, and I am bound to regard myself as very fortunate to have won the hand of so fair a bride. There are many also who think that the Princess herself has been equally fortunate—and I, for one—ahem—will not contest that opinion."

Once again he cast a shrewdly-quick glance in Anthony's direction only to discover thereby that his story was being received with impassive attention. When he chose, Mr. Bathurst's face could be supremely enigmatic. He chose at this moment! The result was that the Crown Prince seemed less sure of himself than ever.

"What I have to say now is not at all easy for me. In fact I am quite prepared to admit that I find it extremely difficult. The Reigning House of Natalia, I need hardly tell you, would not tolerate for one moment a marriage for their only daughter, with a Prince whose 'shield was not stainless'—like the Tunstall of your wonderful literature. Her husband must be *'sans peur et sans reproche'* and his blood of the very purest. They favoured my suit from the first—fulfilling as I did these vitally necessary obligations. Judge of my annoyance then, Mr. Bathurst, to find myself the recipient of these most insufferable letters, which I will confess, it was not my original intention to show you." He took from his breast-pocket a packet of letters. "There are five of them in all and they date from nine weeks ago until now—the latest you will observe according to the postmark on the envelope is dated June 22nd—a week ago. Perhaps you would read this last one, first of all."

Anthony extended his hand for the letter in question. "Westhampton postmark," he observed—scrutinizing the somewhat blurred stamp on the envelope. His visitor nodded in agreement. Anthony took out the letter itself. It was undated and bore no address. He read it. The handwriting spoke of education and culture. "The disinclination of His Royal Highness to reply to the four letters that he has already received is neither to his credit nor will it be to his advantage. At this period of negotiations he should realize that the writer is not penning these communications simply *'pour passer le temps.'* Unless the £50,000 already demanded is forthcoming by the 9th of next month the writer will be reluctantly compelled to add yet another Royal personage to his circle of epistolary acquaintance—the Princess Imogena of Natalia. But he assures His Royal Highness that the course of conduct thus indicated would occasion him extreme regret. His Royal Highness is fully aware that he is still allowed to choose his own method of transmitting the required sum—provided that such method is communicated to the writer through the 'Agony Column' of the 'Times.'" Bathurst wrinkled his brows. "This doesn't tell me all," he exclaimed. "May I look at the first letter of the series?" He extended his hand. The Crown Prince looked through his packet of envelopes and handed over the required letter. "Tranfield postmark this time," declared Anthony. "What date is this?" He looked at the postmark very carefully. "April twenty-third—'Tranfield.' Let me think for a moment—Tranfield is only a few miles from Westhampton, I fancy."

"You are right," replied his Royal visitor, "nine—to be precise."

The opening letter of the batch was much less shadowy—and far more to the point. "My dear Crown Prince," it ran with cavalier camaraderie, "you are entering the matrimonial state next December. That is to say—perhaps—for 'there's many a slip!' What would the Princess Imogena of Natalia say to a full story of your disgraceful *'affaire'* of the last year or so with a certain lady, whose identity for the time being need not be disclosed. However, my gay and gallant lover, there is no especial need for uneasiness on your part. £50,000 will seal eternally my rosebud lips." Similar directions to those in the letter that Anthony had just previously read were laid down concerning the transmission of the money. Bathurst looked at his client with judicial thoughtfulness.

"Far be it from me," he murmured, "to trespass on Your Highness's—shall we say—confidence"—he tapped the letter with his forefinger interrogatively waiting quietly—yet with determination. Mr. Bathurst was nothing, if not delicate in affairs of this nature.

A dull red colour suffused the cheeks of the Crown Prince. "I am a man," he declared with a touch of petulant anger in his tone, "who has always proved a strong and irresistible attraction to the opposite sex. But believe me, I am no Lothario. This incident—for I have no doubt in my mind that I know the *'affaire'* to which reference is made here—was perhaps unfortunate but certainly cannot with truth be termed 'disgraceful.' The lady and I parted upon perfectly agreeable terms some months ago now and upon that happening I imagined that the incident was permanently closed. I trust that you will not find it necessary to ask the lady's name. I am a man of honour."

Anthony pulled at his lip. "Are there any—er—documentary indiscretions relative to the affair still in existence?"

The Prince moved uneasily in his chair. "The lady may have kept the letters," he responded; "women are notoriously careless in these matters."

"Anything else?" queried Anthony.

"There was a photograph," replied His Highness, lamely.

"Of you?"

"Of the two of us—taken together—unfortunately."

"Dear me," ventured Anthony, "how indiscreet of you—that does complicate matters, to be sure!" He held out his hand for the three remaining letters and read each one through with care. "These three bear the London postmark, I notice," he declared; "there's nothing to help me much there, Your Highness! Westhampton and Tranfield, as we agreed, are adjoining. It is quite feasible therefore that the starting-point of our investigation may lie in that district. Have you any reason to believe that this may be so? Possibly, if you are frank, you can help me."

His visitor hesitated a moment or two before framing his reply. "Mr. Bathurst," he declared, "I want you to ferret out this dirty blackmailer and put matters right for me. I realize therefore that it is incumbent upon me to be *quite* frank. In reply to your question then—as to whether I can help you. I have only been to Westhampton once in my life. That was a year ago last February. I attended the Hunt Ball there—but my incognito was strictly maintained. To Tranfield I have never been!"

Anthony went straight to the point. "Did the lady in question accompany you?"

"No," replied the Crown Prince, "she did not. But I—" he stopped—seemingly at a momentary loss for words.

"Was she there?" asked Anthony, quick to seize the point. The Crown Prince bowed his head in assent. "It would appear then—that, as I foreshadowed—the root of the matter lies at Westhampton? Do you agree?" He eyed the Crown Prince with intentness.

"It may—very possibly," came the answer. "On the other hand it may be merely a coincidence. I visited many more places with the lady than Westhampton—as I stated, I have only been in that particular place once."

"You may be right, of course," conceded Anthony. "Where was the photograph taken?"

"At Seabourne—last summer."

"By—?"

"A gentleman who was staying in the same hotel. With my own camera. He obliged me by taking it. It was a wish of the lady."

"Can you recollect this gentleman's name?"

The Crown Prince of Clorania frowned as though he found the questions distasteful and disconcerting. "I think it was a Captain Willoughby. I'm not altogether sure. Naturally I wasn't taking a prominent part in the social life of the hotel at the time."

"What was the name of the hotel?"

"The Cassandra."

"Your Highness still desires to keep the identity of the lady a secret?"

"I have no option."

"Very well," said Anthony. "Leave these letters with me and I will do my best for you. Firstly, however, will you permit me to make a suggestion?"

"Yes, certainly!"

"Set a trap for your unknown correspondent. Lure him into it—then leave him to the tender mercies of Scotland Yard."

The Crown Prince shook his head. "I've thought of that, but I fear the consequences. Some of the story would be certain to become public. I cannot afford it to. I must avoid that at all costs."

"Pay the sum demanded, then," ventured Anthony.

"Fifty thousand pounds?" exclaimed his client in amazement, anger conflicting with incredulity in his voice. "You must be unaware of my very limited resources. Comparatively speaking, Mr. Bathurst, I am a poor man."

"You will give me *'carte blanche'* naturally?" said Anthony.

"As long as you maintain the strictest secrecy—you may act in whatever way you choose. Personally, I shall let nothing stand in my way. And if you are successful—rest assured that your services will never be forgotten. I am a Vilnberg—we have long memories for those who serve us well. Only remember—time is getting short. December is not so very far ahead."

He bowed, turned pompously and Anthony heard his decisive step descending the stairs.

Walking to the window, Bathurst watched the magnificently-liveried chauffeur open the door of the car usher his master to his seat therein with perfect obsequiousness, then drive off quickly and almost noiselessly. With a semi-humorous shrug of the shoulders Anthony returned to his desk. Then he read through the five threatening letters again—with even more care and attention than before. After a little time thus expended, one fact began to stand out clearly from the correspondence and make a deep impression upon his mind. The threats contained in the letters were all indefinite—limited to the "telling of a story," to "forwarding information of a most interesting and important nature," "to acquainting a certain Royal lady with highly-important facts," "to extending a circle of epistolary acquaintance." He was unable to find any mention whatever of the possession for instance, of such a definite thing as a photograph—also there was no hint of the existence of compromising letters. "Seems to me," muttered Anthony to himself, "that the strongest weapon this letter-writing gentleman possesses is the Crown Prince's conscience—and he probably knows it." He reached down for his A.B.C. and quickly flicked the pages for Westhampton. Then he turned back to Tranfield, which place he discovered was served at intervals by a local train service from Westhampton. "I can't run down before next Friday," he said to himself after consulting his diary; "it's impossible for me to touch it till then." He filled the bowl of his pipe and watched the flame of the match curl fiercely round the brown shreds of tobacco. "What happened exactly," he asked himself, "at the Hunt Ball at Westhampton a year ago last February?"

Chapter III
CHIEF-INSPECTOR BANNISTER GETS A "BUSMAN'S HOLIDAY"

ALTHOUGH the "Big Six" of Scotland Yard are invested by an admiring public with superhuman powers, and attributes that border upon the magical, they are for all that, as human as that same circle of admirers. Which fact, doubtless, has brought comfort to the heart of many a hunted criminal when he has brought himself to realize it. In this relation, probably the most human of "the Six" was Chief Detective-Inspector Richard Bannister—known to his colleagues and to a host of friends as "Dandy Dick." One of the most certain and regular indications of this humanity, to which allusion has just been made, is the desire at intervals, to rest from the exigencies of work and to take a holiday. At any rate, that was the particular trait that usually manifested itself in the case of Chief-Inspector Bannister. Three years of strenuous activities had seen him bring during their passing at least half-a-dozen of the "Yard's" "biggest" cases to successful and triumphant conclusions. On that account, therefore, he had no compunctions in taking a month's vacation at Seabourne. The place had always attracted him exceedingly when he had been in a position to enjoy short stays there on previous occasions, and now on a much longer spell it seemed to possess for him an even greater measure of attraction. On the July evening in question he shifted his body to a more comfortable position in the deck-chair which he was occupying and lazily inclined his head to catch more clearly the strains of the Military Band playing in the band-stand on the magnificent promenade of which Seabourne is so justifiably proud. It was a perfect summer evening—the true fulfilment of a perfect summer day. A day of blue sky and majestic sun! The sea was beautifully calm and lapped the beach in a ceaseless creaming succession of lazy, indolent ripples, and now the stars were flashing into the night-sky one by one, as though they were tiny lights turned on by a giant hand. Bannister stretched his long legs from his deck-chair in complete physical enjoyment. As he did so a tall man came down the superbly-kept lawn that fronted the "Cassandra" Hotel and sank comfortably into the deck-chair next to Bannister. He nodded genially. "Glorious evening—I told you last night we were in for a perfect day to-day."

"I remember," replied Bannister. "You did." He went on: "My luck as regards weather is absolutely in. I've actually had a week of uninterrupted sunshine—which I should imagine—speaking without the book—approaches a record for a summer holiday in England. Certainly, I've rarely been so fortunate in the past." He removed the horn-rimmed glasses that he had been using as a protection against the glare of the sun and carefully wiped them with a silk handkerchief.

Captain Willoughby's white teeth flashed in a smile of cordial agreement. "The same here. I've spent a good deal of time down here at Seabourne during the last year or two, but I haven't often had the good luck to get weather like we are experiencing now. It's almost equal to the Riviera. Been far to-day?"

"No," answered Bannister, with a shake of the head, "I've taken matters very easily to-day. Purposely! I came down here for a thorough rest and I intend to stick to my resolve. I'm a firm believer in the idea of a restful holiday."

Willoughby grinned. "Mind you keep it up all the time you're here, then! I always think that those intentions are very similar to 'New Year' resolutions. They're something like keeping a Diary, for instance. You know what I mean. Everything goes swimmingly from the first of January until about Epiphany. We carefully chronicle our petty personalities for just those few days—then our enthusiasm wanes and the remaining days in our Diary calendar are usually quite innocent of ink or even indelible pencil." He tossed away the end of his cigarette. "But I expect you've been guilty of that sort of thing yourself?"

"Perhaps not as much as you think. I've a lot of will-power. I can discipline myself to do things that are irksome—as a rule what I mean to do—I do. It's my way," Bannister concluded rather abruptly.

As he spoke one of the maids came from the Hotel and crossed the grass to where he was sitting. By his chair she stopped. Bannister turned and looked up at her. "Yes?" he questioned. "Are you wanting me?"

"Pardon me, sir," came her reply, "but you *are* Mr. Bannister, aren't you? There's somebody here wants to speak to you—I was to tell you it was very important, he said, sir."

Bannister knitted his brows, as though puzzled at the interruption; the maid waited by his chair, irresolutely.

"Are you sure he asked for me by *name*?" he demanded.

"Yes, sir—he said it quite distinctly—the name was 'Bannister' all right, sir."

"Who is it?" he asked again. "Do you know him at all?"

The maid hesitated a moment before giving him her answer. Then she spoke rather haltingly. "As a matter-of-fact, sir, I think it's Sergeant Godfrey from the Seabourne Police Station—I know him, you see, sir, through seeing him about the town."

"Sergeant Godfrey from the Police Station," frowned Bannister. "What the dickens does he want me for—at this time of the evening?"

He looked at the maid's face as though he expected to find there the answer to his question.

"I don't know, sir, only as I told you before he said that it was very important."

"Oh very well, then," exclaimed Bannister, with an expression of infinite resignation, "but tell him where I am and ask him to come along out here if he wants me as badly as you suggest."

She turned quickly and tripped back across the lawn. Bannister grunted to himself something inaudible and noticed that Willoughby was watching him closely.

"Couldn't help hearing something of what she said," he volunteered semi-apologetically, "hope it doesn't spell trouble for you."

Bannister's eyes glinted through his glasses but before he could reply a tallish man with a brisk step had crossed the grass-plot and reached his chair.

"Good evening, sir," he said somewhat deferentially; "may I have just a few words with you in private?"

Bannister glanced at him keenly and detected at once from the grim expression on his face that it was no petty trifle that had prompted this unexpected visit. He rose from his chair quietly. The Sergeant motioned him on one side and they withdrew about a dozen paces.

"I'm Sergeant Godfrey, sir, of the County Police and firstly I must ask you to excuse this disturbance I'm causing you. But the fact is I had the tip that the famous Chief-Inspector Bannister was staying in Seabourne and I've come to him for help." He dropped his voice to a very low tone and almost whispered to the Inspector. The latter started suddenly.

"*Murder*—are you sure, Godfrey?"

"Not a doubt about it, sir, as far as I can see. Or any of the others for that matter. Let me tell you the facts of the case," he supplemented eagerly. Scarcely waiting for the Inspector's assent he embarked impetuously upon his narrative. "At twenty minutes past two this afternoon, we received a 'phone message at the station, asking us to proceed at once to Mr. Ronald Branston's dental surgery. Mr. Branston, I may tell you, is a dental surgeon who has resided in Seabourne about three years. His place is at the corner of Coolwater Avenue—in the best and most secluded part of the town—quite a 'posh' dentist's—I can assure you—Mr. Branston himself was speaking on the 'phone. All he said was 'Come at once.' Constable Stannard went up and what he found when he got there made him immediately send for me. Mr. Branston's story was as follows. A young lady entered his operating room about two o'clock this afternoon for an extraction. He gave her an ordinary local anaesthetic and according to what he says took out the tooth very smoothly and comfortably. He handed his patient a tumbler of water and left her in the chair for a few moments to recover. His reason for so doing he explains like this. At half-past two another customer of his was calling for a set of artificial teeth that he had promised should be ready at that time. His workroom, you must understand, is about twelve yards away from his surgery—just across a landing. He was anxious to make sure, he says, that these teeth were thoroughly satisfactory and he admits that he may have been in the workroom a matter of seven or eight minutes. When he tried to leave—he found he was bolted in! A brass bolt on the outside of the workroom door had been slipped—to imprison him. For a few moments he scarcely realized what had happened—he shook the door thinking the catch or something had gone wrong and that it might perhaps open under pressure. But it was fastened securely. When the truth came home to him, that he was very effectively locked in as it were, he banged on the door with his fists and shouted for assistance." Godfrey broke off and looked at Bannister. "Interested?" he queried.

"I am that," replied the Inspector, "get on!"

"After a time, Branston's cries attracted the attention of his housekeeper, a Mrs. Bertenshaw—she rushed up to the workroom, undid the bolt and let him out. Unable for the moment to fathom the affair—he dashed back to the surgery. To his utter consternation and horror the young lady he had just left there—was dead. She was sitting in the operating chair exactly as he had left her about ten minutes previously, except for the fact that the tumbler was on the stand by the side of the chair. She had been *murdered*, Inspector! Poisoned! By Prussic Acid!"

Chapter IV
A CASE OF IDENTITY

"Certain of that?" queried Bannister. "How do you know she didn't commit suicide?"

The Sergeant nodded vigorously in affirmation of the Inspector's first question. "It's murder for certain! All her personal belongings seem to have been taken and all around the poor girl's mouth hung that unmistakable bitter almonds smell. You couldn't mistake it. I was sure that's what it was before Doctor Renfrew, the divisional surgeon, arrived. When he did he quickly confirmed my idea. He says she had a pretty considerable dose of the stuff, too. Enough to kill three people. The murderer, whoever he was, didn't intend taking any risks. Besides Branston's story rules out the idea of suicide."

"H'm," said Bannister fingering his chin reflectively, "it certainly seems an extraordinary case. At first appearances to all events. It all seems to have been done in so short a time. Still it may turn out quite a simple affair before you've done with it."

A grim smile played round Godfrey's lips. Albeit he strove hard to conceal his disappointment. "I was hoping you would say 'before *we've* done with it,'" he ventured.

Bannister frowned. "You were—were you?" Then he turned to his companion with a mixture of impatience and ill-temper. "Can't you leave me alone when I'm on a holiday? For a time at least, that is. As I said it may be quite an easy case to solve when you get all your data!"

Godfrey looked dismayed at the Inspector's remark. "No chance of that, I'm afraid, sir," he said. "The fact is I can't see any light at all. I'm up against it from the very commencement. I don't even know *who the young lady is*."

"What?" interjected Bannister. "Surely she has something on her or with her that will help to identify her—it's inconceivable to me that she hasn't."

Godfrey shook his head. "She may have—some of her clothes may have marks that will lead to her identity. I haven't examined any of them yet. I considered my best plan was to leave her almost exactly as she was when Stannard sent for me to come to the Surgery. I thought if I did that, sir, better intelligences than mine might read something into the case that was not apparent to me. I was thinking of you, sir. All the same—not knowing who she is means losing valuable time."

Bannister was temporarily proof against the flattery.

"Who told you I was here?" he demanded curtly.

"I've a cousin at 'the Yard,' sir," explained the Sergeant, "he happened to mention the fact in a letter I had from him a few days ago."

"Like his damned interference," interjected Bannister, "why couldn't he mind his own business and let me finish my holiday in peace?"

"I'm sorry, sir—but if I may make the suggestion—you're suffering from what I should describe as the penalty of fame, sir."

Bannister grinned cynically. "Oh—naturally—and all that." Then he reluctantly resigned himself to his fate—the Sergeant's last remark had been in the nature of a *"coup de grâce."* He submitted himself to the inevitable. "How far away is the place, Godfrey?"

"I've a car outside the 'Cassandra,'" Godfrey answered—relief manifested in every tone of his voice. "It will get us there in ten minutes easily." The car proved equal to the task.

During the short journey, Bannister remained silent. Two attempts that Godfrey made to reopen discussion of the crime were waved aside unceremoniously. "Let me wait," he declared. "Otherwise my brain will be full up with other people's impressions and observations, which is a condition I always try to avoid, if at all possible."

Ronald Branston's Dental Surgery lay at the corner of Coolwater Avenue and the Lower Seabourne Road in the direction of Froam, a watering place some eight miles away. The entrance to the Surgery for the use of patients was situated in Coolwater Avenue, the outer door being open. The Inspector and Sergeant Godfrey made their way to the main entrance which was in the Lower Seabourne Road and rang the bell. A woman with a scared face answered their summons and admitted them, with a suggestion of reluctance in her manner. She addressed Godfrey, however, with a certain deference.

"Doctor Renfrew has come back," she announced. "He's upstairs with Mr. Branston."

Godfrey turned to the Inspector. "Constables Stannard and Waghorn are on duty up in the room, sir," he explained, "they had instructions from me to stay till I returned."

Bannister nodded in understanding. "Take me up," he ordered, decisively. Godfrey obeyed.

Bannister noticed that the operating room lay nearer to the left-hand side of the house—that is to say, the Coolwater Avenue side. As Godfrey had stated in his first account of the case—Branston's appointments and furniture-equipment were, without exception, of excellent quality. The stair-carpet was luxuriously thick and heavy and everything about the place denoted unmistakably that no expense had been spared in the matter of its furnishing and decoration. Doctor Renfrew came out of the larger room—a spacious front room overlooking the Lower Seabourne Road and glanced inquiringly at Godfrey's companion.

"This is Chief-Inspector Bannister of Scotland Yard!" Godfrey was quick to introduce them. "*The* Bannister," he supplemented rather grandiloquently. The Doctor shook hands.

"Proud to meet you, Inspector."

"Good evening, Doctor."

Doctor Renfrew, a tall, thin, nervous man, with watery eyes that blinked repeatedly behind gold-rimmed spectacles motioned to the door of the surgery.

"Will you go in at once?" he asked. Bannister nodded curtly and the three men entered the room. Constables Stannard and Waghorn sprang to their feet and saluted.

"Wait downstairs, you two men," ordered Godfrey. He turned to the Doctor. "Where's Mr. Branston?"

"Downstairs—he had dinner very late, I believe. I told him he'd probably be wanted before very long."

Bannister in the meantime had walked across to the motionless shape that lay huddled in the dentist's chair. He removed the silk handkerchief that covered the face. As far as he could judge from her appearance she was in the early twenties and in life must have been very beautiful—the face having an exquisite delicacy of line. She was dressed in what is usually termed a "three-piece suit"; of jumper, skirt and sleeveless coat. The coat and skirt were of a fine wool, in colour cedar brown—the jumper being striped to tone. Her brown shoes were semi-brogue; like her stockings they were of the very best quality. She wore no jewellery and her fingers were ringless. Doctor Renfrew walked out of the room and returned a moment or two later carrying a hat and a pair of gloves.

"She left these in the ladies' waiting-room," he explained. "Mr. Branston has a separate room for ladies in which to wait if they so desire—it opens out of the front room, which is used more as a general waiting-room."

Bannister nodded and looked at the hat. It was a pull-on waterproof felt with a pleated crown and turned-down brim. He glanced inside at the maker's name. "Moore—Knightsbridge! A lady in very comfortable circumstances, I should say," he declared. Godfrey nodded in agreement. "I think so too!" "Well, Doctor Renfrew," continued the Inspector, "what have you got to tell me?"

Doctor Renfrew wasted no time in telling him. "When I examined the deceased, it was apparent to me at once that death had been caused by narcotic poisoning—hydrocyanic acid to be precise. It was impossible to mistake the odour round the lips and mouth. She had had a big dose administered."

Bannister pursed his lips. "How was it administered—any idea? For instance—can't it be suicide?"

The doctor's reply came quickly and readily. "In my opinion—judging from the position of the body—the poison was given from a small hand-syringe. After locking Branston in, the murderer entered the room through the door here—she heard him—turned in his direction and he used the syringe immediately. Her face would be right in front of him. Quite an easy matter—he had doubtless worked out all the details beforehand."

"Cold-blooded business," muttered Godfrey. "The kind of man I should take a delight in hanging."

"Any purse or anything with her?" demanded Bannister.

"Nothing," answered the Sergeant. "Everything seems to have gone except the hat and this pair of gloves."

A knock sounded on the door and Doctor Renfrew crossed the room to open it. Ronald Branston stood outside. "May I come in?" he queried.

Bannister beckoned to him. "I was just about to send down to you, Mr. Branston," he commenced; "you must have read my thoughts to arrive so opportunely."

Branston bowed. "A dreadful affair this," he declared, "dreadful from whatever point of view you look at it. Pretty rotten for me, you know—in the business sense. It sounds frightfully callous, I know, but self-preservation's the first law of nature. This job isn't going to do my business any good and every man has to think of himself." He flushed under his dark skin.

Bannister eyed him sternly. "I am Chief-Inspector Bannister," he said, "of 'Scotland Yard.' Sergeant Godfrey has requested my assistance. Tell me exactly what happened."

Branston's nostrils quivered slightly as he began to tell his story but he rapidly regained control over himself and his words came clearly and without a shade of tremor in his voice. "I can only repeat to you," he stated, "what I have already told Sergeant Godfrey here. This unhappy lady entered the room in which we are now standing a few minutes before two o'clock this afternoon. I had just attended to a previous patient who was my first of the afternoon. She asked me to perform an extraction. I administered a simple local anaesthetic and extracted a left-hand bicuspid. The lady seemed quite comfortable after the extraction. I gave her the usual glass of water as a mouth-wash—there's the very tumbler on that stand—just as she must have put it down before she was murdered—and then went along to my workroom. I had a special job on this afternoon as I've previously explained to the Sergeant and it's my customary practice to let a patient alone for a moment or two after an extraction."

"One minute," broke in Bannister. "Was the extraction a necessary one?"

"Oh, undoubtedly—the tooth had been filled on a previous occasion and the filling had worn away. The patient had been in considerable pain, she informed me, and I could well understand it. She had probably caught cold in the bad tooth."

"Thank you," observed the Inspector. "Please proceed."

"Well, here comes the extraordinary part of the story." Here Branston's nervousness began to show itself again. "The job took me a little longer than I had anticipated—when I turned to open the door of the room in which I was working, I found to my complete astonishment that I was shut in. Somebody had shot the brass bolt on the outside of the workroom door. I called out and banged on the door but there I had to stay until my housekeeper heard me yelling and released me. I rushed back to the operating room and discovered—this."

"How long were you away—as accurately, now, as you can possibly place it?"

Branston knitted his brows in reflection. "I wouldn't put it at more than seven minutes," he answered, calculatingly.

"Did you hear any step at all when you were in the workroom?"

He shook his head decisively. "No! I didn't! The carpet on the stairs and along the landing to the workroom is very thick, you know."

Bannister went to the door and looked out. "This back staircase leads to the patients' entrance in Coolwater Avenue—I suppose?"

"That's so, Inspector."

The Inspector closed the door and came back. "The lady, of course, was a chance patient—not an appointment case?"

"A complete stranger."

"Were any other patients waiting, do you know?"

"I had no definite appointment till half-past two. I couldn't say if there were any other chance cases waiting in either of the waiting-rooms. Certainly I can remember nobody coming out when we discovered what had happened."

Bannister thought hard for a moment. "Did the expected client arrive at half-past two?"

Branston smiled for the first time. "'Pon my soul," he exclaimed, "I've never given him another thought. It was twenty minutes past two when I 'phoned up for the Police—I must have clean forgotten him. If he came—he probably cleared off in the 'schemozzle.'"

"What's his name?" demanded Bannister.

"He's a Mr. Jacob Morley—a local gentleman—I rather fancy he styles himself a Turf accountant." Branston permitted himself the suggestion of a smile.

"Sound man?"

Branston shrugged his shoulders. "I know nothing to the contrary."

"All right, then, Mr. Branston," put in Bannister after a slight pause, "I don't think I need detain you any longer. That is all I want to know for the moment."

Branston bowed and withdrew, Doctor Renfrew following him.

Sergeant Godfrey caught his superior's eye and understood the intended meaning. "I've told Stannard and Waghorn to watch points in that direction—that will be all right."

"Very good," rejoined the Inspector, "let's hear Mrs. Bertenshaw's story."

The housekeeper corroborated Branston in every particular and was allowed to withdraw. Bannister looked at his watch. "It's so confoundedly late, that it will be extremely difficult to get anything much done to-night. Tell me all you've done, so far, Godfrey."

"I've had the body photographed and I've sent round to all the hotels and boarding-establishments to try to trace by discreet inquiries any young lady visitor who's been missing, say, since luncheon time to-day."

The Inspector showed his approval. "That's all right as far as it goes. But she may be a new arrival to the town. She may have just come in. Stay—what about luggage?"

"She might have left it somewhere," responded Godfrey. "At the railway station or at an hotel. The latter, I should be inclined to suggest as the more likely, taking into consideration the class of girl she appears to be."

"Yes," conceded Bannister. "I think perhaps you're right. Now about this workroom Branston has been telling us of—have you taken a look in there—I suppose his story is authentic—eh? I can't help feeling there's something 'fishy' about it somewhere."

"I've seen the room—you can come along and see it yourself before we go—I'll say this—I found nothing there that seemed in any way to contradict his story. I've also had the brass bolt on the door treated for finger-prints."

"Good man," smiled Bannister. "You should certainly find Mrs. Bertenshaw's there—I suppose you've taken hers and Branston's?"

"You bet I have, sir," grinned the Sergeant. "I've got them tucked away all serene."

Bannister frowned and walked across to the stand where stood the tumbler of water. It was almost full. He smelt it. "The purest of pure water, Doctor Renfrew says. Seems like it," said Bannister. "No odour, certainly."

The Sergeant who was watching him seemed suddenly struck by an idea. "By Jove, sir," he exclaimed, "I ought to have treated that glass for 'prints' as well as the bolt—don't you agree?"

Bannister held the glass high up to the electric light and carefully examined it. "Perhaps you had," he replied, "if it isn't too late now to be effective."

Godfrey went through the insufflating process in his usual workman-like manner. With a small insufflator or powder-blower, he exhaled a cloud of light yellow powder which settled on the glass in an even coating. Then he blew at it sharply. Most of the yellow powder was blown off, but a number of smeary yellow impressions were left behind, standing out in strong saffron relief against the white glass.

"Something to work on here," he said. "I'll have the job completed." He slipped out but was quickly back. "I suggest we get Mrs. Pearson up here from the station," he said after a short interval.

"The female searcher?" queried the Inspector.

"Yes—then we can have the body removed in the morning. If the poor girl's still unidentified by then, perhaps the under-clothes—"

"Sergeant Godfrey!" Branston's voice sounded outside. "You're wanted on my telephone, downstairs."

"I'll come with you," said Bannister. "It may be news."

Godfrey took off the receiver, listened and replaced it. "It's the 'Lauderdale Hotel'—they think they can identify the lady. At my suggestion they're sending the reception-clerk along to us immediately. He will be here any moment—the Manager's coming along with him."

"Good," said Bannister. "We are moving at last." He offered his cigarette-case with a gesture of satisfaction to Sergeant Godfrey.

And judging from the manner in which he selected a cigarette—Sergeant Godfrey thought so too!

Chapter V
JOHN MARTIN'S EVIDENCE

For a few moments the two men smoked in silence, grateful doubtless for the short respite. The silence was soon disturbed by the ringing of the front door bell. Godfrey rose with an alert expectancy that he took no trouble to conceal. Bannister carefully shook his left trouser in an attempt to stabilize an immaculate crease. Mrs. Bertenshaw's steps were heard hurrying to the front door to admit the two people whose visit had been so recently heralded by the telephone. Godfrey went to the door of the room and called down the hall.

"Bring the two gentlemen in here, Mrs. Bertenshaw."

It was easy to see that the Manager of the "Lauderdale Hotel" was the man who entered first. A short, broad-shouldered, florid-faced man, he wore his dress-suit with that air of aggressive opulence that can only be captured with complete success by hotel managers, Sheikhs of the Box-office, and the gentlemen who hold undisputed sway in those cinemas usually designated as "super"—whatever that may mean. The reception-clerk was tall and thin and to all appearances, worried by the singular turn that events had taken.

"Sergeant Godfrey?" questioned the first of the newcomers. Godfrey came forward to meet and to greet him.

"I'm your man—Mr. Maynard—isn't it?"

"That's right—and I'm pretty certain I've some news for you. Very likely the information you're wanting. After your men had been round making those inquiries for you, I guessed it was something pretty serious that was engaging your attention. So I put a few feelers round my staff, off my own bat, so to speak, and I reckon that Martin here has got something important to tell you. Of course, it may be a mare's nest that I'm bringing you—but somehow I don't think so." He shifted his cigar from one corner of his mouth to the other with an adroitness that could only have been cultivated by assiduous practice. "Now, Martin," he ordered rather imperiously, "spill your bibful."

Martin fidgeted uneasily on the chair that he had immediately sought upon his arrival and got even nearer to its edge. He twisted his shabby hat in his hands with a circular movement and seemed at a loss to begin. His eyes sought those of Maynard—then wandered away until they encountered those of Chief-Inspector Bannister. Bannister's glance afforded little encouragement however, so they travelled on again, waveringly and uncertainly until they reached those of the Sergeant.

"Come," said the last-named, "don't waste any time—tell us what you know."

Martin licked his lips, cleared his throat, gulped once or twice and commenced his story. "Well, sir," he started, "it isn't very much that I've got to tell you, but I've the glimmering of an idea that the young lady you're inquiring about came into the 'Lauderdale' about half-past one this afternoon. You see it was like this. About ten-fifty on Wednesday evening a 'phone message came through booking a room for a Miss Daphne Carruthers who was arriving the next day. About the time that I've just mentioned—half-past one of an afternoon—things are pretty quiet as a rule. A car drew up outside the hotel and a young lady alighted and walked into the vestibule. She came straight up to me and said, 'I want a room please, for a fortnight—I believe it was booked last night for me—by 'phone. I'll leave my luggage here now, although I've an important call to make. You might send out for my case—it's in my car. Put it up in my room, will you please? I shall be back in about an hour.' 'Certainly, miss,' I answered, 'your room number will be sixty-six.' I sent the porter out for her suit-case and sent him up to the room with it, confirming the name from the labels on it. 'Thank you,' she replies, trips out of the hotel, jumps into her car and drives off."

"In what direction?" snapped Bannister.

"Towards Froam, sir."

"Go on."

"Well—a lot of other people came in and some went away and the young lady that was to come back in the hour went clean out of my mind. When your man came round this evening making those inquiries it all came back to me. Gentlemen—that young lady has never come back. Her suit-case is in Room Sixty-six just where I told the porter to put it." He stopped and wiped his lips with his handkerchief and the perspiration from his brow.

Bannister interposed again—authoritatively. "Would you be able to remember this young lady, if you saw her again?"

Martin answered the question very readily. "Why, yes, sir, I stood talking to her face to face for quite a matter of a minute or two. She was a real beauty, I can tell you, sir. I haven't forgotten her and no mistake."

Bannister motioned to Godfrey to lead the way upstairs. Then he turned to the clerk. "Come with us, then—and prepare yourself for a shock."

Martin's white face went whiter as they ascended the stairs, Bannister leading and the hotel manager, Maynard, bringing up the rear. The Inspector waited to close the door of the surgery behind them.

"Let him have a look at her, Godfrey," he said, turning to the Sergeant.

Godfrey uncovered the face again for Martin to see. The latter gave a low gasp of horror. Then he uttered an exclamation. "I was right, sir! It's her right enough—as I was afraid it was when I came along. That's the identical young lady that came to the 'Lauderdale' about half-past one this afternoon that I've been telling you about. Just fancy—to think of her as she was then in the best of health, as you might say—and now—"

Bannister abruptly put a stoppage upon his sentimental reminiscences. "You're certain—absolutely certain—of what you say?"

"Positive, sir—you don't see two like her every day of the week."

The Inspector turned to Sergeant Godfrey. "You hear what he says? We'll get along up to the 'Lauderdale' at once. What name did she give, Martin?"

"I've copied the name from the reception-book just as I entered it when she arrived. I thought I'd better do that in case it should turn out as I feared."

He fumbled in his breast pocket for a moment—produced a slip of paper which was far from being clean and handed it to Bannister. The latter read it aloud, "'Miss Daphne Carruthers.' This will save you a lot of trouble, Godfrey. Here's your identification! No need now to broadcast the news or publish a photograph or anything—it's a great help, this evidence of yours, Martin. It will save the police very valuable time at the most important stage of the case—the very beginning. Just where we looked uncommonly like losing it."

Maynard was obviously pleased at the Inspector's tribute to a member of his staff. "Are you coming to the 'Lauderdale' now?" he inquired.

"This very minute—lock the door, Godfrey, put the key in your pocket and station your two men outside."

A matter of a few minutes saw the journey accomplished. "Show these gentlemen the entry you made in the admission register, Martin," said Maynard with a show of authority. The reception clerk ran his finger along the particular line. The name was as he had given it. Bannister glanced over his shoulder—then turned away—seemingly satisfied. The next step was an inspection of Room Sixty-six. The suitcase that had figured in Martin's story lay on the floor between the wardrobe and the dressing-table. Bannister lifted it on to the bed. It was of good quality although of common type. There were, in all probability, hundreds similar to it in various places in Seabourne, on that very night. Two labels of the "tie-on" variety were attached to the handle. The handwriting on each of them was the same—suggestive certainly of a girl's hand—"Daphne Carruthers, 11, Lexham Gardens, Kensington." He tried the catches.

"It's locked. Where are your keys, Godfrey?" Godfrey produced several bunches of keys—unavailingly.

Then the manager came to the rescue. He slipped from the room quickly—to return almost immediately with a large key-ring bearing keys of all shapes and sizes. Bannister's attempts to open the case were eventually successful. He gave a grunt of satisfaction. Its contents were almost entirely clothes and toilet requisites. Clothes that one would reasonably anticipate finding in the suit-case of a young lady upon holiday in the summer. There was no letter, no card—nothing more personal than hair-brushes and face powder. The Inspector tossed the stuff back into the case.

"Your job, Godfrey, will be to get into touch with the place from where this girl's come. Send a 'phone message through to Kensington as soon as you can and use the Press for all you're worth. Get the London papers humming to-morrow morning like flies. We shall soon get information about Daphne Carruthers, you mark my words, even if we can't get it from the place where she lived." He turned to Maynard. "I'll take charge of this"—he patted the suit-case—"you Godfrey—get those strings to work at once. By the way, Martin—the motor-car that the young lady was driving—did you notice what it was?"

Martin scratched his chin—then shook his head. "I didn't, sir, and that's a fact. I was too much taken up with the young lady herself."

"H'm," muttered Bannister, "that's a pity—we must see what we can do in that direction to-morrow morning. That car must be traced, Godfrey. I expect we shall have a pretty ticklish day to-morrow—with one thing and another."

In which opinion Chief-Inspector Bannister was entirely accurate, although the day was destined also to have its compensations for him. Not the least of these compensations was his introduction to a certain Mr. Anthony Lotherington Bathurst. Even though Seabourne is a hundred and nine miles from Tranfield, and a trifle more than that from Westhampton—two places in which Mr. Bathurst had fully expected to be!

Chapter VI
MR. BATHURST CHANGES HIS DESTINATION

ANTHONY BATHURST read the telegram that had so summarily interrupted his breakfast, with much more than the suspicion of a frown. Not that it was at all ambiguous or in any way difficult for him to understand. Indeed it was completely the reverse of these things. "Come at once to Hotel Cassandra, Seabourne," was the message it conveyed and the sender's name was shown at the end of the message as "Mr. Lucius." "His Royal Highness seems to imagine that I'm thoroughly at his beck and call," he murmured to himself softly. "This will put the tin hat on my going to Westhampton—as I had intended." He lit a cigarette and thrust his left hand into the pocket of his dressing-gown. Mr. Bathurst was a staunch adherent of the theory of breakfasting in comfort. "Seabourne?" he thought to himself. "Seabourne? What caught my eye in this morning's paper concerning Seabourne?" He picked up the paper that had already been read and tossed aside—and eagerly sought the more prominent head-lines. "Ah!" he exclaimed, "I thought I wasn't mistaken." His eyes swept the paragraph with its sensational notice. The headings were—"Strange Tragedy at Seabourne. Young Lady Murdered in Dentist's Chair." The paragraph below the head-lines ran as under. "About half-past two yesterday afternoon the Seabourne police were called to the Dental Surgery of Mr. Ronald Branston which is situated at the corner of Coolwater Avenue and the Lower Seabourne Road. A lady patient upon whom Mr. Branston had just previously attended had been discovered poisoned in the Dentist's chair. Doctor Renfrew, the divisional

Surgeon was called and gave it as his opinion that deceased had died from an administration of Hydrocyanic Acid. Mr. Branston himself has told the authorities a remarkable story. Sergeant Godfrey of the Marlshire County Police had charge of the case but has now had the good fortune to obtain the active co-operation of Chief-Inspector Bannister, one of the famous 'Six' of New Scotland Yard, who happens to be spending part of his annual holiday in Seabourne. Thanks to the untiring assiduity of the latter gentleman, the lady, in regard to whose identity the Police were at the outset without the vestige of a clue has now been identified as Miss Daphne Carruthers of 11, Lexham Gardens, Kensington, a visitor to Seabourne staying at the Lauderdale Hotel. Taking into consideration certain facts that Mr. Branston has communicated to them, the Police have no doubt that a brutal murder has been committed. Surprising developments are hourly expected." Mr. Bathurst put down his paper, and pulled at his top lip—"I wonder," he murmured.

Two hours later he stood outside the big railway station that introduces Seabourne to thousands of visitors. He hailed a "taxi." Five minutes longer saw him inside the "Cassandra."

"Mr. Lucius," murmured a gentleman superbly tailored and faultlessly barbered, "suite 17, if you please. Have you then the business with him? But yes? Then I, myself, will personally conduct you to him." He shrugged his perfectly-fitted shoulders with a shrug that betokened much to a receptive mind. "Mr. Lucius—he is indeed a personage. But yes!"

Mr. Bathurst appeared to be in no mood to contradict him. He followed the gentleman upstairs. Mr. Lucius was in! Mr. Lucius was pacing the floor of his room after the manner of an infuriated tiger. It was evident that Mr. Lucius was very much annoyed!

"Ah, Bathurst," he exclaimed, with a shade of relief in his tone, "so you're here at last. I am indeed pleased. Sit down. This terrible business is wearing my nerves to pieces. In fact I'm thoroughly nerved and nearly worried out of my life. Doubtless you've seen this morning's paper?"

Mr. Bathurst had. "Did His Royal Highness allude—" Mr. Lucius's hand stopped him with a dramatic gesture.

"Please respect my incognito. You have a saying, 'The walls have the ears.' Pardon my seeming insistence on the point."

Anthony murmured what he considered was a dignified apology. Then he completed his unfinished sentence, "Did Mr. Lucius allude to the matter that the Press were calling 'The Seabourne Murder'?"

Mr. Lucius clapped the palms of his two hands together in uncontrollable emotion. Anthony realized at once that His Royal Highness was certainly in a highly-nervous state and that his previous protestations to that effect had strong foundation. He had been frightened by something and frightened badly. Anthony remembered his parting words at their interview of a week ago. He had threatened to let nothing stand in his way—and at the moment was badly rattled. Anthony decided upon reflection, that it promised to turn out a distinctly interesting case. His host stopped his nervy pacing of the room and plunged himself ill-humouredly into an armchair. "I will be very frank," he commenced. "Although it goes against the grain of my inclination—yet I will tell you all." He laid his finely-shaped hand upon Anthony's arm with an imperious movement. "After I left your rooms, Mr. Bathurst, at the end of last week, I drove straight to my hotel 'The Florizel.' And although I was very much preoccupied on the journey, nevertheless I was convinced when I reached my destination that I had been followed. By two men! They were hanging about outside your rooms when I left there— and I am positive that they followed me in a small two-seater car to my hotel. However, it is of the smallest importance, perhaps. What I am going to tell you now belongs to what you will call—a different category. *'Une autre galère!'* By the next morning's post I received another surprising communication. Not in the atrocious handwriting of that 'detestable'—no—from a lady." He paused to see the effect of his words but Anthony's face was as inscrutable as ever. "In fact, Mr. Bathurst, from *the* lady."

"Really," murmured Anthony with the suspicion of a smile. "I take it you were extremely surprised?"

"Most assuredly," replied Mr. Lucius, "I had not heard from the lady for a considerable length of time, as I informed you last week. And if I was surprised to receive the letter, I was still more surprised at the nature of its contents. Unfortunately—in the light of after events—I destroyed it."

Mr. Bathurst lifted his eyebrows—was His Royal Highness, the Crown Prince of Clorania always a stickler for veracity, he wondered?

"But I can remember it *verbatim*,—every word, Mr. Bathurst." The Crown Prince leaned back in his armchair, closed his eyes, placed his finger-tips together and proceeded to remember the contents of his letter. "It was as follows," he announced pompously. "'Dear Alexis, I am perfectly aware, you will be surprised to know, that you have made two unsuccessful attempts to transfer a certain particular object from my possession to your own. Advices received to-day, that I cannot disregard, tell me that you have sought the professional assistance of Mr. Anthony Bathurst. I happen to know something of that gentleman, you see, as my solicitors are "Merryweather, Linnell and Daventry." Upon mature reflection therefore, I have decided to discontinue what would be a hopeless struggle. I liked you once, Alexis, very, very much. Because of that, and because I'm a silly idiot as well, I'm going to give the photo back to you and burn all the letters. Meet me at the Hotel where we stayed in Seabourne before. I will give it to you there. Will some time next week suit you?'" His Highness turned in his chair. "That, Mr. Bathurst, is reproduced as accurately as I can recall it." A spirit of uneasiness appeared to take possession of him. "It was signed," he added in an apparent afterthought and undertone, "by a pet-name that I had used upon previous occasions when addressing her. It would not assist you at all to know it. To cut a long story short, Mr. Bathurst, I came to this Hotel on Tuesday last, met the lady, as she had suggested, on the following day and as a matter of fact was able to bring the affair that was so important and interesting to me to a highly-satisfactory conclusion. The lady concerned left the Hotel on Wednesday evening—I stayed on."

His Royal Highness sprang to his feet as he finished his story. His excitement and anxiety had temporarily mastered him. He approached Anthony and his face was white, shaking and uncontrolled. "Mr. Bathurst," he exclaimed, "when I called upon you at the end of last week you will remember I refused to divulge the name of the lady in the case—I told you that I was a man of honour." His voice shook with emotion. "Now I feel myself as compelled to reveal it, even though at the risk of injuring myself. Fate has taken a hand in the game, Mr. Bathurst. The lady's name was Daphne Carruthers—and I learn from the Press this morning and also from a medley of cursed, gossiping tongues in this infernal seaside town—that she was murdered here in Seabourne—yesterday." His voice was now completely hoarse. With grief or with anxiety, Anthony was unable to decide. But he went on. Standing erect in the middle of the room, he raised his right hand dramatically over his head. "And I myself, it is more than possible, will be the 'suspect.' I would not have had such a terrible affair happen for the world. It will ruin me." He gestured helplessly in Mr. Bathurst's direction, then sank into his chair again—his head in his hands.

"When did you last see Miss Carruthers?" demanded the latter.

"On the evening of Wednesday—we dined together—early—settled our little differences, and parted—to go our own ways and to lead our own lives. We understood each other."

"You had possession, then, I take it, of the photograph?" remarked Anthony.

"But certainly—I had come to get it. It is destroyed."

"And the letters—!"

"We burned them together," rejoined the Crown Prince.

"Where?"

"In a wood that lies off the road to Froam."

Anthony looked grave.

"The letters you had threatening blackmail—those you left with me—what had Miss Carruthers to say regarding them?"

"But that is remarkable! I taxed her with them—she denied all knowledge of them."

"Did you believe her?"

The Crown Prince shrugged his shoulders eloquently. "Can a man ever believe a woman with whom he's once been in love?"

Anthony shot a quick glance at him. He was not an amorist and supremely contemptuous of the professional philanderer. To him, *"le pays du Tendre"* was far too sacred a country for such light imaginings. "You're more qualified to answer that question than I, Your Highness. *Did you believe her?*"

The Crown Prince sulkily reflected for a brief moment. "Well—on the whole—I think I did. Her denial of the affair seemed to me to be transparently honest."

"Tell me," said Anthony, "was it, as far as you know, the intention of Miss Carruthers to return to her home at once—or did she intend to stay anywhere else in Seabourne?"

"She intended to return to London by the last train on Wednesday evening—she told me so."

"Of course," suggested Anthony, "her plans may have been altered—an attack of violent toothache, for instance, has a lot of force behind it."

"No mention was made to me of any toothache. She had none while she was with me," grumbled His Royal Highness.

Anthony couldn't resist the feeling that the Crown Prince regarded it as most inconsiderate on the part of Miss Carruthers to have been murdered. "You have been seen together here, of course?" he queried.

"But naturally! We dined *'à deux'* in the hotel on Wednesday evening. There is for example, a Captain Willoughby staying here who was also here in the hotel when we stayed before. They say he lives here permanently. If you remember—"

"He was the taker of the particularly-important photograph," interjected Anthony. He made a point of remembering most things—did Mr. Bathurst.

"That is so," supplemented the Crown Prince; "you see Captain Willoughby will be certain to connect us."

Anthony could find no reason to contest the point. "Undoubtedly," he responded.

His Highness came over to him again. "Tell me," he said, rather more imperiously than Mr. Bathurst considered commendable, "what steps had you taken in respect of my own case? Had you made any investigations?"

"It was my intention to have started to-day—strangely enough. I was on the point of starting for Westhampton this morning—your telegram calling me down here was the thing that stopped me. I was convinced, you see, that a judicious inquiry in the Westhampton district might yield good result."

The Crown Prince nodded in corroboration. Putting his right hand on Anthony's shoulder he looked very carefully round the apartment—then sank his voice to a mere whisper. "Mr. Bathurst," he said softly, "I take it you are quite familiar with the facts?"

"Of yesterday's tragedy?"

"Yes—of the murder."

"Only so far as I have been able to read the morning papers."

The Crown Prince nodded again. "Quite so—and you will agree I feel sure that it appears to be a most remarkable case. You will have been able to glean sufficient from the accounts in the Press to admit that. Listen—I have a theory—an idea has persisted in my brain since I heard of the affair in the first place. Those letters that were addressed to me. Vile blackmail! Mr. Bathurst—supposing that blackmailer is also the murderer of Miss Carruthers. It fits! It is on all four legs as you English say. Supposing he knew that Miss Carruthers and I had met amicably—that the affair was settled—that she had returned the photograph to my keeping—that the letters were burned—it would be clear to him that I could snap the finger-tips to him— that I could treat his threats with scorn—with disdain—in short that I could say to him, 'Go to Hell.' Well, then—assume that he knows what I have just said—he follows Miss Carruthers whose arrangement with me has spoiled his little game and in a rage and passion at being thwarted—he kills her at this dentist's to whom she had gone. Why not—I say—why not? Find my blackmailer, Mr. Bathurst—and you'll find the murderer of Daphne Carruthers." He paused—his face and lips tremulous with anxiety and excitement—and took out a cigarette. Anthony watched him closely—the affair had got badly on his nerves—there was no denying the fact.

"It's feasible, certainly," he conceded. "But it would be extremely injudicious of me to debate the case, with so little first-hand evidence upon which to go. The worst mistake any investigator can ever make is to let his brain run away and play mental Badminton with fanciful theories. It might pay, perhaps, once—or even twice—but I can hardly see it bringing consistent success. And as, in this case, I am not likely to obtain any first-hand evidence—"

His host interposed eagerly. "But you are, Mr. Bathurst. You are! Permit me to explain. I am privileged, as you may guess, by reason of my rank and powerful influence, to know many who sit in high places. I have this morning spoken to the Chief Commissioner of Police—Sir Austin Kemble," he indicated the telephone on the table in the corner of the room; "he has given orders for you to have access to anything you desire in your handling of the case upon my behalf. Chief-Inspector Bannister of Scotland Yard who was called in by the local police has already been informed to that effect. I am very anxious that my interests should be in the very ablest hands. I may need them."

Anthony waved aside the very direct compliment. "Really, Your—Mr. Lucius, rather, I am not at all sure that my engagements will allow me to do what you wish. As I pointed out to you previously, I am not a professional inquiry-agent."

The Crown Prince extended what was almost a suppliant hand. "But you took those letters of mine—you were going to investigate the secret that lay behind the writing of them—and I am sure that the affairs are connected. I would esteem it as the very greatest of favours if you—"

"What makes you so positive of the connection between the two things?" demanded Anthony, with strong curiosity.

Mr. Lucius shrugged his shoulders even more eloquently than before. Then he placed his two fingers upon where he imagined his heart to be. "I feel it *here*," he explained—it was an un-English gesture, and to Mr. Bathurst, was far from satisfying.

"The whole affair is puzzling," declared the latter, "but one feature of it puzzles me very considerably. At the moment, that is. You have just informed me that Miss Carruthers has been staying here at the 'Cassandra.' That is so, isn't it?"

"Why yes. As I told you just now she wrote to me—it was her idea—asking me to meet her here—at the Cassandra! What is it exactly that mystifies you?"

"Simply this," exclaimed Anthony; "the Press report that I read at breakfast this morning stated that Miss Carruthers was a guest at the 'Lauderdale' Hotel—certainly no mention was made of the 'Cassandra.'"

The Crown Prince looked startled out of his skin. "What!" he exclaimed, "the 'Lauderdale'? It is impossible. You must be mistaken. That was not reported in my paper. How can it be? What paper was it—*surely* you must be mistaken?"

Anthony demurred very quietly but firmly. "You will find I am not. It was the 'Morning Message'—send for one and see for yourself."

His Royal Highness touched the bell. "A copy of this morning's 'Message,'" he said to the attendant, "as quickly as possible. I cannot believe it," he muttered, as he paced the apartment after a minute's silence. "The 'Lauderdale'—it is incredible that— thank you." He broke off and opened the newspaper that had been brought to him. "I ask your pardon, Mr. Bathurst, for seeming to doubt you—you are quite correct—the report says 'a visitor to Seabourne, staying at the "Lauderdale" Hotel.' It is inexplicable—it must be the misprint—or at any rate false information."

"I doubt it being that," ventured Anthony, "the London Press is pretty accurate as a rule upon details of that nature. In murder cases especially. After all we may be puzzling our brains needlessly—the explanation of the tangle may be perfectly simple when we hit upon it. Miss Carruthers may have had a second assignation. She may have intended to stay in Seabourne longer than you thought. She may have simply moved her quarters from the 'Cassandra' to the 'Lauderdale' intentionally."

"Never," cried His Royal Highness Alexis of Clorania, "never." He brought down one of his palms upon the other in the same manner that he had employed before. The suggestion assailed his vanity. "I am quite certain of what I am saying. Miss Carruthers left me, as I informed you, to return to London. She had no assignation in Seabourne beyond her assignation at the 'Cassandra' with me."

This time it was Anthony's turn to shrug his shoulders. "With all deference—I don't know how you can be so certain on the point. May I remind you in your own words, 'Can a man ever believe a woman with whom he has been in love?'"

The Crown Prince winced slightly at the aptness of Mr. Bathurst's reply. Then the wince gave place to a frown which in its turn was superseded by a distinct tendency to sullenness. "I *know* Miss Carruthers left me to go back to London. This toothache or neuralgia or whatever it was must have come on suddenly and perhaps caused her to alter her plans very quickly. That is the only explanation I can offer at the moment."

"We shall have to wait," supplemented Anthony, "until we get more reliable information—that is all we can do. But the two facts certainly do not tally—they contradict each other rather—you must see that."

"The 'Morning Message' has its facts wrong—that is the explanation," said the Crown Prince pettishly; "it's the only explanation that there can possibly be—their reporter has confused the two hotels." He was interrupted by the sharp ringing of the telephone on the table in the corner. He walked to it—obviously angered at what he considered an interruption that need not have happened. "Yes—yes," he said irritably as he picked up the receiver. "Yes, it's Mr. Lucius speaking. Who is it . . . a trunk call . . . all right . . . yes . . . yes . . . Lucius speaking . . . I can't hear properly . . . you're very indistinct . . . speak up . . . what . . . *you*. . . ."

Anthony watched him curiously as he listened, his face white as death. Suddenly he gave a quick gasp, took the receiver from his ear and covered the mouthpiece with his disengaged hand. . . . "Mr. Bathurst," he said tremulously, turning to Anthony. "What on earth is the real meaning of all this ghastly business? . . . I'm speaking to *Daphne Carruthers*."

Chapter VII
GENTLEMEN AND PLAYERS

"I suppose there can be no doubt about it," ventured Anthony; "you recognize the lady's voice?"

"Of course," retorted the Crown Prince, somewhat testily—still showing signs of the shock to which he had been subjected so suddenly.

"Better see what the lady has to say then," suggested Anthony decisively. "She at least will be able to clear up some of the parts that have been puzzling us. That's very apparent!"

His Royal Highness spoke a few sharp words through the telephone and then listened attentively for the lady's answer. Anthony noticed him nod repeatedly at what he heard and a sudden look of complete amazement cross his face. "Hold on, Daphne, for a moment," Anthony heard him say. "Miss Carruthers says she left Seabourne at three minutes past ten on Wednesday evening and that her train arrived at Victoria at a quarter past eleven." His voice contained a note of triumph that he made no attempt to conceal. "You will notice, Mr. Bathurst, that she had no other assignation."

"I notice that she says she hadn't," replied that gentleman, "but go on."

"She tells me that she arrived at her home in Lexham Gardens, Kensington, at twenty-five minutes to twelve. She has occupied a flat there for some time now. Yesterday evening she had been to the theatre and reached home about the same time as the previous evening. As she entered she states that she heard her telephone ringing. Before she could get into the room to answer it the ringing ceased and was not again repeated. Being very tired and attaching no particular importance to it, she didn't trouble to make inquiries, she says, but went straight to bed. Early this morning the Police called with the fantastic story (to her, of course) that Daphne Carruthers had been found murdered in a dental surgeon's operating room at Seabourne. Naturally she was able to laugh at their story and to convince them that they were at that moment actually talking to the supposedly murdered girl and that the story to which she was listening must be all wrong somewhere. They've informed the Police at this end, she says, of the dreadful mistake that has been made. She 'phoned me to find out if possible how the ghastly error could have occurred and also to allay any fears that I might have had on her behalf." He coughed. "She's coming straight down here by the first fast train."

"She can't account in any way for the mistake, then?" queried Anthony.

The Crown Prince shook his head gravely. "No—she's as much in the dark, she tells me, as the Police themselves."

"Did she tell you what time it was when the Police up the other end sent the news down here? I mean the news that the first idea was all wrong—that Daphne Carruthers was alive and that the murdered girl had still to be identified."

"'Early this morning,' was the phrase she used."

"H'm!" rejoined Anthony. "I wonder why—how about your theory of the blackmailer—it won't quite answer now, will it?" He broke off abruptly as this new aspect of the case came home to him.

His Royal Highness shook his head again. "It won't—what shall we do?"

"Do you still want me to take the case?"

"Yes, please, if you will. I am far from satisfied and I shan't feel easy in my mind till it is all cleared up." He looked at Anthony. "Why has Miss Carruthers' name been dragged into the case? Tell me that. For some wicked and malicious reason, doubtless. Yes, Mr. Bathurst, I do want you to take the case . . . if for nothing else to protect my interests."

"In that case, then," said Anthony, "our best plan will be to await Miss Carruthers' arrival."

The fast train that Miss Daphne Carruthers had indicated in her telephone message did not fail either its reputation or its description and within an hour and a half she was inquiring from the before-mentioned gentleman of faultless attire and magnificent bearing who graced the entrance to the "Cassandra," if she could be escorted to Suite 17.

"It was extremely kind of you to meet me at the station," she exclaimed, turning charmingly and impulsively to the dignified man that accompanied her. "I expect you had the biggest shock of your life this morning—when you heard the news—didn't you?"

Bannister smiled gravely as the escort announced them. "I certainly sat up and took notice—and I'm still attempting to puzzle things out. Sir Austin Kemble—the Chief Commissioner—he's had a 'pow-wow' with me early this morning—and taking into account the particular details that he arranged—well—your 'resurrection' fairly mystifies me."

The Crown Prince himself opened the door that admitted them, with a gesture that bordered on the imperious. He raised his eyes inquiringly as he observed the lady's companion. "This gentleman?" he queried.

Daphne was quick to bridge the situation with an immediate introduction. "Is the celebrated Chief-Inspector Bannister of Scotland Yard," she declared.

"He is the gentleman in charge of this terrible business and when he heard that I wasn't dead—he arranged for me to come down to Seabourne again and to meet me at the station. I know it sounds awfully mixed up," she concluded with a little *moue*, "but you know what I mean."

Bannister bowed, it was a situation in which he felt adequately "at home." "Sir Austin Kemble 'phoned me this morning, Your Royal Highness, as I expect you are well aware. Therefore I was not surprised when Miss Carruthers expressed her desire to have an interview with you before coming along to the Police Station with me."

The Crown Prince looked unhappy and a trifle apprehensive.

"Strangely enough," proceeded Bannister, "I've also been, as it were, roped into the case. I've been staying here—at the 'Cassandra' for over a week—Your Highness possibly—" His eyes for the first time travelled the length of the room and caught sight of the tall figure reclining negligently in the armchair. His Royal Highness, eagerly seizing any favourable opportunity to closure any discussion upon his own personal sojourn at the "Cassandra," produced Mr. Bathurst from the depths of the chair and introduced him, regardless of etiquette. It was easy for an onlooker to observe that he found more favour in Daphne's sight than in that of the famous detective. It was obvious that Richard Bannister, acclaimed hero of a hundred difficult cases, required no assistance from Mr. Anthony Bathurst to carry the hundred and first to a triumphant conclusion. Sensing an inimical atmosphere, Anthony grinned at him cheerfully. He had had experience of this kind of thing before—although never from one placed quite so high in the Police service.

"I cannot describe the extent of my relief, my dear Daphne," exclaimed the Crown Prince, "to know that you are alive—after so many hours of such deep sorrow—I am unable—"

"Cut it out, Alexis," said the young lady abruptly; "these gentlemen aren't interested in your feelings—let's get to work. From what Mr. Bannister has told me in the car on our way down from the railway station—the poor girl that's been murdered went to the 'Lauderdale Hotel' and booked accommodation there in my name. I want to find out why—and quickly—at that."

Anthony threw her an approving glance. She seemed eminently business-like; but the Crown Prince made no appreciable attempt to emerge from the state of comparative subjection into which Miss Carruthers' opening cold douche had sent him. He sat there the picture of offended dignity.

"I entirely agree," declared Bannister. "First of all—I want you to accompany me to Seabourne Police Station—doubtless you gentlemen would like to come too."

"I'm sure you'll pardon me, Mr. Bannister," ventured Anthony. "Have you taken any further steps this morning to identify the dead girl—since you heard that Miss Carruthers was alive—I mean?"

"That will be my next step," was the reply. "I considered the matter and decided to wait till I'd seen Miss Carruthers and heard if she could throw any light on the mystery. I thought that would be my best course."

"Thanks—yes—I see your point." Anthony followed the three people into the big car that was waiting. Bannister took the wheel and threaded his way through the thronged streets of the town.

"It will be in the nature of an education for me," murmured Bathurst in his most engaging of tones, "to watch your methods, Inspector. As an amateur, I have long looked up to you, if I may use the phrase, as perhaps our premier crime expert. I've always regarded your handling of the affair of the murder at 'Mawneys Crossing' as little short of masterly. The way in which you were able to connect the blood shed by the raven—" He paused as he saw "Dandy Dick's" eyes glisten at this homage to his vanity.

"That was a nasty case," said Bannister, "and I don't think I unduly flatter myself when I say that I certainly did handle it well."

"The peculiar part of the present case," went on Anthony—his eyes twinkling, unobserved by the Inspector—"up to now—that is—is this apparent 'masquerade' on the dead girl's part."

"H'm," rejoined Bannister, non-committally.

"How did it happen?" queried Anthony.

The detective glared at a pedestrian that ambled across the road in the track of the fast-travelling car and sounded the horn twice before replying to the question. "The 'Lauderdale' people brought us the news last night—very late. The reception-clerk there—name of John Martin—took a telephone message on Wednesday evening—the evening before the actual murder—mind you—from a lady who gave the name of Daphne Carruthers. She booked a room at the hotel and told him, I understand, that she would arrive some time on the following day. At half-past one yesterday—less than an hour, mark you, before the murder—the lady concerned arrived at the 'Lauderdale.' She referred to the booking of the previous evening—as might have been expected—gave Martin her suit-case to send up to her room and told him she had an important call to make but would return in about an hour. The suit-case was all in order, apparently, and labelled just as Martin expected it to be—'Miss Daphne Carruthers—11, Lexham Gardens, Kensington.' When she failed to return—he connected her, after a time, with the inquiries that Sergeant Godfrey had caused to be made immediately after the discovery of the body. He was right—his fears were only too well founded—when we showed the body to him—he identified it—unhesitatingly—as the girl of the hotel incident. There you have the reason why we described the dead girl as we did. I don't see that we could have done anything else."

Anthony drew thoughtfully at his cigarette. "How did she come to the hotel—by car?"

"Yes," replied Bannister, "and drove away by car. What is more—Martin says—she herself was driving. The car was otherwise unoccupied."

"Should be a comparatively simple matter to trace the car," ventured Anthony.

Bannister pushed out his lower lip as he swung round the corner of the road in which was situated the Seabourne Police Station.

"It ought to be, but unfortunately Martin can't say what make of car it was, neither can he remember the number. In all probability, he never saw that. I've had investigations going on all day, trying to trace any car that's been abandoned anywhere round about, but up to the present no news of anything has come through. Here we are. Jump out."

The Crown Prince and Daphne fell in behind them.

"Come through into the private room," said Bannister.

The constable on duty in the charge-room saluted promptly as they passed through.

"Is Sergeant Godfrey in?" demanded Bannister, authoritatively.

"Yes, sir."

"Tell him I want him—at once."

The constable disappeared even more promptly than he had saluted, to return in a few moments with the Sergeant behind him.

"Any more news, Godfrey?"

"No, sir—I should think the news first thing this morning was sufficient," he added—rather lugubriously.

"I want the dead girl's suit-case," said Bannister, briskly.

"You took it—!"

"It's in that cupboard," rapped Bannister indicating the cupboard with a gesture of the forefinger. "I put it there last night—you've got the keys."

Godfrey nodded and quickly unlocked the cupboard door. Bannister pulled out the case and stood it upright on the table. As has been previously stated, it resembled hundreds of others, which very obvious fact made Anthony shake his head with a feeling of misgiving. But not so—Daphne Carruthers. That lady left the Crown Prince's side and excitedly pulled the two tie-on labels down to the level of her vision. Her eyes flashed with her excitement. *"They're my labels,"* she cried, *"in my handwriting."* She fished impetuously in her vanity-bag and produced a key. It fitted. The catches clicked and the case swung open as she pulled at it. "And they're my clothes inside," she cried in increased amazement. "What on earth is the meaning of this? She's taken all my things as well as my name." Her eyes were wide-opened and wondering, as she stood there waiting for one of them to answer. Nobody obliged her—but Mr. Bathurst noticed that the Crown Prince was trembling with excitement; the ash of his cigarette was shaken to the floor.

Chapter VIII
DAPHNE DRAWS UP THE BLINDS

HE GAZED at her—amazed and incredulous—fascinated at the sudden and unexpected turn that she had given to the march of events. But his emotion at the news was such that he sought for and sank weakly into a convenient chair. Anthony then turned his attention to Bannister and to Sergeant Godfrey. Bannister's eyes were gleaming with a strange mixture of curiosity and satisfaction. Here was a witness at last upon whose evidence he felt that he could thoroughly rely.

"This is most extraordinarily interesting, Miss Carruthers. Please explain how your luggage comes to be in the dead girl's possession and in Room 66 at the 'Lauderdale' Hotel?"

Daphne turned upon her questioner two round eyes of beautiful astonishment. "I should very much like to be in a position to do so," she exclaimed. "I am just as eager to know as you yourself are. Those two questions are just the two that I can't answer," she supplemented.

"When was this suit-case last in your possession?" demanded Bannister.

"On Wednesday evening," she replied, "when I was on the point of leaving the 'Cassandra.' I left the hotel about twenty minutes to ten in order to catch the ten-three from the station. But as I had a handbag and two novels to carry, I left my suit-case to be forwarded to my home address. I labelled it—just as you see it now—and left appropriate instructions at the 'Cassandra.' It's my usual practice if I'm travelling alone—I just hate to be lumbered up with heaps of things to carry."

"Where did you last actually *see* it?" queried Bannister with a *soupçon* of impatience.

Daphne puckered her brows. "One of the hotel porters took it downstairs for me—I tipped him—I didn't see it again after he'd taken it from my room."

"Pardon me a moment, Inspector," intervened Anthony. "I should like to ask Miss Carruthers a question. Are the labels as you see them now tied in exactly the same manner and in exactly the same positions as you yourself tied and placed them?"

"Absolutely," replied the lady, "one at each end of the handle."

"There's only one explanation that will fit the case," broke in Alexis of Clorania, hoarsely. "The suit-case was stolen by this other girl—whoever she is—for some malicious motive that hasn't yet been fathomed—it's all part of the same dark plot—commencing with the—" He caught a warning glance from Anthony and summarily stopped.

Bannister broke in sharply. "I beg to differ. There's more than one possible explanation, Your Royal Highness, come to that. Besides the possibility of the suit-case having been stolen by the dead lady—there's also the rather likely possibility of an exchange of luggage having been effected *unintentionally.* We shall have to find out what the procedure is with regard to luggage at the 'Cassandra.' The exchange may even have taken place in some way at Seabourne Station and it may have been quite an innocent one."

"The dead girl came by car, Inspector," ventured Anthony.

"True—but from where? She may have met the car at the station—asked a porter there to put her suit-case in for her—and the man may have picked up Miss Carruthers' by mistake—waiting on the platform somewhere, ready to be despatched to town."

Bannister paused—then went on again directly. "Very likely the dead girl's suit-case is still kicking its heels on the platform at Seabourne, for all we know to the contrary."

"There is yet another likely possibility it seems to me," said Anthony, quietly.

"What's that, Mr. Bathurst?"

"That the suit-case *was stolen by the murderer.*"

Bannister contemplated the suggestion for a moment or two. "For what reason?"

"It's impossible to say for the moment," replied Anthony, "but you must admit that it's a distinct possibility."

He turned to Daphne Carruthers. "How many people knew you were staying at Seabourne?" he queried.

The lady blushed rather charmingly. "Two only," she answered, "a very special girl-friend—Lois Travers—and—" She hesitated and looked round the company.

Bannister noticed her hesitation. "Yes?" he interrogated, "and?"

"The Crown Prince here," she answered with a certain amount of dismay.

"I see." Bannister made an understanding motion with his head and Sergeant Godfrey relaxed his attitude of tension for the moment and permitted himself the luxury of a fugitive smile. "This young lady you mentioned—Miss Travers—I presume that I can regard her as a *confidante* of yours—yes?"

Daphne nodded. "Yes—she has my complete confidence. It was she who recommended the 'Cassandra' to me originally—when I came to Seabourne last year. Her fiancé stays here quite a lot, you see."

"Oh," muttered Bannister, "that's rather interesting—what's his name?"

"Captain Willoughby."

"Really," replied the Inspector, with a smile, "that fact, perhaps, is still more interesting—he's by way of being an acquaintance of mine."

"You've met him here, I take it, Inspector?" interjected Anthony.

"I have that," answered Bannister with a set expression. "I was actually in conversation with him when Godfrey here 'barged in' and lugged me from a restful holiday into this."

Anthony was beginning to realize that he was confronted with a curious combination of circumstances. The obstinate contention of the Crown Prince concerning the implication of the murderer with the blackmailer might not be so fantastic after all. Here was a certain Captain Willoughby already fitting into the pieces of the puzzle at both ends. He had taken the photograph of Daphne and her Royal admirer during the year before and now he cropped up again in the same place at the very time coincident with the murder. Mr. Bathurst came to the conclusion that the matter would have to receive definite attention.

"Give me the address of this Miss Travers, will you?" demanded Bannister.

"Forty-four, Crowborough Mansions, Maida Vale."

Anthony glanced across at the Crown Prince who was showing decided signs of discomfort at the turn the investigation had taken. Evidently he could see by now—almost as clearly as Mr. Bathurst did—that it was going to be extremely difficult, to say nothing of being, perhaps, extraordinarily indiscreet and risky to keep Bannister and Godfrey completely ignorant of the matter of the blackmailing letters. This last love-escapade of Alexis had certainly proved to be most unfortunate for him! He was inclined to rail at Fate for the maliciously-mischievous trick that she had played him. After all, look at it any way you like—he was a Royal personage—heir to a throne—not by any means an ordinary person—he should have been immune from trouble of this kind—Fate should have recognized—

Bannister broke in upon his rebellious musings. He turned sharply towards Godfrey and the statement and question he put to him were sufficiently startling to rouse even Anthony himself to an acuter alertness. As the Inspector spoke Anthony recognized that here was a Police-Officer of imagination far beyond the ordinary. Of course he had been aware all the time of Bannister's almost International reputation. But Mr. Bathurst it must be observed was not a slavish believer in the value of mere reputations. He knew the strength of the hand that Dame Fortune frequently played towards their establishment. In emphasis of this point he had been known to quote more than once, "Reputations are what people think of us—character is what God and His Angels know of us." Bannister's question proved to him conclusively that whatever qualities might be lacking in the Inspector's composition—imagination was not one of them.

"Godfrey," rapped Bannister, "you'll find that the dead girl in the mortuary yonder is Lois Travers—what do you say to my idea—eh?"

The audacity of the theory appeared to take Godfrey's breath away for he was some appreciable time before he replied.

"Can't say, sir." He shook his head. "I think I see the direction your thoughts are taking, but—"

He shook his head again—doubtfully.

The idea struck Anthony as containing great possibilities. He rose from the chair in which he had been seated. "It's certainly worth testing, Inspector," he exclaimed. He jerked his head almost imperceptibly towards Miss Carruthers. Bannister caught his meaning.

"Do you feel that you could submit to the ordeal of viewing the body, Miss Carruthers?" he asked.

The lady thus addressed shuddered. "Please don't ask me to do that," she replied—white to the lips. "But I can't believe it's Lois. It's terrible to think that—" She stopped as a sudden thought appeared to strike her. "Ask Captain Willoughby to look," she exclaimed. "He's almost certain to be at the 'Cassandra'—'phone from here."

"That's certainly a good idea," said Bannister grimly. "Captain Willoughby—the lady's fiancé—will be able to settle the point at once. Get on to the 'Cassandra,' Godfrey, and tell him we want him down here at once, will you? Wrap it up a bit. Break it to him gently."

Godfrey went out, to return in a matter of a few moments.

"Did you get him?"

Godfrey nodded. "He's coming straight down here."

"How did he take it?" demanded Bannister.

"Seemed very upset at the possibility—naturally—I only hinted at it, too."

The Crown Prince twirled the ends of his moustache. "After all, Inspector," he contributed, "say what you like—you've nothing really tangible towards this theory of yours. You may be alarming Captain Willoughby needlessly—it seems to me—"

Bannister interrupted him. "Outside yourself, sir, Miss Travers was the only person who knew anything of Miss Carruthers' whereabouts. Now this dead girl knew something about Miss Carruthers—that's conclusive to my mind—*she's actually in possession of her suit-case*. That's one thing, at all events, upon which I can base a theory."

Anthony found himself partly in agreement with Bannister's contention. The Crown Prince, however, seemed very much inclined to reject it; Daphne Carruthers herself could visualize only the horror of the idea.

"At any rate," continued Bannister inexorably, "we shan't have to wait very long to know for certain. Then we shall see who's right. Captain Willoughby should be here at any minute, now." He glanced at his watch.

"It seems a very remarkable thing to me, Inspector," declared Anthony, "that this dead girl had nothing *with* her or *on* her by which she could be identified. For instance—a purse—where was her money—where was her money, for instance, with which she intended to pay Branston, the dentist, for the extraction that she had just had?"

"Exactly what appealed to me, Mr. Bathurst. What you're asking me was one of the first questions that I asked Godfrey. She only possessed what she stood up in. Let us say, rather, what she sat down in, plus a hat and a pair of gloves."

The lines of his mouth relaxed a little as he uttered this grim pleasantry.

"Which makes it pretty obvious to me then," exclaimed Anthony, "that she was not *meant* to be identified—for as long a period as possible. Things that would have identified her were taken from her—there's not a doubt about it—the murderer—or murderers—there may have been two of them for all we know—wanted *time* to do something during this period of non-identification—they're doing it now—at this minute—very possibly—the question is 'what'?" He paced the small room anxiously—his face betraying his excitement. "That's our problem, Inspector," he concluded turning to Bannister.

The latter smiled at Bathurst's keenness. "Perhaps," he rejoined. "For the moment I would rather concentrate on my own little idea and stick to that. You're inclined, if you'll allow me to say so, Mr. Bathurst, to *imagine* 'data.' I prefer to work upon the 'data' that lie in front of me. It's usually a more profitable proposition, I find." He glanced at the Crown Prince and thence to Daphne Carruthers and Anthony read unmistakably the marks of approval in their eyes. Before he could reply to Bannister's sally—a smart young constable entered and announced Captain Willoughby. Mr. Bathurst eyed the newcomer with more than ordinary interest. He saw a tall, well-groomed man who was plainly not looking at his best. His finely-cut features, beautifully even teeth and glossy raven hair gave him a patrician appearance that was marred on this particular morning by the pallor and anxiety of his face.

"Chief-Inspector Bannister?" he inquired—then as his eyes caught sight of the Crown Prince of Clorania and Miss Carruthers, his apprehension seemed to increase. "Good morning"—he bowed to the two whom he knew.

"Good morning," said Bannister. "Sergeant Godfrey has told you what I want of you—hasn't he?"

Willoughby nodded—then broke in quickly and impetuously. "I feel certain you're on the wrong track, Inspector," he urged. "Miss Travers, my fiancée, is miles away from Seabourne—"

"We shall see," said Bannister interrupting him. "For your sake—I sincerely hope you're right—naturally—but personally—I'm not so sure! Come this way." He conducted them across the stone-flagged station-yard to the small building in the corner that served Seabourne as a mortuary. Anthony and Sergeant Godfrey followed—separated from Bannister by Captain Willoughby, his fingers working nervously round his silver-knobbed stick. The Crown Prince and Daphne brought up the rear—the lady apparently having to some extent overcome her reluctance. The Inspector gave orders for the door of the mortuary to be unlocked and they passed in—the Crown Prince and his lady still last. Captain Willoughby braced his well-knit shoulders and walked to the white slab bare-headed—hat in hand. For one nerve-shattering second his shoulders remained braced. Then the rigid tension of his body relaxed.

"No—Inspector," he said very quietly—his face ashen-pale—"this is not Miss Travers. This lady is a complete stranger to me."

Bannister threw him a shrewd and challenging glance. "Then I'm glad and sorry," he declared. "Sorry, of course, to have troubled you so needlessly."

Willoughby bowed his thanks and as the light caught his face Anthony was able to discern the extent to which the ordeal had tried him. Then he noticed with surprise that the Crown Prince and Miss Carruthers had approached the white slab more closely. Daphne's eyes were agleam with a mingled horror and excitement. "That girl, Inspector," she cried uncontrollably, "I *can* identify her—I know her well—it's Sheila Delaney!!!"

Chapter IX
MR. BATHURST LOOKS AT A PAIR OF SHOES—AND A LUGGAGE-WAGON

Bannister's eyes blazed! Whatever chagrin he may have felt at the failure of the theory that he had put forward was momentary. It almost instantly gave place to the excitement of the chase. The hunt was up!

"Sheila who?" he exclaimed.

"Sheila Delaney," replied Daphne. "I—"

"How do you come to know her?" demanded Bannister peremptorily. "Was she a friend of yours?"

Daphne shook her head—her own excitement had passed for the time being and she was now feeling quite calm—stunned almost with the horror that she had been the first to unveil properly.

"Hardly a friend," she replied. "Although I knew her very well. She was a very great friend of my late uncle—Major Desmond Carruthers. I expect you have heard of him—he died in March of last year—he was killed in a motoring accident. He was Chief Constable of Westhamptonshire." She looked at Bannister inquiringly.

Anthony was stung into the keenest attention. Westhamptonshire! Another coincidence or another link in the chain—which? He caught the Crown Prince's eye and instantly formed the opinion that the mention of Westhamptonshire had increased that gentleman's agitation. But Bannister was pressing eagerly for information.

"I remember the name, I think. Although I never connected you with him. Can you give me her home address?"

"Oh yes," replied Miss Carruthers simply. "Rest Harrow, Tranfield, near Westhampton."

Mr. Bathurst's grey eyes flashed back to the Crown Prince. Westhampton and now Tranfield—the two places of the postmarks on the Crown Prince's letters! Alexis had apparently appreciated the point just as quickly as Mr. Bathurst himself—

his fingers were toying nervously with the ends of his bellicose moustache. Bannister noted the address in his book.

"Why was this young lady in Seabourne, Miss Carruthers?" he inquired. "Any idea?"

Daphne's answer was a negative. "None whatever, Inspector. I haven't set eyes on her for months."

"What are her people?"

"Her father and mother are dead. Her father was Colonel Delaney of the Westhampton Regiment. She lives with a kind of family retainer—her old nurse, I think." She knitted her brows.

"Shall have to get into touch with her," muttered Bannister. "Do you happen to remember her name?"

Daphne pondered, the tip of her forefinger pressed to her dainty lips. "Carr, I think," she answered after a moment or two, "but Sheila always referred to her by a nickname or something—now what was it?—I can remember hearing Uncle Desmond use it when he mentioned her." She screwed up her eyes—as people sometimes do when attempting to remember something particularly elusive. "No," she concluded regretfully, "I can't remember what it was."

The Crown Prince looked across at Anthony in such a meaning way that that gentleman formed the opinion that he wished to communicate something to him. Mr. Bathurst judged that the existing conditions might be far from favourable for an interchange of the Royal confidences—he therefore rather adroitly avoided the Royal eye. Whatever it was it could wait and, which was more, would probably be all the better for keeping. Bannister turned to Sergeant Godfrey as they left the building.

"Get through to the Westhampton police as quickly as possible. Tell them as much as you consider expedient—tell them I hope to be up there with them by tea-time this evening."

Godfrey vanished—a load was taken from his mind—Bannister was taking hold! That to him meant considerable relief. Anthony approached the Inspector.

"I should be tremendously obliged, Inspector," he spoke very quietly, "if I could have a glance at the clothes this poor girl was wearing."

"Don't think you'll learn much from them," rejoined Bannister. He obtained them and tossed them over to Anthony. The latter turned them over and picked up the hat. "The only name to be found is inside the hat—you'll see it if you look."

But Mr. Bathurst appeared to be more concerned with the external. He looked carefully at the brim—turned down as it was all the way round—Bannister watching with some amusement. Anthony looked away quickly and caught his critical eye. He gave Bannister smile for smile; then picked up the dead girl's brown shoes. He ran his finger-tips across their glossy surface. First across the right shoe—then across the left. He looked at his fingers.

"Well?" queried his audience, "Cherry Blossom or Kiwi?"

Mr. Bathurst ignored the interruption. He could afford to—he had managed to establish his first point. He looked at the soles of the two "semi-brogues." With the help of his magnifying-glass he scrutinized the tops of the two shoes and the sides of the two soles with the most meticulous care.

"There's one thing I can tell you, Inspector," he said, as he put back his glass in his pocket, "this lady had travelled some considerable distance by car—she had driven it, I should say, all the way from her home at Tranfield."

"We know she came by car," returned Bannister. "The 'Lauderdale' people—"

"With all deference, Inspector—we didn't know *how far* she had come in that car. She might have come by train as you yourself suggested and picked up the car here in Seabourne. However, she didn't. Look at the brim of this hat—it is distinctly dusty—and if you look at the dust very carefully, you will see that it is not all quite the same shade of colour. Now the curtains will protect you on a comparatively short journey, but over a distance of a hundred miles or so—a car-driver usually picks up *some* patches of dust. Much more than a person travelling by train, for instance. The different shades of dust suggest to me for example, two separate counties many miles apart. Let us say, just for example, Westhamptonshire and Marlshire. Now look at the surface of these shoes. A person who had walked even a small part of that distance would have much dustier shoes than these!" He held them out to Bannister who nodded his acceptance of Mr. Bathurst's theory.

"No doubt you're right," he conceded.

Anthony continued his explanation, warming to his work. "Now there are certain parts of the soles of these two shoes that show unmistakable signs of friction—of rubbing. I am pretty certain that Miss Delaney had driven a considerable distance in that car when she drove up to the 'Lauderdale' Hotel."

"Yes—I think you're right. One of the questions we have to face is the tracing of that car."

He turned to address the Crown Prince and Miss Carruthers. "I won't detain you any longer, Your Royal Highness, if you'd care to go. If I want you again I'll see you at the 'Cassandra'—I shall be calling there again before leaving for Tranfield." He thought for a moment. "Get Godfrey to drive you up and tell him to come back here for Mr. Bathurst and me."

The Crown Prince accepted the dismissal with evident pleasure.

"Seemed very sure the dead girl *wasn't* Miss Travers, didn't he?" contributed Bannister meaningly—"did you notice that?"

"I did—on the other hand so did Captain Willoughby—so there might be nothing in that—it's an extraordinary case altogether—it's difficult to know where to begin."

Bannister put the dead girl's clothing back in the cupboard from where he had taken it and carefully locked the door. "If we walk up to the 'Cassandra' we shall meet Godfrey in the car on the way back here. Fit?"

Anthony acquiesced.

He couldn't resist a strong feeling that Bannister's recent allusion to the Crown Prince's attitude towards what he himself had termed the "Lois Travers theory" was in the nature of a warning to him. Bannister knew from Sir Austin Kemble that he represented the interests of the heir to the throne of Clorania—so that Anthony was disposed to think that the Inspector had given him an initial hint as it were that the Law is no respecter of persons—"or personages." They soon spotted Sergeant Godfrey with the car and were quickly back in the "Cassandra." Bannister immediately sent for the manager.

"I want some information," he said, when the latter appeared, "concerning your procedure with regard to the transport of visitors' luggage."

"Certainly, Inspector. What is it you wish to know?"

"I want to know exactly what occurs when luggage is left here to be forwarded to a visitor's home. I want full details of the procedure."

"I'll send for the head porter. He will tell you." The manager despatched a messenger to find the man required. In a few minutes he stood before them. "This gentleman wishes to ask you some questions about luggage-transport," said the manager; "tell him all he wants to know."

"Let me take an actual example," illustrated Bannister. "Suppose when I leave to-morrow, I leave my cabin-trunk behind in my room to be forwarded to my home. The trunk in question we will assume to be labelled properly and correctly addressed—understand?" The porter nodded. "Well," proceeded the Inspector, "tell me exactly what happens after that."

"The trunk would be brought down here, sir, and placed on the luggage-wagon. From there, I should superintend its removal to our own hotel motor-lorry which would convey it to the station. The driver of the lorry sees it on to the platform."

"H'm," said Bannister; "how long usually elapses between the trunks going on to the wagon and being put on the lorry?"

"That depends, sir," said the porter, pushing his cap back from his forehead, "and it varies, too. Sometimes, a matter of a few minutes, sometimes in the afternoon, perhaps, the luggage might stand on the wagon down here for a couple of hours."

"As it might on the platform, too," declared Bannister. He turned sharply to Sergeant Godfrey. "You say there's nothing been found on the platform that appears to have been substituted for Miss Carruthers' case?"

"Nothing, Inspector."

"Suppose we have a glance at this luggage-wagon, Inspector," ventured Anthony. "I suppose it's on duty to-day, isn't it, porter?"

"It is, sir."

"Very well, Mr. Bathurst, I'm perfectly agreeable." They trooped along the corridor.

"There's the wagon," pointed out the porter, "standing there by the door. We load the lorry up from here."

Bannister and Godfrey and Anthony walked up to it.

"Easily accessible from the street," demonstrated the last-named with a motion of the hand.

"Too easily," agreed the Inspector.

"Tell me," said Anthony to the porter, "did you see this wagon first thing on Thursday morning?"

"Yes, sir."

"Was there any luggage on it?"

"It was empty."

The Inspector dismissed the porter curtly and thanked the manager for his assistance.

"Anybody intending the changing of those cases or alternatively the stealing of Miss Carruthers' suit-case—had ample opportunity both here and at the station. All the same—as I said before to the Crown Prince—we may eventually discover that it's the result of a pure accident."

He turned smartly on his heel.

"It's not an accident, Inspector," declared Anthony.

"Look at the accumulative force of evidence that we have already managed to collect. Not only is Miss Delaney's suit-case or trunk missing—and it's reasonable to suppose that she had something of the kind with her—but also her purse and the motor-car itself, which brought her. The idea is obvious. She was to remain *unrecognized*; and from the murderer's point of view, the longer that situation remained in force the better. There's no possible doubt about it."

"You're very confident, Mr. Bathurst," smiled Bannister; "but I shouldn't be overwhelmingly surprised if you're right." He looked at his watch.

"My next move is 'Tranfield,'" he announced.

"And if you've no objection, Inspector," remarked Anthony, "I'll accompany you."

Bannister was on the point of replying when he remembered his telephone conversation with Sir Austin Kemble.

"Please yourself," he said a trifle coolly. "I'll meet you on the platform at Seabourne in an hour's time." Anthony waved his assent as Bannister left the hotel; then turned to seek the Crown Prince and Miss Carruthers. They had returned to the Crown Prince's suite, he was informed. On his way to the apartment he passed Captain Willoughby carrying a suit-case.

Chapter X
A ROOM IS RANSACKED AT "REST HARROW"

"A GREAT DEAL of my success in cases that have seemed to be at first sight, both intricate and baffling," remarked Bannister as the train ran through Bletchley, "has been due to my appreciation of the value of care allied to imagination. Apply the maximum of the one to the maximum of the other; and when you get the combined *maxima* judiciously concentrated upon the problem in hand, they should eventually yield a minimum of trouble." He removed his horn-rimmed glasses—wiped them studiously—and replaced them. "I've worked on those lines ever since I can remember," he continued, "and I've never had any reason to alter my plan of campaign."

Anthony took the offered cigarette from the Inspector's heavy silver case and lit up.

"A thoroughly sound plan, too," he concurred.

Bannister elaborated his point. "Care and finely-controlled imagination should take most men as high as they can reasonably wish to rise—they are two admirable servants. Now in this present case," proceeded Bannister, "all efforts to trace Miss Delaney's car have failed—to all intents and purposes it might have been spirited away—it's not been abandoned on the highway anywhere that we can find. Similarly with her luggage." He took a cigarette for himself. "Care then having failed to produce me anything—I shall have to give flight to imagination."

"Go on," said Anthony; "I'm most interested."

"I'm coming to Tranfield in the hope that something I may happen to pick up here will stimulate my imagination and eventually supply me with the answer to this riddle that has been set me. By the way, Mr. Bathurst, we change at Westhampton for Tranfield. It lies on the branch line to Easton Favell—I expect we shall find one train on it every six hours or thereabouts."

Bannister was wrong in his prophecy. They discovered upon arrival at Westhampton that trains to Tranfield and Easton Favell were scheduled to run at regular intervals of twenty minutes. The station-master at the little station of Tranfield was delighted to direct them to "Rest Harrow."

"It's Miss Delaney's place you're wanting," he announced. "You've a walk of about eight minutes. Go down the hill that leads from the station and you'll come to a field on the left that belongs to Farmer Peasland. Cut across by the footpath—you can't miss seeing it—go over a stile and then through a swing gate. That will bring you to the road running to Easton Favell. 'Rest Harrow' is about one hundred and fifty yards down on the right."

Ten minutes' walk brought them to it. Anthony immediately placed it as one of the most charming bungalows he had ever seen. It nestled back from the road with a kind of old-world shyness that did much to enhance its appeal. The garden in front was a mass of varied bloom and colour and the air was heavy with the scent of its many flowers. As they made their objective a man who had been standing fifty yards or so further up the road came towards them.

"Inspector Bannister?" he inquired with an interrogative glance.

"Quite right," said Bannister. "You got my message, then?"

The newcomer nodded. "I'm Sergeant Ross," he added, introducing himself. "I've been waiting for you here as instructed."

"Very good," said Bannister. "I'm sorry to say, Sergeant, that Miss Delaney—the lady who lived here, I believe—has been murdered in Seabourne."

Ross whistled. "We guessed as much from your message," he exclaimed. "You're going inside I take it?"

Bannister's reply was to ring the bell at the front entrance. Anthony heard it peal through the building but could hear no step in answer to it.

Bannister turned to Ross. "I understood that Miss Delaney lived here with another lady, a companion or something. Is that so?"

"So I believe," returned Ross.

"Not in, that's evident," retorted the Inspector.

Anthony strolled round the right-hand side of the bungalow to the back. Then he called to the others.

"We ought to be able to get in this way," he said.

Bannister broke a pane of glass, pushed his hand through and lifted up the catch of the casement window. A few moments saw them inside. There were no signs of very recent occupation showing in the kitchen-scullery in which they stood. Everything was tidy and orderly. Bannister gave it a sweeping glance.

"Looks to me as though the other lady's away," he remarked. "Let's get along to the other rooms."

On the left lay the dining-room and the lounge. On the right were three bedrooms. Suddenly Bannister gave a sharp exclamation and walked to the front door. From the mat he picked a postcard. "That explains this other woman's absence," he said to Anthony as he tossed it over to him.

Anthony read it. It was a picture postcard of the seaside-view variety. The view was of Budleigh Salterton. Its message was brief. "4, Rolle Cottages, Otterton. July 3rd. Dear Miss Sheila, I am having a lovely time and it's so nice to be home again. The weather is beautiful—I only hope it will continue so for you. Much love from 'Pinkie.'"

"One thing—you've got her address, Inspector," remarked Anthony.

"I have that," replied Bannister with a touch of tolerant cynicism. "And I'm afraid she's going to be the second person to have her holiday rather ruthlessly disturbed."

"Evidently the companion went away first, and Miss Delaney went down to Seabourne afterwards."

"Intended staying there, too, Mr. Bathurst. The clerk at the 'Lauderdale' stated that she booked her room for a fortnight. This card to a certain extent confirms his statement. 'I hope it will continue so for you'; the sentence certainly implies that Miss Delaney intended being away for some time."

Anthony assented.

"What about having a look over the rooms?" suggested Ross.

"That's what I'm here for," returned Bannister grimly.

The doors of the respective rooms seemed to be locked; with the respective keys left in the locks. The Inspector turned the key in the door of the dining-room and went in. Like the previous room that they had entered there were no signs of disorder or of very recent occupation. Everything was just as could be expected, quite consistent with the facts as Bannister and Anthony knew them. The occupants of the bungalow were away for a holiday, the rooms had been uninhabited for a matter of a few days. There was nothing whatever so far to excite comment. There were no papers, documents or letters lying about anywhere. Bannister walked to the open grate. It was beautifully clean. "Ross," he said, after two or three seconds' thought, "see if there's a refuse-bin at the back of the bungalow. Keep your eyes open for any correspondence that may have been torn up and found its way in there. Unlikely," he added—turning to Anthony—"but it's just a chance. I've known it happen before now, especially when the number in a household is small. When you've only one other person living with you—especially a person of the type that we have here—it's almost the same as living alone. There's always a certain privacy." Anthony saw the Inspector's meaning and said so. "While Ross is out there," continued Bannister, "we'll glance at the other rooms." The lounge was as reticent as the dining-room. "Nothing here," grunted the Inspector. Anthony's eyes examined it keenly and saw nothing to arrest his attention.

The two men crossed to the other side of the hall. The door of the first room was almost exactly opposite to the door of the lounge. Bannister tried the handle. The door instantly yielded. "That's funny, Mr. Bathurst." Bannister shot the remark at him. "All the other doors have been shut; the keys turned in the locks. The key was in this lock but this door is open." Anthony followed him in. "Good God!" exclaimed the Inspector; "something's been happening here." The dressing-table was without its drawers. Anthony pointed to the bed. It was easy to see what had happened. The contents of the drawers had been turned out on to the bed which presented an appearance of indescribable chaos and confusion. The drawers lay on the bed. Gloves, handkerchiefs, ribbons, silk scarves and stockings, powder, toilet requisites of all descriptions, lay scattered there in a shapeless heap. From the manner in which the various articles had been tossed aside it was evident that the drawers containing them had been subjected to a rigorous examination. "Looking for something, Mr. Bathurst! The question's 'what?'"

Anthony nodded. The case was getting trebly interesting to him. On the pillow at the head of the bed lay a lady's hand-bag and several keys thrown in all directions. For a moment he regarded them intently, while Bannister busied himself with an examination of the Wilton hair-carpet that covered the floor. Anthony picked up the hand-bag and opened it. At the first glance it seemed to be empty, but Mr. Bathurst, in examinations of this kind, always made a point of being extremely thorough. A thin card nestled in one of the corners. Anthony drew it out carefully. It was a man's visiting-card of the usual kind, "Alan Warburton, 19, Crossley Road, Westhampton." He turned it over. On the other side another address had been carefully scrawled in pencil.

"Ronald N. Branston—Dental Surgeon—Coolwater Avenue, Seabourne."

"Inspector," he called quietly. Bannister came round immediately from the far end of the bed.

"What do you make of this?" he demanded. "Look at the back!"

Bannister's eyes shone through his glasses with quick interest. "This is important, Mr. Bathurst, exceedingly important. Where did you find it?"

Anthony held up the bag in explanation. Bannister frowned; then stretched out his hand for it. Anthony walked to the bed and picked up several of the keys that had lain there.

"Have to see this gentleman," exclaimed the Inspector; he tapped the visiting-card with the back of his finger-nail. "It's just possible that we've got the threads of the affair in our hands at last."

"Yes," smiled Anthony, "just 'on the cards' as you might say. If he recommended Miss Delaney to visit the Coolwater Avenue Surgery, it could certainly be argued against him that he might have known when to find her there. But look here, Inspector," he paused—looked at the keys in his hand—then back to the hand-bag that Bannister was still holding.

"Well?" said Bannister, invitingly. Anthony smiled again. "It's like this, Inspector. Imagination is a skittish sort of filly to ride, I'm well aware. But it seems to me that the hand-bag, the visiting-card, and these keys tell us a lot." He looked quizzically at Bannister.

"I'm listening," said that gentleman with the same touch of tolerant cynicism that Mr. Bathurst had observed before. "What's the big idea?"

"Were there any signs, Inspector, when we entered 'Rest Harrow' just now, that any forced entrance had been effected?" Bannister promptly shook his head. "Well, then," proceeded Anthony, "how did the people who played high jinks in this bedroom *get in*?" He went on without waiting for Bannister to answer. "*They got in with these keys, Inspector!* And in my opinion this hand-bag containing these keys and this visiting-card, was taken from Miss Delaney at Seabourne either just before her death or just after."

Bannister rubbed his chin thoughtfully with the fingers of his left hand. "I think you're right, Mr. Bathurst. If only we knew what the devils were looking for. Get on the track of that and we shall be two-thirds of the way towards a complete solution. Yes, Ross—what is it?"

"No luck, sir, out in the garden. The dust-bin is empty. All the refuse that was here when the people went away must have been burned."

"I was afraid so," replied the Inspector. "Come and look in here!"

As Ross obeyed the behest, Anthony tried the doors of the other bedrooms. They were locked and when opened presented no appearance beyond the ordinary. He called Bannister's attention to them.

"They knew where to look, Mr. Bathurst, for what they wanted, didn't they?" said Bannister.

"I don't think, somehow, that we're dealing with ordinary thieves. There's something special about this."

"You think there was more than one then, Inspector?"

"I'm inclined to think so! There are a few traces of dried mud on the carpet—nothing to speak of—can't be sure whether they were left there by one man or two. Still, on the whole, I fancy there is more than one in it." He looked at Anthony critically. "What can this young lady have possessed of such value that these people wanted it so badly?"

Anthony considered the question. "And was its value intrinsic or extrinsic?" he added to Bannister's query. He was thinking now of such things as a photograph. The Inspector raised his eyebrows interrogatively.

"Just what are you thinking of?" he asked.

"When I spoke," rejoined Anthony, "I wasn't exactly thinking of anything in particular. Since you've pressed me, however, I'll give you an example. In some circumstances, for instance, a photograph or a bundle of letters might possess an extraordinary value."

Bannister caressed his top lip. "H'm," he commented. "I suppose there's something in what you say. But where we're handicapped so tremendously here at the moment is in the fact that there's nobody here can tell us anything about the dead girl. Until we get into touch with this 'Pinkie' person—or with the gentleman whose visiting-card we've found—we're working in the dark." He swung round on the local man. "Ross," he exclaimed sharply, "can you tell me anything personal or intimate about this Miss Delaney?"

Ross responded to the invitation with a certain amount of eagerness. "I'm a Westhampton man, although I only came to my present job a year ago," he said, "and I've known Miss Delaney ever since her father came to live in Tranfield. I've watched her grow into the beautiful young woman that she undoubtedly was. I knew her father, Colonel Delaney, well. He died while home on leave in 1917, I think it was." He knitted his brows, then continued his story. "He was drowned, if I remember rightly, up at Nillebrook Water—that's about four miles from here—and the police weren't altogether satisfied with the manner of his death. It was a most unsatisfactory business. In fact—for a considerable time, too—foul play was strongly suspected. But nothing ever came to light that properly justified their suspicions and it was brought in 'Accidental death.' I wish I could remember the details but it's eleven years ago and a lot of things have happened since then. Still, the best man for information about Colonel and Sheila Delaney is Sir Matthew Fullgarney, the Lord Lieutenant of the County. He and Major Carruthers were great pals of the Colonel, officers together, I believe, years before in the same regiment or something."

Bannister showed signs of corroboration. "That would be the Major Desmond Carruthers to whom Miss Carruthers referred this morning," he announced to Anthony. "He's dead, also, I believe. Tell me, Ross, is Miss Delaney's mother dead, too?"

"Yes, sir," replied Ross. "She survived the Colonel for some years but died, I think, about four years ago."

"Which leaves only Sir Matthew Fullgarney," soliloquized Anthony. He turned to Inspector Bannister. "Quite a chapter of fatalities, isn't it?" he suggested. "How did Major Carruthers die, Ross?"

"In a motor accident, sir, somewhere about the early part of last year."

"H'm," said Anthony, "nothing to arouse suspicion, eh?"

Ross shook his head. "Nothing that I can remember, sir."

"Perhaps you can tell me something else, Ross," remarked Bannister. "Do you know anything about a gentleman living in Westhampton—Alan Warburton by name?"

Ross nodded eagerly. "Know him well, Inspector. He's the only survivor as far as my knowledge goes, of the famous Warburtons—the big banking family. You remember the celebrated 'Mutual Bank Frauds' of about two years ago. Sir Felix Warburton was arrested and sentenced and afterwards committed suicide in his cell. He was Alan Warburton's uncle—Alan being the son of his only brother, Murray Warburton. Alan's father died when Alan was a boy. It's rather a coincidence that you should have introduced his name."

"Why?" snapped Bannister. "Where's the coincidence?"

Anthony watched Ross's face carefully and awaited his reply with much more than ordinary interest.

"Well," proceeded Ross, "what I meant exactly was this. Up to the time of the 'Mutual Bank' scandal, local gossip in Westhampton and Tranfield was inclined to couple Alan Warburton's name with Sheila Delaney's."

"Really now," said Bannister; "that's most interesting. And what happened *after* the Bank scandal?"

Ross shrugged his broad shoulders non-committally but the movement was expressive. "The lady didn't appear to be anything like so keen. At least rumour has it so."

Bannister eyed Anthony significantly. Evidently an idea was beginning to assume very definite shape within his mind. "I see," he said quietly. "The family reputation was tarnished, eh?"

"Possibly," smiled back Ross; "the Delaneys were always people to hold their heads high."

He gave Anthony the impression that he was very much more inclined to be confidential than to be reserved. But Mr. Bathurst kept quiet, he was content to let Bannister do the questioning.

"And after that?" continued Bannister, "was there another Richmond in the field? Another lover, eh?"

"I can't answer that," declared Ross. "Local gossip hasn't reached that stage yet."

"But it's quite likely, eh?" urged Bannister.

"I should imagine so, considering what a charming girl Miss Delaney was."

"H'm. What sort of a chap is this Alan Warburton, pretty steady? Or does he inherit the tendencies of Sir Felix?"

"I know nothing against him," declared Ross. "No whisper against him has ever reached me."

"How did he take the lady's change of feelings?"

"No idea. As I said just now, I'm only repeating local gossip." With that the Inspector was forced to be content.

It was obvious that the local man's knowledge was largely founded upon hearsay. Anthony realized this and turned once again to the miscellaneous heap upon the bed. He picked up a long silk scarf, with what definite object at the time he scarcely knew, when to his surprise a postcard fluttered from the folds and fell to the ground. He stooped to pick it up. It was undated and the sender had omitted to put his or her address. It ran as follows: "Dearest Sheila, If only you were here instead of those miles away! Then I should love the Spring (and you) still more. The garden is looking splendid, nearly equal to that at 'Rest Harrow.' All the flowers have made a fine show but the irides are simply wonderful." It was signed with one initial only—"X." Anthony held it out to Bannister. "Came out of this scarf," he said. "Do you think it's of any importance?"

Bannister looked at it very attentively; read the message; then attempted to decipher the postmark. Anthony looked over his shoulder. "Looks to me like Dulwich," he said.

"I think so too," said Bannister.

"It's a peculiar handwriting, Inspector," added Anthony. "You very seldom see a hand slope quite like that."

"Very peculiar indeed, Mr. Bathurst. I'll hang on to this; you never know in cases of this kind. The least thing may turn the scale."

Anthony walked to the window of the bedroom and looked out on to the front garden. He stood there for perhaps a minute. Then he turned quickly round and addressed Bannister again. "An idea has just come to me, Inspector. I should very much like to test it. What do you say?" Bannister stared. "I'm going to bring all these larger keys into the garden and find the garage. I want to have a peep inside. Come along with me." He suited the action to the words and within a few minutes swung open the garage doors. A car stood inside, a "Standard." Anthony waved his hand towards it. "There, Inspector," he exclaimed dramatically, "is the car that took Miss Delaney to Seabourne."

Bannister regarded him incredulously. "Then how the devil did it get back here?" he demanded.

"That certainly is a poser," replied Mr. Bathurst, "but we'll find the answer before we've finished. Come in and have a look at her, Inspector. I would suggest that somebody drove it back."

"Go on!" said Bannister.

Chapter XI
A NEWSPAPER AND A SECOND SUIT-CASE

"Much petrol in the tank, Inspector?"

Bannister looked. "Very little, Mr. Bathurst." Anthony bent down and took a good look at each one of the tyres. Bannister watched him.

"There's one thing," he added, "she hasn't been cleaned up lately, certainly not since the last time she was taken out. I'd bank on that!"

Anthony agreed. "Doesn't look like it, Inspector. I'll tell you though what does strike me," he went on. "What's that?" queried Bannister.

"The top and the side-curtains are up." Anthony pointed to them.

"What about it?"

"Well," remarked Anthony slowly, "there's been no rain for over a week, and the temperature has been decidedly high for several days now, hasn't it? I should have thought that anybody driving that car would have been only too glad to have kept it open. That's the point I've been considering. Of course they may have been put up after the car returned."

He paused and rubbed his forehead with the tips of his fingers. Bannister regarded him with the semblance of a grin playing round the corners of his mouth. He translated it into words. "I haven't yet accepted as final your theory that this is the identical car that Miss Delaney had at Seabourne," he reminded Anthony.

The lines of Mr. Bathurst's mouth were firmly set.

"You can take it from me that it is, Inspector," he announced with an unmistakable air of determination, "and I hope in time to be able to prove it to you."

"Perhaps you will. I shall want some convincing though. Still—even so—assuming for the moment that your idea is correct—the car after all may have been used late at night, when the air begins to feel a bit cold."

"That's perfectly true," conceded Anthony, "and there's yet another possible explanation; one which I'm disposed to think may eventually prove to be the correct one. The person that drove this car back to Tranfield from Seabourne wanted to be screened from observation as much as possible. So he or she had the side-curtains on and the top up."

"That's certainly a point, Mr. Bathurst," admitted Bannister, "I grant you I hadn't thought of that." He rubbed the ridge of his jaw with his finger-tips. "Give me a hand, Mr. Bathurst," he said, "let's get the top down, we shall be able to see things more clearly then. Mind your fingers! That's the ticket! Now get these side-curtains off."

Anthony pulled the rods from the sockets prior to opening the door of the car.

"Hallo!" exclaimed the Inspector sharply, "what's this under the seat?" Anthony watched him as he bent down to pull an object out from beneath the farther seat. It was a suit-case bearing the initials "S. D." "What do you make of this, Mr. Bathurst? The *second* suit-case we've encountered!"

Anthony smiled whimsically. "Two ladies, two suitcases, Inspector. I don't know that I'm overwhelmingly surprised to run up against this second one. If Miss Delaney intended to stay in Seabourne for any length of time as the people at the 'Lauderdale' testify—and as the postcard from Otterton indicates also—she would almost certainly carry something in the nature of a suitcase. No," he shook his head as though attempting to measure the situation thoroughly, "I'm not surprised, Inspector."

"I grant you all that," replied Bannister, "but I don't know that I expected to meet it in a motor-car at Tranfield. It's locked," he added, trying the two catches.

"You'll find the key on the bed in all probability, Inspector," cut in Anthony jerking his head in the direction of the room that they had just left. "The murderer—if it were a man—took all Miss Delaney's keys and brought them back with him from Seabourne. Nothing of hers was found in Branston's surgery, remember."

Bannister grunted thoughtfully. Anthony picked up the suit-case. "Was this case actually right underneath the seat, Inspector?" he asked.

"It was, Mr. Bathurst—why?"

"Does it suggest anything to you, Inspector?"

"Only too true! This car was pretty full up on the return journey."

Anthony regarded him curiously. "Funny thing that didn't occur to me. It's strange how people see different explanations. Two heads are better than one; you can't get away from the truth of that. No, what I was thinking was that the suit-case had been pushed under the seat to hide it."

Bannister turned slowly, his eyes narrowing. "By Jove, now that possibility certainly might mean—" he strode to the doors of the garage rapidly and decisively. Anthony's idea seemed to have given him a new and definite impetus.

"Ross," he called, peremptorily. The local Sergeant came up quickly. "Ross," went on Bannister, "get a telegram despatched at once to '4, Rolle Cottages, Otterton,'" he referred to the postcard they had found on the mat, and then turned to Anthony. "I think Miss Carruthers said the nurse's name was 'Carr,' didn't she?"

"Quite right, Inspector."

"I'll write the name and address down for you, Ross." He suited the action to the words and handed the Sergeant a slip of paper. Ross placed it carefully within the leaves of an expansive pocket-book. "Right you are, sir," he said, saluting, "I'll attend to it at once."

"I want you to," confirmed Bannister, "and when you've sent it off—you see what I've said—come back here."

Ross swung down the garden path and they heard the gate shut behind him.

"I've sent for the old companion, Mr. Bathurst—this 'Pinkie' person. If she's lived with Miss Delaney for as long as we've been informed she probably knows more about her than anybody else."

Anthony nodded in agreement. Suddenly he walked to the front of the car and looked intently at the dashboard. "The car has no speedometer," he pointed out. Then he thrust in his hand and drew out a newspaper, folded carefully. He opened it, then smiled and handed it to his companion. "Let me call your attention, Inspector, to the name and the date."

Bannister turned eagerly to the title-page. "The 'Seabourne Herald,' Thursday, July 5th. Well, I'm jiggered."

"I told you I would convince you that this car was the car that was seen in Seabourne," declared Anthony.

"Copies of that stupendous publication that is inflicted upon a long-suffering public under the title of the 'Seabourne Herald' are not likely to have been on sale in Tranfield or Westhampton for instance. I don't think the 'Seabourne Herald' circulates as far as that."

Bannister polished his glasses very thoughtfully and carefully. "You're right, Mr. Bathurst," he said after a moment or two spent in this thought-stimulating occupation. "I believe the 'Seabourne Herald' is on sale in Seabourne on Thursday mornings. But I'll tell you frankly, I'm damned if I know what to make of it. Why was the car brought back to Tranfield and then left here? Speed would surely be equally important after the search had been made here? What were they after? Again—did they succeed in finding it—whatever it was?" He looked at Anthony.

Mr. Bathurst shrugged his shoulders. "Also, Inspector," he contributed, "there's another point that I'm considering. Who is 'X'?" He knitted his brows in thought. "Tell me again," he said, "what was the exact wording of that postcard we found in the bedroom?"

The Inspector fished the card from his pocket and handed it to Mr. Bathurst. Anthony read it for the second time. "Why did Miss Delaney keep a seemingly unimportant card like that? I can only think of one reason. What do you think, Inspector?"

Bannister's reply was in the nature of a half-grimace. "There's no accounting for what women will do. With one it's a whim, with another it's just temperamental, with a third, the caprice of a moment—you can't generalize. On the other hand this particular card may have escaped destruction by a pure accident."

"That's all true, to a point," intervened Anthony, "but many things are kept for years by a woman—entirely valueless in themselves—just because they have certain definite associations. Flowers, a theatre-program, a dance-program, a letter, a postcard—because they have sentimental values. They may be relics of long-ago romances. And articles of the nature that I've just indicated are usually kept in a very private place, such as a special drawer in the bedroom."

Bannister opened the newspaper again. "I suppose there's nothing marked anywhere in the paper, is there?" He scanned the columns without success. "No," he remarked after a few moments, "I couldn't imagine the 'Seabourne Herald' publishing anything deemed worthy of marking."

"Let's look at the card again, Inspector, will you?" Bannister handed it to him again and watched him over the top of the newspaper. "The slope of this handwriting is most unusual and yet—"

"And yet what, Mr. Bathurst?"

"I can't help a strong feeling that I've seen something like it before."

"You have? Where?"

Anthony shook his head doubtfully. "Can't place it for the moment; but there's a decorative flourish about it that at times seems to strike a familiar note. It's the kind of thing that's difficult to associate—one's mind is groping as it were," he stopped and frowned, as he strove for elusive association. "It will come back to me," he asserted, confidently.

"Don't you think we often imagine that we can see resemblances between things when none really exists?" argued Bannister. "I mean this," he continued, "the existence of a general resemblance is very often mistaken for something much more particular. Don't you think so?"

"It's possible," conceded Anthony.

"There's Ross back," declared Bannister listening to the sound of approaching footsteps. "All right?" he queried.

"Everything O.K., sir," answered the Sergeant.

"Any news come through for me from Seabourne?"

"None, sir."

"I asked Sergeant Godfrey to keep me posted if anything important transpired."

"Did you expect anything?"

"I gave Godfrey instructions to try to trace the purchase of the hydrocyanic acid. Not that I think he'll succeed," he added sternly. "I'll wager my kingdom that little dose of poison was bought a good many miles from Seabourne."

Ross nodded wisely. "Something to kill a dog, if you please, chemist?" he quoted sarcastically.

Bannister grinned in satirical appreciation. "Every time!" he exclaimed. "Well, Mr. Bathurst, what's our program now?"

Anthony closed the doors of the garage and locked them again. Then he handed the keys and the postcard to Bannister. "It's getting on," he said glancing at his watch, "I think I'll stay the night in Westhampton. Can you recommend me to a hotel, Sergeant Ross?"

"The Grand should suit you, sir, just up the High Street on the right."

"I think I'll accompany you, Mr. Bathurst, if you've no objection?" put in the Inspector. "I've seen all I want here, Sergeant. Fasten the place up, and we'll get away."

"The Grand" was of the solidly-comfortable type. The dining-room to which Bannister and Anthony repaired gave promise of substantial refreshment. It was some time since either of them had tackled anything in the shape of food and the meal that the waiters placed before them proved singularly acceptable. Anthony ordered a bottle of "Pol Roger" and Bannister expanded under its inspiring influence. Four or five other tables were occupied, in most instances by a pair of people. Suddenly two young men, in morning dress, entered the room and made their way to the left-hand corner of the dining-room, to the table nearest to the fireplace and directly behind where Anthony was seated. They seated themselves and gave their order to the waiter. Shortly afterwards Anthony caught the sound of a familiar name. "Alan Warburton?" he heard. "Haven't seen him at all this journey, and I've called at one or two of his favourite haunts, too." Anthony half-turned in the direction of the speaker. He was just in time to see the man addressed lean across the table and speak in low tones. The first man paled, lifted his hand and then stopped suddenly short, his glass half-raised to his lips. "Good God!" he gasped. "Never! Daphne Carruthers?! That's a Westhampton name."

Chapter XII
MR. BATHURST LISTENS TO A LITTLE LOCAL GOSSIP

ANTHONY MOTIONED Bannister to lean over the table in his direction. Bannister needed no second bidding. He had noticed that Mr. Bathurst had displayed a more than ordinary interest in the two gentlemen and he guessed that there must be good reason for this interest.

"Friends of young Warburton, behind," he whispered. "It's just possible we might pick up some information if we handle them judiciously. What do you think?"

Bannister nodded vigorously. He had only a few months to run before reaching a well-earned retirement and it was far from his intention, if he could help it, to complete his career with an unsuccessful "case." Everything that touched upon the affair at all he meant to investigate with the utmost thoroughness, even though it might appear at first blush to be of the most unimportant and trivial nature.

"Good idea," he muttered. As he spoke the door of the room opened again and a stout, jovial-faced man entered and crossed the room. He came straight to Bannister's table.

"Good evening, Inspector," he said with outstretched hand.

"Good evening," replied Bannister, rising quickly, "you are Mr.—?" He paused.

"Falcon," announced the newcomer.

"Why, you're the—?"

"Proprietor of the 'Grand Hotel,'" came the answer. "What is it this—?"

"Just the man I wanted," interjected the Inspector, cutting short his sentence. "This is a friend of mine—Mr. Anthony Bathurst."

Falcon smiled across at Anthony. Mr. Bathurst bowed his acknowledgment. Bannister motioned Falcon to a seat beside him. "Something you can tell me. Who are the two young fellows at the table behind?"

Falcon indulged in a sharp sidelong glance. "Two young salesmen," he declared. "They're frequently here. They come in here pretty regularly towards the end of the week."

Bannister pulled the hotel-proprietor towards him. "Did you see any news in the paper this morning about a tragedy at Seabourne?"

"Can't say that I did," said Falcon. "As a matter of fact I've had a downright busy day and haven't had too much time to spare for actual newspaper reading. I looked at the parting news, it's true, but I think that was about all. What about it?"

Bannister dropped his voice to its lowest possible pitch. "We have reason to suspect," he announced very gravely, "that the murdered lady is an inhabitant of these parts."

"By George," cried Falcon with excitement, "I remember now. You've refreshed my memory. I heard a couple of customers discussing it in the bar early this evening. I remember I heard the name Carruthers mentioned."

"That's the case," continued Bannister capturing an elusive olive, "and a Miss Carruthers *was* originally believed to have been the victim."

"Major Carruthers' niece that would be?" interrupted Falcon.

"Yes, Daphne. But latest information that we have managed to pick up proves that that is not the case. There has been a confusion of identity. The murdered girl turns out to be another young lady." He crumbled a piece of bread on to the white tablecloth. "In the greatest confidence, Mr. Falcon, I'll tell you what we have discovered and what brings me on the hunt to Westhampton. The murdered girl is a Miss Sheila Delaney of 'Rest Harrow,' Tranfield." He paused to watch carefully the effect of his somewhat curt announcement upon Falcon's jovial face.

"Sheila Delaney?" he cried. "Colonel Dan's daughter. Oh, but that's bad. Is there any chance that you're mistaken?"

"None, I'm afraid," replied Bannister gravely.

"What a dreadful business! Dreadful! Dreadful!" He wiped his forehead with his handkerchief. "Everybody liked Sheila Delaney."

"Now, Mr. Falcon. These two young men here,—your two salesmen. I have reason to believe that they are acquainted with a Mr. Warburton; a Mr. Alan Warburton of Crossley Road, Westhampton."

"Sir Felix's nephew, Inspector," intervened Falcon. "*The* Sir Felix, the Mutual Bank—"

"So I understand. Now could you arrange for me to have a little chat with them? Don't tell them who I am."

Falcon's face wore a new horror. "Surely you aren't going to tell me that Alan Warburton's the murderer? I can't believe that. Why—"

"Why—what?"

Falcon shifted uneasily in his chair and knew that despite all he himself could achieve to the contrary, Bannister meant to have his question answered. He caught the Inspector's eyes fixed unwaveringly on his own and realized that there was going to be no escape for him.

"Well," he said eventually—semi-apologetically—"what I was going to say exactly was this. Miss Delaney and Alan Warburton were, a short time ago by way of being very great friends; that was all." As he spoke his eyes sought Bannister's again in the hope that the Inspector would be able to find satisfaction in his statement. But Bannister had by this time scented his quarry and refused to be in any way denied the swift exultation of the hunt.

"What do you mean exactly by the expression 'great friends'?"

Falcon's tongue played round his lips nervously before he answered. "Well, Inspector, let me put it like this, they were seen about together a rare lot. Went to dances together, went motoring together, theatres, you know; the usual companionships of a young fellow and a young girl. People began to look for one with the other."

"Did that state of affairs exist what you might term recently?"

"That's a question I couldn't properly answer, Inspector. Certainly, I believe they were nothing like as intimate as they had been in the past. That's what I've been told; and from what I've been able to see for myself it was perfectly true. It was noticeable."

"Had the lady other admirers or formed other attractions?"

Falcon shrugged his ample shoulders. "I couldn't put a name to one, Inspector, if that's what you mean, but I should think it extremely likely."

Bannister turned to Anthony. "Very much on a par, Mr. Bathurst, with what Ross told us just now. This much seems to be plain. If Miss Delaney had decided to turn young Warburton down in favour of another lover, nobody here seems to be able to give the successor a name. Nobody seems to have seen him."

Anthony lit a cigarette and tossed the match into an ash-tray. Bannister, however, had not yet finished his inquiries with Falcon. "I suppose you see quite a fair amount of this Alan Warburton, don't you, Mr. Falcon? I suppose he's a pretty prominent figure in Westhampton, eh?"

"Not so much since the Sir Felix business, as you may guess, Inspector. That seemed to put the family under a bit of a cloud. Still, I can own to seeing a good deal of him."

"Quite so," purred Bannister, "now tell me this. Did the sudden change in Miss Delaney's attitude affect him to any extent? Did he seem upset at all over it?"

Falcon extended a protesting hand. "Now you're travelling too quickly, Inspector! I told you just now that I didn't know what had happened. I think you're assuming something. I don't know if any definite understanding ever actually existed between the two young people. I don't know what happened at all. If I said that Warburton was upset at the change that came over the young lady, I should be exceeding my duty as a fair-minded citizen and I don't want to do that." He rose from his seat and walked over to the table behind. Anthony saw a flush of annoyance pass over Bannister's distinguished features but it soon passed and the Inspector flicked an imaginary crumb from his immaculately-creased trousers with a grim smile. Falcon quickly returned with the two young salesmen.

"Mr. Rogers and Mr. Davidson," he announced, "Mr. Bathurst and Mr. Bannister."

Bannister signalled to a waiter and ordered drinks. "I understand from Mr. Falcon here," said the elder of the two young men, "that you gentlemen want to get into touch with Alan Warburton."

"Yes, that is so," said Bannister, "could you let me have his present address?"

"I haven't his address," said Rogers. He looked at Davidson inquiringly.

"I can't help you either," replied his companion, "but I think I could put you on to somebody who—"

"Never mind—don't trouble—it's of no special consequence to-night—I can get it quite easily to-morrow, I've no doubt. I thought perhaps though that you knew Mr. Warburton very well."

Rogers shook his head. "Not well. We've only met him on the several occasions when we've stayed in Westhampton on business. But we run across him so regularly then that we've got into the habit of looking out for him every time we come. By the way, talking about Westhampton, that's a terrible thing in this morning's papers—that murder at Seabourne. I hear in the town to-day that the lady murdered—a Miss Daphne Carruthers—was the niece of Major Carruthers. I met Major Carruthers some years ago on my first visit to Westhampton. He was a splendid fellow—a 'pukka' gentleman."

"I understand then," Anthony interjected quietly, "that you haven't seen Mr. Warburton during your present visit?"

Rogers and Davidson shook their heads energetically.

"Devil a glimpse of him," said Davidson. "We haven't run him to earth anywhere—and we've called at more than one shrine where he's wont to worship." He grinned cheerfully at his friend and Rogers found the grin infectious.

"And we haven't confined ourselves to one call at some of the extra-special places, either," he added in support of his statement. "Have we, Rodge?"

"I should say not."

"Last time we were in Westhampton," went on the irrepressible Davidson, "we had a proper old 'binge' with Warburton. We fairly hit the high spots that night." He chuckled at the gratifying reminiscence with such profound amusement that Rogers took up the thread of the narrative with an exuberant gaiety.

"You're right! I remember. We had a hot time in the old town that night. Old Warburton was properly down in the mouth too when we blew in. I can remember that perfectly. In a regular Slough of Despond he was, poor old blighter. He seemed to have turned 'Bolshie' or something. Absolutely shouting Red Revolution. Goodness knows what had upset him. Don't know whether it was the sequel to his uncle's trouble or what? Anyhow when we drifted in on that particular evening in question old Warburton was blowing off a lot of hot air about exterminating Royalty and a lot of proper silly ass tripe of that kind. Quite the soap-box thumper style. Can you remember him, Davey?"

"You've said it," said Davidson, "you've brought it all back to me. I can remember how he was going off the 'deep end.' He'd got a particular grouch against some Foreign Johnny, some Prince of God knows where. He wouldn't let on why when we pulled his leg about it—in fact he was inclined to turn sulky—but from what I could gather he fairly ached to present this Prince-person with something lingering with bags of boiling oil in it."

Bannister sat transfixed in his chair as Davidson concluded his remarks and Anthony could almost see a question trembling on his tongue. Davidson, however, was sublimely oblivious of the fact. He rattled merrily on. "Can't think of the particular merchant's name," he murmured with an air of attempted, but abortive reminiscence, "but it reminded me at the time of geraniums."

Inspector Bannister leaned over the table and held him lightly by the forearm. "Think very carefully," he said quietly, "was it by any chance the Crown Prince of Clorania? Was that the name?"

Davidson sat back in open-mouthed astonishment. "'Pon my solemn soul," he exclaimed with a look of complete mystification, "you've holed in one. You're sure some little laddie—what?"

Chapter XIII
RE-ENTER MR. X

It seemed to "Pinkie" Kerr that her entire world had come tumbling hopelessly about her ears. That she had been relentlessly caught in the mesh of misery. The news that had awaited her upon her arrival at Tranfield had produced in her a species of mental paralysis. Her brain was numbed. The telegram that had summoned her from her Devonshire home and holiday had not told her all. Bannister had deliberately tempered the blow to her by partly preparing her for the inevitable shock. She sat in the dining-room of "Rest Harrow" with the brilliant July sunshine pouring through the windows and tried hard to realize that she would never see her beloved Miss Sheila again in this transitory world of hopes, doubts and fears. And the mental paralysis that had so completely taken hold of her mercifully prevented her from experiencing this bitter realization to its full poignancy. To her, representative as she was of her class, a telegram was always regarded as the harbinger of evil and when it had reached her on the evening of the previous day, she had felt instinctively and assuredly that this particular telegram would prove no exception to the sinister rule. She had obeyed its startling summons almost mechanically—dumbly as it were—making no articulate complaint against the bludgeoning of Fate and accepting the scroll of punishment with a bowed head and the better part of a contrite heart. As she sat in the comfortable chair in the room at "Rest Harrow" and faced Chief-Inspector Bannister, supported left and right by Anthony Bathurst and Sergeant Ross, her sixty-odd years weighed heavily upon her but she tried hard to collect the best qualities of her intelligence for the sake of her "bairn" that had been so foully struck down and so ruthlessly taken from her. The only real consciousness that she possessed was clamouring for vengeance. She was half Devonian and half Scots and for the moment the Scots strain had struggled for the mastery and after the habit of its kind had succeeded in obtaining it. One thought was being registered clearly in her sorely-afflicted brain and one thought only. She might be the means of bringing Miss Sheila's murderer to the penalty of Justice. An idea here or a suggestion there might well prove to be a shaft of enlightenment to the skilled brains that were waiting to question her. She sat there, fighting hard again the chaos of her mind. There was not only Miss Sheila's memory for her to serve! There was also Colonel Dan's! Colonel Dan to whom she had ministered faithfully for more years than she cared to remember. Colonel Daniel Delaney had been a gentleman—more than that even—he had been an Irish gentleman and as his faithful servant had informed more than a few persons in her time, an "Irish gentleman was the finest gentleman in the world." When the news was brought home to her years ago that he had been found drowned it had plunged her into genuinely deep distress—distress that persisted—but her supremely loyal nature after a time asserted itself and the distress became alleviated by the loving care that she showered upon the dainty blossom that Colonel Dan had left behind. When Colonel Dan's widow followed him a few years later to "the bourne from which no traveller returns," this care became even more assiduous—it became in the nature of a Religion. But now she was assailed by a black and devastating sense of complete and utter loneliness. All her loving care had been brought to naught—she had laboured in vain! The edifice that she had built so lovingly had been eternally shattered. As she sat there sobbing convulsively her tall spare frame shook with the paroxysm of her grief. She dabbed continually at her streaming eyes with her handkerchief and Bannister was sufficiently sensible to let the first flood of her sorrow run its full course before he attempted to put any questions to her. Gradually it began to show signs of subsiding and as the intervals between her shuddering sobs grew more lengthy he saw that before very long she would quiet down considerably. He waited patiently and Anthony could not help admiring his dignified control—so many men would have rushed their fences and achieved in the rushing entirely inadequate results.

"We want you to help us," he commenced very quietly, and with a delicate suggestion of sympathy, "we understand your feelings thoroughly. But please do your best to control them. If you do you will not only help us in our investigations but you will also help the poor girl who has gone. Please understand that," he added sympathetically.

"What is it you want to know?" she asked listlessly.

"We want to know as much as you can possibly tell us," said Bannister, "about your young mistress; about her life here with you; what friends she had in her life: you know the kind of things I mean."

She nodded. "I've lived with poor Miss Sheila ever since she was born. I was with her mother when she came. My name is Agnes Kerr; my home is in Devon. I had gone there for a holiday, the address on your telegram is my home." She stopped for a moment and pushed the buff envelope on to the edge of the table. It would have fallen but for the agility of Mr. Bannister who gallantly retrieved it. Bannister nodded encouragingly.

"We found the address here. We got it from your postcard to Miss Delaney," he explained.

"I see," murmured "Pinkie." "I thought perhaps that was how it came about. When Colonel Delaney died some years ago I stayed on with Mrs. Delaney and when Mrs. Delaney was taken too, I had to be mother and father to Miss Sheila, sort of combined. What else do you want me to tell you?" she inquired of him, plaintively.

"Who were her friends? With whom did she mix?" demanded Bannister. "Who was in the habit of visiting here?"

"Since Major Carruthers was killed, scarcely anybody," came "Pinkie's" answer.

"Come now," said Bannister, gently and persuasively, "surely somebody came here sometimes?"

"A few girl friends—very occasionally—and a year or so ago young Mr. Alan Warburton was a pretty frequent visitor. Up to the time, say, that the Major's accident took place. But he hasn't been near here for a long time now. Sir Matthew Fullgarney and Lady Fullgarney would come perhaps once every two or three months but latterly there was no one at all who came here anything like regularly. You can rest easy on that," she added.

"You say Alan Warburton was a regular visitor a year or so ago. Why did he suddenly cease to come—any idea? Was there any trouble between them that you know of?"

"I don't know about trouble exactly—Miss Sheila told me though in the early part of last year that Alan Warburton needed 'putting in his place.'"

"Putting in his place, eh?" exclaimed Bannister with interest. "And what did you understand by that remark?"

"I thought perhaps he had presumed on his friendship with Miss Sheila."

"How far had this friendship extended?"

"What do you mean?" "Pinkie" looked a trifle scared.

"I mean this. Rumours have reached me from more than one source that Miss Delaney and Alan Warburton were looked upon as lovers at the time of which you speak. Would you subscribe to that opinion?"

"Pinkie" demurred, vigorously shaking her head. "No! Mr. Warburton admired her very much—it's true—a blind man would have been able to see that. And Miss Sheila liked him a great deal, too. I can tell you that much. But I wouldn't admit anything beyond that. Sheila, in my opinion looked upon him as a close friend, but I wouldn't say that it was anything more than that." She repeated her denial.

"I see," soliloquized Bannister. "So that it would be altogether an unfair statement to say that Miss Delaney's attitude changed towards Mr. Warburton consequent upon the Bank scandal in which his uncle—Sir Felix Warburton—was involved?"

"Utterly untrue," responded Miss Kerr, vehemently. "A thing like that wouldn't alter Sheila's feelings in any way towards anybody she regarded as a friend. She would have scorned to do such a thing. Such conduct would have been completely foreign to her nature." She began to sob again, engulfed once more in a tide of poignant memories. Her mention of Sheila had brought them all rushing home to her again.

"Please calm yourself," entreated the Inspector, "there's something else I want to ask you."

She pulled herself together as the result of a supreme effort and faced him confidently. "Had your mistress a lover?"

"Pinkie" shook her head but in such a way that Bannister was quick to see it and follow up his question with another.

"No? Are you absolutely certain that there wasn't a secret lover in her life? Would you swear to it?"

She hesitated; then framed her reply. "No one to my knowledge—but—"

Bannister pounced. "But what?"

"I am *not* absolutely sure."

The admission seemed to have been wrung from her. Her reluctance was plain to behold. The Inspector looked her over keenly—obviously wondering what it was exactly that was in her mind. "What do you mean?"

"I have noticed a change in her."

"What kind of a change?"

"She was just a little bit secretive over one or two small things—didn't confide in me so much."

"Give me an example."

"Pinkie" bent her head for a moment, thinking.

"Well—just this. It's hard to explain to anybody else. She has been to London about half-a-dozen times within the last twelve months. When she has returned here she hasn't been so full of what she had done, like she used to be. In the past she had always confided in me and told me everything. Then she has had letters from time to time in a handwriting that was strange to me; also I can remember a few postcards. I don't know where they came from."

Bannister frowned, but Mr. Bathurst evidently considered the point of some importance.

"Did you ever actually see one of these?" he inquired with his most engaging smile.

"See one?"

"Read one, if you like? I'm not accusing you of spying on your mistress's correspondence, if that's what you fear, but sometimes it may be hard to avoid seeing something that isn't intended for us."

"Pinkie" nodded in acquiescence. "On two occasions I did happen to notice an initial at the foot of the card," she contributed.

"And what was it?" inquired Anthony.

"Just the one letter 'X', that was all."

Anthony looked across at the Inspector and waited for his next move. The latter caught Mr. Bathurst's meaning. He produced the postcard found among Miss Delaney's belongings in the bedroom and handed it across to the woman. "Is this one of those to which you are referring?"

"Pinkie" gazed at it with wide-opened eyes. "Yes—yes! This is one of the cards I mentioned. That's in a handwriting I don't know. Where did you get this?"

"I'll show you later on," observed Bannister with a touch of severity, "meanwhile you can definitely state that Miss Delaney has received several communications in the same handwriting as this postcard—yes?"

"Pinkie" nodded, "Several, sir."

"How long would you say they had been coming? Could you give a time?" questioned Anthony.

She puckered her brows as she sat there and thought over the question.

"Let me help you with a suggestion," broke in Anthony. "Would it be correct to say that they commenced to come somewhere about the time that Alan Warburton's visits began to get less frequent? Could you agree with that?"

"Let me think," she answered. The three men watched her closely. "As far as I can remember the first time I saw this handwriting was about Eastertide last year. I think it was on the Maundy Thursday. Yes, it was about then when young Warburton stopped coming here. Let me think again. If I've given you the impression that his visits *gradually* dropped off, I'm afraid I've confused you. They didn't—now I can think more clearly. They stopped quite suddenly. I should say a month or so before I noticed these letters and things coming. I know!" she concluded on a note of triumphant remembrance. "He hasn't been here since the Hunt Ball at Westhampton early last year."

Mr. Bathurst felt his blood course a little more fiercely through his veins. He remembered the trenchant query that he had put to himself upon the occasion of his first visit from the Crown Prince of Clorania. "What was it that had happened at the Hunt Ball at Westhampton in the February of the previous year?" Find the right answer to that, he argued to himself and he would go a long distance towards solving the entire mystery. Bannister's thoughts were evidently following similar lines for the expression on his face showed that he thought "Pinkie's" statement to be extremely important.

"That was in the February," she continued, "only a few weeks before Major Carruthers was killed in his motoring accident. I'm certain, now I come to think of it, that young Mr. Warburton hasn't been here to see Miss Sheila since then." She spiced her statement with unmistakable emphasis and certainty.

"Did you notice this change in Miss Delaney that you speak of immediately after?" queried Anthony.

"After when?"

"After this Ball that you have mentioned?"

She thought for a while before she answered. "Yes, I think I can say now that it *was* after that, that she began to alter. Just a little. Perhaps some people wouldn't have noticed it. But in small ways—"

Anthony interrupted her. "So that it might be a perfectly reasonable inference for one to make—that Miss Delaney met somebody at the Ball whom she preferred to Mr. Alan Warburton? What would you say to that?"

"Yes, it might," she conceded with a quick movement of the hand.

"Let's ask her to have a look at the bedroom," put in Bannister, "she may be able to help us there too."

Ross crossed the corridor and opened the bedroom door; Bannister piloted her to it and showed her the indescribable scene of confusion in the room itself.

"Any idea what they were looking for?" he demanded of her sharply. "Pinkie" slowly shook her head.

"None whatever! All Miss Sheila's valuables—except her own personal jewellery of course—were always kept at the bank."

"H'm," grunted Bannister, "you're sure she kept nothing valuable in any of these drawers?"

"I'm quite sure—although—"

"Although what?"

"Well, she was in the habit of keeping that small drawer on the right there always locked. I've often noticed that." She pointed to the drawer she mentioned.

"Why?" ventured Anthony, "do you know?"

"I am sure that she kept nothing that you could call *valuable* there—in the real sense of the word—that is—" She hesitated again. "I think that she just kept private things in there. Things that she considered valuable, let us say, but that nobody else would."

Anthony nodded. "And I think I agree with you, Miss Kerr. I think it extremely likely that she would do so."

"Another point," Bannister cut in, "when you went home to Otterton for your holiday the other day were you aware then that Miss Delaney was intending to go to Seabourne?"

"No. I knew she intended going away *somewhere*—as my card showed you—but I didn't know to what particular part of the world she was going. I understood when I left her here, that she didn't know for certain, herself, that she hadn't made up her mind. She was always inclined to leave holidays till the last minute."

"Had Seabourne been mentioned between you?" persisted Bannister.

"To my knowledge," she answered, "never, that is to say, in connection with this last holiday of Miss Sheila's."

"Now think, Miss Kerr," exclaimed the Inspector, still quietly persistent, "has anything at all unusual or abnormal happened here, lately?"

"How do you mean?" she returned.

"In any way," he reiterated, "in the country one day is very like another, full up with the 'trivial round and common task.' Has *anything* happened recently to disturb this? Has anything occurred that you could call unusual?"

She thought. "All I can think of was the Indian's visit about a month ago," she declared.

"The Indian!" cried Bannister, "what Indian?"

"I think his name was Lai Singh or something like that. He called here one afternoon to see Colonel Delaney. He had been the Colonel's body-servant years ago in India and said he didn't know that the Colonel was dead. He was a big tall man, getting well on in years. Miss Sheila interviewed him here and I fancy helped him financially. I was glad to see the back of him, he rather frightened me. He asked after Major Carruthers and also Sir Matthew Fullgarney. He had known them as well, when they were with the Colonel in India. I think that Miss Sheila thought he intended to call upon Sir Matthew from what she told me he said to her. I don't know whether he actually did."

"Strange thing him turning up," observed Bannister musingly; "did you see him again at all?"

"No," replied "Pinkie," "I haven't ever seen him since."

Anthony turned this new piece of information over in his mind. The case certainly became more puzzling as it progressed. He couldn't forget that he had two trails to follow. Would the trail that led to the blackmailer of the Crown Prince also lead to the murderer of Sheila Delaney? He couldn't feel sure . . . yet something seemed to tell him that they were intertwined. He heard Bannister put another question to the woman who sat in the room.

"How long did this Indian chap stay with Miss Delaney?"

"Not long—less than half an hour, I should say."

"Did you hear any of the conversation?"

"No. None at all. All I heard was his greeting to her when I took him into her. If Miss Sheila had wished me to hear what he came to see her about she would have asked me into the room where the interview took place. She didn't, so I heard nothing. All I know is what she was pleased to tell me of it afterwards. She gave him money. That's all I can tell you." "Pinkie" tossed her head rather defiantly; she was unable to rid herself of the idea that she had been suspected of eavesdropping.

Bannister turned to Ross. "Seen anything of this Lai Singh in the neighbourhood; heard of him anywhere?"

Ross shook his head. "Not so far as I know, I've heard nothing. But I'll inquire for you if you like when I get back?"

"Do," said the Inspector, "it may be worth following up. I should have thought he would have been a pretty conspicuous figure."

"There was an Indian chap found about ten years ago wandering round Nillebrook Water but the doctors reckoned he was 'queer'—bats in the belfry—you know. They brought him in as a lunatic 'without settlement' and bunged him in the County Mental Hospital. The Nillebrook ratepayers have had the somewhat doubtful pleasure of maintaining him ever since." Ross chuckled and proceeded. "Perhaps he's escaped," he added, jokingly.

Bannister made no reply to what he considered an extravagant and inappropriate suggestion but returned to the woman. "You can assure me, I suppose, that your mistress had no money troubles?"

"Pinkie" scouted the idea on a strong note of indignation. "Absurd! You can clear your mind on that point," she declared. "Miss Sheila was left very comfortably off—and with a considerable reserve," she hinted darkly.

"That's all right then," put in Bannister, "I can rest easy on that score, eh?" He watched her carefully for a moment.

"Where will you be staying during the next few days?" intervened Anthony, "in case the Inspector or I should want a word with you?"

"I thought about going to stay with some friends in Westhampton—the name is Lucas—they live at—"

Anthony handed her an envelope that he took from his pocket. "Address this to yourself, would you mind? Then I can use it if I should find it necessary." He handed her his fountain pen, and carefully put the envelope inside his wallet when she had addressed it. Later on, in the privacy of his bedroom he carefully studied it. A careful observer might have imagined that the handwriting afforded him some peculiar fascination. For a grim smile played round the corners of his lips as the words leaped vividly from the paper to his inquisitive eyes, "Miss Agnes Kerr, c/o Mrs. Lucas, 21, Crossley Road, Westhampton." "Now that gives me much food for thought," he soliloquized.

Chapter XIV
THE PEACOCK'S EYE

Mr. Stark—the manager of the Westhampton branch of the once ill-starred Mutual Bank—sat in his spacious private room on the Bank premises and thoughtfully stroked his chin with his long supple fingers. He then picked up the morning paper again and read a paragraph therein with much more than ordinary interest. This done he put the paper down on his table and resumed his previous occupation of chin-stroking. He was a man of striking appearance—tall—and of fine physique generally—debonair and always dressed in the height of good taste. When he had suddenly entered the industry of Westhampton—a matter of about fourteen months ago—he had caused something akin to a sensation in Westhampton social circles, and many Westhampton hearts surrendered to his fascination. Rumour had it that he was extremely highly-connected and that he had been sent to Westhampton immediately following upon the scandal caused by Sir Felix Warburton's downfall—upon a special mission. Banks must be like the wife of Caesar! Rumour also had it that he was or had been intimate with such people as Sir Matthew Fullgarney, the late Major Carruthers and even with Lady Brantwood herself. Brantwood Castle, it may be observed, was the biggest house for many miles around and Lady Brantwood suited it. It was evident that upon this particular morning something had occurred to worry him, and to cause him disturbance. Suddenly he came to what was obviously an important decision. He pressed the bell that communicated with the outer office. A junior clerk obeyed the summons.

"Tell Mr. Churchill that I want him, at once. If he's busy tell Mr. Jennings to go on the counter in his place. Churchill must come to me."

Within the space of a few moments Mr. Churchill—the first cashier to designate him accurately—stood in front of the manager. Mr. Stark picked up the paper and handed it to him. He indicated the paragraph that he had read so many times with a gesture both graphic and eloquent. "Pretty dreadful, isn't it?" he remarked when Churchill had finished reading it. Churchill nodded his head slowly in agreement. "Now, Mr. Churchill," went on Mr. Stark, "what I want to say to you is this. Miss Delaney called here on the morning of the day that she appears to have been murdered. That's a fact, isn't it, Churchill?"

Churchill nodded again. "Quite right, sir."

"Did you attend her yourself?"

"I did. Don't you remember that I brought her in here to see you? She requested the interview."

"Yes, I felt pretty certain it was you who ushered her in here. Now tell me, what was the nature of her transaction with you at the counter?"

"I cashed a cheque for her amounting to a hundred pounds. The cheque was drawn to 'self.'"

"Notes—all of it?"

"Every penny, sir."

"Remember what you gave her?"

Churchill knitted his forehead. "Five 'tenners,'" he said slowly as the remembrance came to him—"that's fifty—eight 'fivers'—that's ninety—the rest in currency notes—pounds and halves. I couldn't say to those exactly."

"Good," declared Stark, "here's another one for you; got the numbers of the big stuff?"

Churchill disappeared with alacrity to return to the room after a brief absence. He noticed that his Chief looked very perturbed. "There you are, sir. I made a note of them when I paid them out across the counter. I remembered I had it out there somewhere."

The manager smiled gravely with just a touch of magnanimous patronage. "Excellent, Churchill! You never took a course in Pelmanism, did you?"

"No, sir, although I knew a man who did. He could remember extraordinarily difficult things—but used to forget the date of his wife's birthday."

"No doubt she reminded him, Churchill. That's all now, thank you. Send Miss Rivers in to me as you go out, will you? No, never mind, it doesn't matter."

Churchill favoured him with a puzzled stare as he departed but the lessons of experience had taught him that there was usually method in his Chief's madness even though at times the latter was very much more discernible upon the surface than the former. Whatever his faults the manager's ability commanded the confidence of his staff. Stark tapped the broad pad of blotting-paper in front of him very deliberately and turned the whole story over in his mind. He rose from his chair, paced the square of the room two or three times and sat down again. Still he seemed dissatisfied—uncertain. Walking to the telephone at the side of the room he suddenly lifted the receiver—then just as impulsively replaced it. He returned to his desk, his mind now thoroughly made up, and quickly wrote a letter. In a few minutes the letter was in the hands of the Westhampton Superintendent of Police. Half an hour later it was being considered by Chief-Inspector Bannister at the Grand Hotel. He passed it over to Anthony Bathurst. This was its message:

"Mutual Bank,
"Westhampton,
"July 9th.

"If convenient I will call and see the Inspector-in-charge at 11.30 this morning as I am of the opinion that I am in a position to place before him important evidence relative to the murder of Miss Sheila Delaney at Seabourne this week. Will the Inspector please telephone Westhampton 29 to confirm appointment?
"Faithfully yours,
"E. Kingsley Stark, Manager."

P. S. "When you 'phone ask to speak to me personally. E.K.S."

Mr. Bathurst tossed the sheet of notepaper back to the Inspector somewhat nonchalantly. "Mutual Bank, Bannister," he said meaningly, "wasn't that the Bank with which Sir Felix Warburton was implicated? The Bank where the frauds were?"

Bannister nodded in affirmation. "That is so!" Then he looked carefully at the signature at the foot of the letter. "E. Kingsley Stark," he muttered, "I wonder if it's really genuine information that's going to prove of help to us or whether he's the kind of man who always thinks he can assist the Police. Very often the story that comes along is nothing less than nonsensical, and two-thirds imaginary. Still, I suppose I'd better 'phone him and see what he has to say."

He descended the staircase that led from the coffee-room, found the telephone and confirmed the appointment. "I've heard from Godfrey," he informed Anthony when he had found his way back, "I heard early this morning. He reports that they're fairly up against it down there. No additional facts whatever have been brought to light at that end. So it's up to us, Mr. Bathurst." He smiled at Anthony in encouraging anticipation.

"Well, we haven't done too badly, Inspector, considering all things. And we may progress a bit farther this morning after this chap Stark's visit."

"That may be," rejoined Bannister, "all the same I've a feeling in my bones that the solution to the affair lies in Seabourne. After I've seen Alan Warburton—and I certainly mean to do that as soon as possible—I'm turning my attention again to the 'scene of the crime.' Of course," he added reflectively, "there may be something in this fantastic story of the Indian calling upon Miss Delaney—my experience as an investigator of all classes of crime teaches me to ignore *nothing*—to disregard nothing—to consider carefully *everything*—no matter how absurd, grotesque, impossible it may appear at first blush to be. I've always worked on those lines."

"With that, Inspector, I'm bound to say that I cordially agree," responded Anthony. "The truth may shine suddenly from the most unexpected quarter. All the same, I'm rather inclined to disagree with your first opinion that the eventual solution will be discovered at Seabourne. In my opinion—I speak with all deference, of course—the answer to the riddle will be found up here."

Bannister shrugged his shoulders. "Time will tell, Mr. Bathurst. Meanwhile here is Mr. E. Kingsley Stark."

That gentleman was punctual to the minute. Half-past eleven saw him ascending the main staircase of the "Grand Hotel." When he reached the top, Bannister met him on the carpeted landing. "Mr. Stark? Come in here, will you? I have arranged that we shall be free from interruption. This gentleman is Mr. Anthony Bathurst. You can speak in front of him with perfect confidence and you can depend upon his discretion. I am Chief-Inspector Bannister of New Scotland Yard. You wished to see me, I believe?"

Stark entered the room that Bannister indicated, fluttering with suppressed excitement and with a sense of tremendous impatience. He had heard of Bannister—who hadn't?—and immediately, for him, the case began to assume greater proportions than ever before. He plucked the lemon-coloured glove from his right hand and bowed to his auditors, somewhat consequentially. "That is so," he opened, "and I think it will not be very long before I am able to convince you, Inspector, that I have information for you of the most—er—paramount importance. For I am sure that I have."

"Let's have it, then," declared Bannister, "my ears are open. Sit down."

"At the present time," proceeded Stark, "I hold the position of Manager of the Westhampton branch of the Mutual Bank. But you know that, of course."

"One moment," came the quick interruption, "how long have you held that position?"

"I came here in May—the May of last year. What I have to tell you will not take me very long. I read in this morning's paper that the young lady found murdered at the dentist's at Seabourne has now been identified as a Miss Sheila Delaney of Tranfield—the village adjoining Westhampton. Am I correct in that statement, Inspector Bannister?"

"We have good and substantial reasons to believe so," conceded Bannister.

"Well then, you may be interested to hear that Miss Delaney, who was a client of ours of some years' standing cashed a cheque at our bank on the morning of the very day that she was murdered, value a hundred pounds. The cheque was made payable to 'self' and was of course drawn against her current account." He paused as though to measure thoroughly the full effect of his statement.

"Go on," said Bannister, a grim note sounding in his voice. Stark looked at him quickly and went on as ordered.

"The notes handed to the lady by my cashier were partly 'tens'—partly 'fives' and the remainder ordinary currency notes. There were ninety pounds in bank notes. Those are the numbers." He handed across to the Inspector an envelope upon which the information was written. Bannister beamed and rubbed the palms of his hands in unmistakable pleasure.

"Splendid," he cried, "you've done us a great service, Mr. Stark, there's no doubt about that. This should help the course of our investigations tremendously."

"I thought it would," said Stark, flushed with pleasure at Bannister's approbation, "but please wait a minute, I haven't finished yet. There's more to come." He rose from his chair and walking to the door opened it and looked sharply outside. Then he closed it again, came back to his chair and drew it a little distance nearer to the Inspector. "After Miss Delaney had received her money," he was now speaking very quietly and intensely, "she asked the cashier who attended to her—Churchill by name—to show her in to me. Into my private room! He did so. She came into my private office and made what I considered to be an extraordinary request. You are doubtless aware that banks often keep in their strong-rooms certain valuables belonging to their clients. Miss Delaney not only has a deposit account with the 'Mutual' as well as the ordinary current account but we have also had lodged with us for some years, I believe, a legacy left her by her father the late Colonel Daniel Delaney. I refer, Inspector, to what is always described in the deposit-note as 'The Peacock's Eye.'"

"What?" ejaculated Bannister. "What the blazes is that?"

Anthony also eagerly awaited the manager's answer.

"'The Peacock's Eye' is the description given to a magnificent blue-shaded emerald of somewhat peculiar shape. It is valued, I believe, at something like twenty thousand pounds. Anybody who has not been privileged to see it can have no adequate idea of its immense size or unique beauty. Miss Delaney asked for the gem, signed for its receipt and took the stone away with her." He passed a slip of paper over to the Inspector. "There's her signature for it," he explained. Bannister pursed his lips in deep thought. Anthony bent over his shoulder. Stark took advantage of their silence to continue his story. "I pointed out to her the foolishness of the procedure as far as I could—consistently that is with my duty and position as her Bank Manager. I foreshadowed the risk she was running and tried to get her to visualize certain dangers to which she was exposing herself and also the stone. To no avail, gentlemen! The lady was adamant."

"What did you do then?" inquired Bannister peremptorily.

"I went to our strong-room, opened Miss Delaney's private safe in which the jewel was kept, took the case containing the 'Peacock's Eye' back to my own room and handed it to her. Whereupon Miss Delaney signed the receipt that you've just examined." He sat back in his chair with a certain amount of self-satisfaction.

"Did anybody else in the service of your Bank know of this transaction?"

"Nobody at all," replied Stark firmly. "I confided the matter to no one, neither then nor since, and nobody could possibly have known what I was doing."

"One moment, Mr. Stark," Anthony broke in sharply, "had Miss Delaney ever made this request before?"

"Never—during my tenure of the Managership. I couldn't say regarding the period before that, naturally."

"If so—if she *had* done it previously—I take it there would be documentary substantiation of the occurrence?"

"I should say so—yes."

"And you haven't come across any?"

Stark shook his head with decision, "None."

"Did the lady seem at all upset, nervous, or frightened, or was she quite normal?"

"Well," answered Stark, "I've seen her several times before and I don't think she's the kind of girl to show such conditions as nervousness or fright. She has always impressed me as very self-reliant and capable. I should say she was a girl that could face the music—could stand fire as you might say. But I'll also say this. On the morning in question she certainly seemed to me to be labouring under a sort of—" he hesitated momentarily and sought mentally for what he considered the correct description, "let me say 'nervous excitement'—perhaps the term 'nervous eagerness,' would fit the situation even better."

"A certain amount of agitation, eh?" suggested Bannister.

Stark shook his head. "Hardly that. As I said just now the best term to use would be 'nervous eagerness.'"

Anthony intervened again here. "I fully realize considerations of professional etiquette, and all that, Mr. Stark, and I appreciate the fact that you were almost debarred from putting any question to the lady—hut did she give you any tangible idea as to her intentions with regard to the stone; why she had asked for it; what she purposed doing with it and so forth?"

"None whatever! As you observe, it was not within my personal province to subject Miss Delaney to any sort of inquisitorial examination. She was entirely within her rights in demanding the stone. I was holding it for her and I had to produce it. I did so. She took it away with her. That's all there was to it."

"Why is it called 'The Peacock's Eye'?" The inquiry came from Bannister.

"By reason of its strange shape. It is very similar to that of the 'eye' of the peacock's train-feathers."

Bannister showed his understanding with a quick nod of affirmation. "Juno made a mistake there"—his mouth set half-humorously and half-satirically—"instead of endowing her peacock with the hundred eyes of Argus she ought to have given them to the members of my profession. A detective with a hundred eyes would stand a better chance," he added. "Two are hopelessly inadequate."

Stark smiled at the Inspector's sally.

"This cashier of yours," went on Bannister, back to gravity again, "I think you mentioned that his name was Churchill. Could he tell us anything more? I suppose Miss Delaney said nothing to him? Very often, you know, in cases of this kind—a chance remark—a word dropped here or there—is sufficient to put us on the track of something big. Was there anything of that kind in this instance, do you know?"

Stark again gave a denial. "I've spoken to Churchill. I obtained the numbers of the notes from him—thanks—er—to a system that I have been instrumental in instituting in the working of my

Branch. But I'm certain that he knows no more than I have told you. He just cashed Miss Delaney's cheque—that was all."

"Very good," said Bannister. "At the present moment then, I don't think I can do better than to communicate these note-numbers to the Sergeant who is in charge of the case at Seabourne. He can then take the necessary steps to get them properly circulated. Mr. Stark, I'm thinking that your evidence this morning throws a new light on this dreadful affair. We have, at last, been able to establish a motive that is clear-cut and definite. Previously we were forced to consider motives that were undeniably shadowy, now we have something upon which to work." He turned towards Anthony Bathurst and his eyes shone with concentrated eagerness. "You agree with me there, I take it, Mr. Bathurst?"

The gentleman thus addressed took a moment or two before replying. Mr. Bathurst never hurried unless necessity demanded. "Yes, perhaps I do. But it's an extraordinarily baffling case, I must say that. I don't think I've ever been called into a problem that presented so many puzzling points. To me at the moment, the question that requires the most delicate answer is, 'why was Miss Delaney's identity so cleverly and so deliberately confused with that of Miss Carruthers?'"

"I think that can be answered quite easily," replied Bannister, with a touch of impatience. "In fact you outlined it yourself at Seabourne. It was done to gain time. To gain time to accomplish something. You haven't altered your own opinion, surely?" Bannister eyed him keenly.

"You don't quite get me, Inspector," said Anthony, unperturbed at the suggestion. "I'm going a step further along the road, that's all. What I mean now is this. Miss Delaney's identity, we are agreed, was hidden under somebody else's. Now tell me this! Was it sufficient for the murderer that the dead girl when discovered should be thought to be *anybody but Sheila Delaney* or *definitely thought to be Daphne Carruthers*? Do you see the point there? It's a distinction with a big difference! You see now what I'm driving at, don't you?" He paused—then went on rapidly, "In other words is Daphne Carruthers a more important card in the pack than we think? Is she *the* card?" He watched Bannister very carefully as he put the question to him. The Inspector thrust his hands into his pockets and paced backwards and forwards as he turned the question over. Anthony had raised a new aspect of the case. Mr. Stark polished the silver knob of his walking-stick most assiduously. He felt honoured to be present at such a conference. He became almost imperial. It was a story that would gain appreciably in the recounting. His already considerable reputation as a *raconteur* would be— Bannister broke in upon the flight of his fancy.

"You've given me a poser, Mr. Bathurst, and I'm quite prepared to admit as much. Certainly Daphne Carruthers can't altogether be ruled out. I'll grant that. Then there's another point to be considered. Where does the Carruthers-Crown Prince-Captain Willoughby interest impinge on the Delaney-Alan Warburton connection?—that's what I can't fathom. I confess it's got me fairly wondering."

Anthony smiled; his slow, quiet smile. The smile that always seemed to contain the quality of assurance. "There's one common factor though to both sides of that equation. Have you realized that?"

Bannister looked a trifle bewildered. "What's that, Mr. Bathurst—I don't quite—?"

"Major Desmond Carruthers, the gentleman that was killed in the spring of last year. He was Daphne's uncle and also I believe a close friend of Colonel Delaney. He fits into each part of your little problem, you see."

"H'm," muttered Bannister. "I see what you mean, but I don't know that I can link them up. I'm working in the dark." He went to Mr. E. Kingsley Stark and held out his hand. "I won't detain you any longer, Mr. Stark," he announced cordially. "You've helped us considerably. If I want to see you again concerning anything, I'll let you know. Good morning!"

Stark rose and bowed his acknowledgment. "Good morning, Inspector. Good morning, Mr. Bathurst. I'm indeed happy to have been of service."

Bannister conducted him to the door and watched him descend the substantial staircase. He then crossed the landing and telephoned to Ross certain instructions that were to be forwarded to Sergeant Godfrey immediately. When he got back to Mr. Bathurst, he found that gentleman ensconced in the most comfortable of all the chairs, his long legs outstretched to the limit. Mr. Bathurst was a firm believer in physical comfort as a stimulant to mental exercise. He turned his head towards the Inspector as the latter entered.

"Well?" he said, "what do you make of him?"

"Stark? Very useful evidence, without a doubt. Why?"

"I'm not gainsaying that, Bannister," murmured Anthony gently, "that little story of the 'Peacock's Eye' rather intrigued me, to tell the plain and unvarnished truth. By the way, though, Inspector, did you happen to notice his initials?"

Bannister raised his eyebrows, then pulled out the letter Mr. Stark had sent. "E.K.S.?" he queried.

"Might conceivably be 'X' as pronounced," suggested Anthony quietly, "it only just struck me, that was all."

Bannister stared. He opened his mouth to answer when a tap at the door destroyed his intention. It was Falcon.

"There's a gentleman wants to see you," he declared. "He's downstairs. Shall I show him up?"

"Who is it?" demanded Bannister. Falcon smiled.

"Mr. Alan Warburton."

Chapter XV
ALAN WARBURTON LEADS TRUMPS

"This is getting more interesting than ever," exclaimed Bannister. "Lo and behold! the man I was about to seek, seeks me. I wonder why. Send him up, Falcon."

"Very good, Inspector."

Both men were quick to see that Alan Warburton looked very much the worse for wear. He was unshaven, his hair anything but tidy, and his clothes unbrushed; so completely unbrushed and creased that they gave the impression of having been slept in. And very recently at that. His collar by no stretch of imagination could be described as clean and his tie had been tied with glaring and almost exaggerated carelessness. He himself was in no different condition from the clothes in which he stood. His not too clean hands were shaking, and in his eyes glittered something that looked exceedingly like a dangerous malevolence. Decidedly Mr. Warburton was looking anything but his best. Anthony had seen a suggestion of the same look before in the eyes of the mentally imbalanced and knew that it bordered upon a state of fanaticism. He was quite prepared therefore to hear startling news. He was not disappointed. He has been heard moreover, more than once afterwards to remark, when this astounding case has been the subject of discussion, that this coming of Warburton enabled him to disentangle the threads perhaps more than any other feature of the affair. Coincidental with Warburton's voluntary entrance into the cast he avers that he began to see a glimmer of light stabbing through the darkness of doubt. He was able to reconcile certain suspicions with actual facts. Alan Warburton came to grips immediately. His self-control seemed to have entirely gone and he appeared mastered and dominated by a kind of raw desperation.

"Chief-Inspector Bannister?" he exclaimed abruptly.

"My name," said Bannister laconically.

"I understand you're in charge of the Seabourne murder case. My name is Alan Warburton."

The Inspector watched him very carefully through his glasses. "Yes?" he murmured encouragingly. "What can I do for you?"

"I've got information for you," went on Warburton, fiercely; "information that only I can give, information that lets daylight into the case. I know the murderer and I'll give you his name and by Heaven may I be there when the swine swings." He brought his fist down on to the centre of the table with a resounding crash.

"Steady, Mr. Warburton, steady. Collect yourself if you possibly can. Tell your story intelligently."

Warburton turned and eyed him with a dull smouldering glare. "What?" he demanded truculently; "what's that you said? Intelligently? You'll find my little recitation intelligent enough; too intelligent, God knows." He buried his face in his hands to conceal the depth of his emotion. When he lifted it he was considerably calmer, but the dangerous light still remained fitfully flickering in his eyes. "Gentlemen," he said, "I ask your indulgence. I'm on edge. My nerves are frayed to threads. I've been through red, blazing Hell these last few days. You see, I loved Sheila Delaney. I am the nephew of Sir Felix Warburton, another unlucky beggar"—he spoke with mordant bitterness—"and you can imagine I used to be in a good deal better circumstances than I am now. I've known Sheila since we were boy and girl together. We grew up side by side. Now she's been murdered," he burst out again. "And murdered by a lascivious blackguard"—he went on heedless of Bannister's restraining hand—"and I'll give the swine a name—Alexis, Crown Prince of Clorania. Now you know," he declared defiantly. Anthony saw Bannister start with astonishment.

"What?" he shouted. Then his professional training asserted itself and he began to reason calmly with the extraordinary situation. "Explain yourself, Mr. Warburton. It's one thing to bring an accusation; it's another thing justifying it."

Warburton waved the challenge away almost imperiously—certainly disdainfully. He seemed very sure of himself and continued unperturbed and untroubled by Bannister's curt demand. "I can justify myself all right, don't you fret yourself. I shouldn't be chatting here with you, Inspector Bannister, if I couldn't do that. Ask Mr. Royal Highness Alexis what he was doing in Seabourne when Sheila went down there this last time. He's been pestering her for months now—the skunk—ever since he met her in the February of last year. I know that and I can prove it."

It was here that Mr. Bathurst took a hand. The date was his positive attraction. "The February of last year? Mr. Warburton, you aren't quite so well placed for information as we are. I'll explain what I mean a little later. But coming back to what you just said. Where did Miss Delaney meet the gentleman you mentioned? I should be interested to know that."

"At the Westhampton Hunt Ball." Warburton shot the answer back in a tone that brooked no denial. "I can prove it, too, as I said. I was there myself and saw him."

Anthony saw from the corner of his eye that Bannister was knitting his brows in perplexity. But only momentarily.

"Suppose you tell us the whole story, Mr. Warburton?" suggested the Inspector persuasively. "Begin at the beginning and marshal your facts in proper sequence so that we may properly understand it. We can then test its strength better."

Warburton flung another defiant glance in Bannister's direction. "Test its strength?" he echoed mockingly. "It's true and you can't get anything stronger than truth. Order me a drink, will you, Inspector, it's confoundedly dry work talking? My mouth's as dry as a lime-kiln."

Bannister frowned, and touched the bell without making any reply. Refreshed, Warburton began at the beginning as he had been directed and Anthony settled himself down to hear something that held a double interest for him. Although he was still agent for the Crown Prince he began to wonder where that gentleman actually stood and it seemed to him that Warburton's story must throw light on the question. For he was beginning to harbour doubts about Alexis.

"There's not much to tell," said Alan Warburton moodily. "In the February of last year I was a guest at the Annual Hunt Ball at Westhampton. It's quite a big thing in its way. I accompanied Sheila Delaney."

"One moment," broke in Bannister; "was there any understanding at that time between you and the lady?"

"Not in so many words, but I was very confident that there soon would be and so there would have been if—"

"Go on," motioned Bannister.

"During the evening, Major Carruthers, who was Chief Constable then and a sort of guardian always of Sheila, introduced her to a man whom I had never seen before. I suspected him to be the Crown Prince. To cut the story short, Sheila fell for him badly, and from that moment I began to slump very badly as an ice-cutter. In fact I disappeared completely from Sheila's map. She told me some weeks afterwards that the man was Alexis, Crown Prince of Clorania. I implored her to give the man up. Showed her how ridiculous it was. I told her she was playing with fire; that she was just providing temporary amusement for him. But she was like the rest of her sex. She wouldn't listen to me. There are none so deaf as those that won't hear! By God, I was right! She went to Seabourne to meet that swine and he murdered her. She'd served his purpose," he declared vindictively. "But he's not going to get away with Bannister had some interrogating to do. "You assert that Miss Delaney informed you that her lover was the Crown Prince of Clorania. You have no doubt on the point?"

"She told me what I've just told you. I couldn't invent the name, could I?" he demanded churlishly.

"Did you attempt to verify her statement in any way? It would have been quite simple to do so, surely—up to a point?"

"I ascertained that it was perfectly true that the Crown Prince had attended the Ball that night, if that's what you mean? I was quite satisfied, more than satisfied."

"Have you ever seen a photograph of the Crown Prince?"

"Never—I'm not interested enough."

"You say that you saw him introduced to Miss Delaney by Major Carruthers?"

"I did!"

"Could you recognize him again if you saw him?"

"I couldn't swear to that. I might if I saw him in evening-dress. But he was some distance down the ballroom when the introduction took place and at other times I only saw his back. I tell you I wasn't interested in the man, curse him!"

Mr. Bathurst leaned across the table. "I should like to ask you something, Mr. Warburton."

"What's that?" replied Warburton discourteously.

Anthony ignored the discourtesy. He made allowances for Alan Warburton's unsettled condition. "Do you know a lady—

niece of the late Major Carruthers, I believe—a Miss Daphne Carruthers?"

"I've met her—I can't say that I know her."

"Cast your memory back to that February evening. Was this Daphne Carruthers present at the Hunt Ball?"

"Yes, she was. I distinctly remember seeing her."

"Good! Now tell me again. Did she meet or dance with the Crown Prince of Clorania? To the best of your knowledge that is."

"As far as I know, certainly not."

"You never saw them together?"

"No, I saw the Crown Prince with Major Carruthers. And as I said, Major Carruthers introduced Sheila to him, I'm positive of it. I'm almost certain he came to the Ball in the company of Major Carruthers."

"Would you be prepared to assert that he didn't come with a lady?"

"Most certainly I would!" Warburton was most emphatic on the point.

"Don't you think it strange, then," went on Anthony, "that, although this distinguished guest came with Major Carruthers as you so positively declare, he never made the acquaintance of Daphne Carruthers—the Major's own niece?"

"I don't think about it. I don't see what any of these questions has got to do with my story."

"Don't you?" interjected Bannister, unable to conceal a note of triumphant sarcasm; "don't you? Would you be interested to know that the Crown Prince whom you are accusing of the murder of Miss Delaney was in Seabourne for the purpose of meeting Miss Carruthers?"

"Who says so?" blazed Warburton.

"I do," rapped Bannister. "If you want to know, I left them there. They were at the 'Hotel Cassandra.' I saw them myself. Mr. Bathurst here can support me, so you needn't start arguing about it."

Warburton went white as a sheet. But he quickly recovered himself. "What's all this talk about Daphne Carruthers, anyway? I don't quite get in on that. Why did the 'Seabourne Chronicle' of Saturday last say that the police had every justification for their first attempt at identification? Why was Daphne Carruthers supposed to have been murdered?"

"And where did you see the 'Seabourne Chronicle'?" thundered Bannister.

"In Seabourne, of course," stormed back Warburton. "Where do you imagine I saw it, in the Westhampton Free Library, or that I found it in a railway carriage?"

"Oh, then," said the Inspector, with an ominous quietness, "so you've been recuperating at Seabourne too. Seems mighty popular just at the moment as a health-resort! What's its special attraction?"

Warburton glared at him insolently. "What took me to Seabourne is no concern of yours, Inspector. You bark up the right tree. And keep barking up it till something comes down. Never mind about me. Concentrate on little Alexis."

"Hold on for a moment. Where did you stay in Seabourne? Give me the address."

"At a dirty little boarding-house, if you want to know. Right at the back of the town and kept by a Mrs. Leach. Damned good name for her, too," he added reminiscently, "judged by the terms she charged in relation to the quality of her *cuisine*."

"Give me the exact address, if you please?" ordered Bannister, with growing impatience.

"'Sea View,' it's about three miles from the sea, to be exact—that's the reason for the name, no doubt. Froam Road."

Bannister made an entry in his book. "Not a very great distance, though, from Coolwater Avenue, Mr. Warburton," he added with a wealth of meaning.

"Too big a distance, by God," raved Warburton. "If only I'd been nearer that swine would never have finished his dirty work. I'd have killed him with these hands!" He swung round on Bannister, passionately. "You can't be such a fool as to think I'd lay a hand on Sheila Delaney of all people. I loved her far too much to hurt a hair of her pretty head. I worshipped the very ground she walked on." His eyes caught Bannister's and held them menacingly.

But the Inspector was rapid and ready to counter him adroitly. "You loved her too much, eh? You loved her so much that you haven't called upon her for months! You've never gone near her. How do you explain that, Mr. Galahad?"

Warburton's reply was contemptuous and emphatic. "Haven't called upon her," he repeated, the contempt increasing with each word uttered. "When a girl doesn't want a man—if he's a sportsman he keeps away. I don't suppose your education has taught you that much. He doesn't hang round her with a whine, does he?"

Bannister's temper, however, was badly frayed by now. "It depends," he blazed. "Your story may be all right, Mr. Warburton. On the other hand it may not. I can assure you, it will have to be pretty strictly investigated."

"When you like and where you like, Inspector Bannister. Go through it with a small tooth-comb. That cackle won't put any wind up me." He flung out of the room leaving Bannister white and furious.

"Well, Mr. Bathurst," he said at length, "and what do you make of that charming gentleman? An extraordinary story, don't you think?"

"He's passing through a phase of deep emotion, Inspector," responded Anthony; "in point of fact, I'm intensely sorry for him. As to his story—it's more than extraordinary—to me it's positively conflicting—yet—"

"Yet what?"

"I think it may prove to be of inestimable help eventually. When I've sorted things out a bit I think perhaps there may be a peep of silver lining shining through the clouds."

"Hope to goodness you're right, although I can't see it myself." He rattled the coins in his pocket.

"What's your next step, Inspector?" queried Mr. Bathurst.

"Don't quite know at this juncture. I'm torn between two or three intentions. There are several things I want to do. On the whole, I think I shall return to Seabourne. I'm confident the kernel of the affair will be found down there. Why do you ask?"

"Well, I rather fancy I shall put in one or two more days up here. It's a county about which I know very little and I feel that I should like to have a bit of a run round. I was always interested in new places."

"Hallo, Mr. Bathurst, the scent getting cold, eh?" Bannister's tone was genially provoking and contained a strong hint of raillery.

"I wouldn't say that," replied Anthony, showing easily discernible signs of discomfiture. "I wouldn't say that. A day or two's rest shouldn't make a huge difference."

"None at all, in all probability," laughed Bannister. The telephone rang and he crossed to it. The call was for him. Anthony listened attentively. "What?" the Inspector yelled. You don't say so? Two 'fives' and a 'ten,' eh? By Jove! That complicates matters with a vengeance. All right! I'll be back to-morrow." He replaced the receiver and turned to Mr. Bathurst. "That message settles me. I'm going back to Seabourne. Three of Miss Delaney's stolen notes have been traced."

"To whom?" asked Mr. Bathurst quietly.

"To a guest at the 'Cassandra,'" said Bannister. "You've met him, too! A certain Captain Willoughby!"

Chapter XVI

OF WHICH MR. BATHURST HOLDS THE ACE

Mr. Bathurst was considerate enough to see Chief-Inspector Bannister off from Westhampton station on the following morning. He was sufficiently solicitous also to procure for him a corner seat; to obtain for him all the newspapers that he desired; and to press upon him a couple of Henry Clays. From which it will be unerringly inferred that they parted upon the best of terms. "I wish you the best of luck down in Seabourne, Inspector," he said on parting. "Keep me posted if anything important pops up, won't you?"

"I will," promised Bannister. "Rely on me. And I hope when I see you again to be on the way to a successful termination of the case."

Anthony grinned. "There's nothing like a note of cheery optimism," he murmured; "just enough to cover a sixpence."

Bannister smiled back and waved his hand gaily as the train drew slowly from the long platform. Anthony made his way back to his hotel. There he sought the seclusion afforded by the smoke-room. Writing materials were to hand. Mr. Bathurst set to work upon what he always called his "Initial Summary of Facts." Completed he snuggled back in his chair and surveyed the epitome complacently. This is how it read. (A) Present at Hunt Ball—*"lever de rideau,"* so to speak—Alexis—Sheila—Daphne—Major Carruthers—Sir Matthew Fullgarney (probably)—Alan Warburton—and the mysterious "Mr. X." (B) Present at "Cassandra" when compromising photograph was taken—Alexis—Daphne—Captain Willoughby—"? Mr. X." (C) Present at Seabourne at the time of the actual tragedy—Alexis—Sheila—Daphne—Alan Warburton—Captain Willoughby—"? Mr. X?" Is "Mr. X" one of these? If so, which one? Or is he another person altogether? A curious point how certain names are like a certain type of decimals—they keep recurring. (D) Sheila is deliberately shrouded under Daphne's identity and provided with her suit-case—why? Arrangements are made in *Daphne's name*—and that luggage is deliberately substituted—again why? (E) Sheila is poisoned at a dentist's of all places. (F) "Pinkie" and Alan Warburton are agreed that there came a lover into her life. When exactly? Crown Prince? Mr. X? (G) Whose was the mysterious correspondence referred to by "Pinkie" Kerr? Who was the ardent horticulturist that wrote concerning the beauty of the Iris? (H) Who wrote Branston's address on the back of Alan Warburton's visiting-card—Sheila herself, Warburton—or another? (I) Why did Sheila want the "Peacock's Eye" on that particular day? (J) What has Lai Singh to do with the picture? Does he really fit in at all? (K) Colonel Dan drowned—Major Carruthers killed while motoring—Mrs. Delaney dead—Sheila murdered—is it just a line of coincidences or a *sequence of intention*? (L) Why exactly did the murderer, murderess, or murderers return post-haste to Tranfield? What did they want if they *had* the "Peacock's Eye"? Anthony twisted the top of his fountain-pen round and round and smiled grimly. It was a smile that boded no good for a very clever criminal. Anthony Bathurst had formed certain conclusions. He added another heading. (M) Did Stark (E. Kingsley Stark) *know Sir Felix Warburton*? He spent another quarter of an hour or so studying his list then folded it carefully and placed it in his pocket. He looked at his watch, obtained his hat and stick from the stand outside the door of the smoke-room and sauntered to the front entrance of the hotel. The porter knew Crossley Road very well. He would assist Mr. Bathurst! Mr. Bathurst should follow the tram-lines, turn round by the "Ram and Raven," pass the statue to Doctor Harvey, and he would see that Crossley Road was the first turning on the left. Mr. Bathurst accepted the instructions with a charming thankfulness and sallied forth. For the moment he had left the main question of Sheila Delaney's murder. As Bannister had implied the day before—he was taking a rest— partly. But he had a shrewd idea at the back of his clever brain that the half-holiday would not prove completely unprofitable. He turned down Crossley Road and it was not long before he stood in front of Number 19. In response to his knock a rather slatternly woman appeared at the door. She eyed Mr. Bathurst with a disfavour that she took no pains to conceal. Which fact mattered but little to him. Mr. Bathurst always appeared to be supremely unconscious of little incidents of that kind.

"Mr. Warburton?" she echoed his request. "Yes, he's in. Would you be wantin' him?" she added unnecessarily.

"Naturally," smiled Mr. Bathurst. "That was why I asked for him."

The lady scowled ungraciously, but Mr. Bathurst could be as charming to scowls as he could be to "wreathed smiles."

"What name shall I say?" she demanded more churlishly than ever.

"Say Mr. Bannister's assistant."

The lady disappeared with the mendacious information and left Mr. Bathurst kicking his heels outside the front door. Within a few minutes she returned.

"You're to come upstairs," she announced with the air of one bestowing the greatest of favours. "Mr. Warburton says as how he'll see you."

Anthony ascended the unpretentious staircase and was shown into a sitting-room that had seen a good many better days.

"Well, my inquisitive friend"—such was the manner of Mr. Warburton's greeting—"to what particular strain of damned curiosity am I indebted for the honour of this visit?"

Anthony waved a deprecating hand. "I beg of you, Mr. Warburton, I beg of you! Do not, please, mistake your man. It would grieve me enormously if you were to do that, and I fear that my recovery from that grief would be extremely tardy. Let me assure you that I have no official connection whatever with the Police. Rest easy on that point."

Warburton stared at him, incredulity and wonderment struggling to find expression. "What the hell do you mean?"

"Precisely what I say. I do not come from the Police."

"What were you doing then with Bannister yesterday, eh?"

Again Mr. Bathurst raised a mildly protesting hand. "Ah! There we do meet on more appropriate terms. I will tell you, Mr. Warburton. I am watching the case on behalf of His Royal Highness Alexis, Crown Prince of Clorania. Does that surprise you? My name is Anthony Bathurst."

Warburton sprang to his feet, furious with anger. "Then get out of here," he cried. "As quickly as you know how or—" He stopped irresolutely.

Mr. Bathurst, as has been observed more than once, was always very fit, thank you, and Mr. Warburton was intelligent enough to note the fact. One glance at the lithe and muscular six feet length of body was ample for him in which to arrive at his conclusions.

"I think not," said Mr. Bathurst, sweetly—as sweetly as he knew how, which is considerably so. "And I'll tell you why, Mr. Warburton, in case you don't know." There was no sweetness in his tone now, rather a grim menace. "Have you ever heard of the Princess Imogena of Natalia?"

"What do you mean?" muttered Warburton.

"I was called into this case, Mr. Warburton, before it assumed the tragic aspect that unhappily it has now." He took a bundle of letters from his pocket. "Your handwriting, I fancy!" He held one out to Alan Warburton.

The latter's lower lip dropped as he gazed at the letter sullenly. "There's no need for you to answer," said Anthony, "your face betrays you." Warburton remained obstinately silent. "There's no fifty thousand pounds for you this journey, my young friend—you may be housed rather as a guest of His Majesty."

"It's of no consequence to me now. You won't frighten me with that."

"Perhaps not! But nevertheless I'm very curious on one point. What bluff were you calling? You had absolutely nothing at the back of you. What was your game?"

Warburton's face twisted into a sneering laugh. "I knew he'd been meeting her," he declared. "That was good enough for me to work on."

"Good enough for blackmail? A dirty word and a dirty trade! However did you imagine you would be able to keep the strings pulled tightly enough when you knew absolutely nothing; when you were groping in the dark? You must be mad."

"I knew he was meeting Sheila Delaney and a word of that in his future bride's ear would have cooked his goose all right, don't you worry. At any rate I frightened the swine. I put the fear of God in his carcass sufficiently for him to call you into the case."

"You'll cut a sorry figure in the dock, Warburton, and you'll get a stiff sentence. You won't have a leg to stand on."

"I'll stand in no dock," sneered Warburton. "And what is more, you know it! I can see dear Alexis cutting almost as sorry a figure as I should—and a bit sorrier—Prosecute?" He laughed with an almost affected bitterness. "He'll never prosecute me, he hasn't got half the pluck."

Anthony folded up the letters preparatory to putting the bundle away in his breast pocket. "I'm going," he announced.

"What the Crown Prince decides to do is entirely his own affair. I can promise you that. I shall refrain from advising him either way. In some circumstances, I might feel sorry for you. Good morning."

Warburton sat sullenly in his chair and made no reply. Anthony stopped on the threshold. "By the way," he declared, "you might oblige me in one little matter, will you? I want the address of an important gentleman of these parts. I have no doubt you can give it to me—Sir Matthew Fullgarney."

Warburton stared wonderingly. "Dovaston Court." He gave the information with surliness. "Two miles out of Westhampton on the Bedford Road."

"Thank you," said Mr. Bathurst. He closed the door gently behind him.

Chapter XVII
BANNISTER STRIKES THE TRAIL

BANNISTER left the Seabourne train with a quickness of step that denoted serious business in front. The express had made excellent time from Victoria, as a result of which the Inspector's spirits had considerably risen. This "note" story that had been telephoned to him was really interesting. At last there had come tangible evidence upon which he and his subordinates could get to work. He walked quickly down the platform, passed the barrier and flung himself into a waiting taxi. When he had heard from Sergeant Godfrey, at Westhampton, that the missing notes had been traced to the possession of Captain Willoughby, he had instructed the Sergeant to take no immediate action but temporarily, at least, to hold his hand. To hold his hand until Bannister himself could arrive upon the scene and direct the plan of operations. He dashed into the Police Station and within a matter of a few minutes was interviewing Sergeant Godfrey.

"Tell me the whole story from the beginning, Godfrey," he ordered. "I mean from the time when I sent you the numbers of the notes."

"That's an easy matter," replied Godfrey. "We circulated the missing numbers as you instructed us in the usual way and within a couple of hours received surprising information. Information from the Seabourne Branch of the Southern and Home Counties Bank. The manager telephoned us here and I went along myself to hear what he had to say. It appears that one of his cashiers remembered taking some five pound notes over the counter on the previous day. He looked at them again just out of curiosity when our inquiry went through to his Bank and discovered to his surprise that two of them corresponded with those taken from Miss Delaney. They had been paid into the credit of the 'Cassandra' Hotel. There was no doubt about it. He showed me the entry on the paying-in slip. I thanked the manager and rolled off at once to the 'Cassandra.' Saw the manager there, saw the cashier, saw pretty nearly everybody concerned. 'Quite right,' they said, 'the notes had come from them certainly.' The cashier was able to remember receiving them, perfectly. They had been paid over in settlement of his weekly account by Captain Willoughby, who has stayed at the hotel for some time. I enjoined absolute silence upon all of them for the time being and 'phoned the news direct to you. Willoughby is blissfully ignorant that the notes have been traced to him! What will you do—see him?"

"Most assuredly," chipped in Bannister. "I can't neglect to follow this up. Say what you like, it's most important. These notes in the first instance *must* have been taken from the dead girl. There's more than one point in connection with this case that I haven't been able to clear up yet, but this note business doesn't look like falling into that category. So, I'm thankful for small mercies."

"Right then," responded Godfrey. "I'll come up to the 'Cassandra' with you. I'd like to hear what this Captain Willoughby has to say."

Captain Willoughby was in and Bannister reflected how strange it was that Willoughby had been talking to him on the very evening that Godfrey had so unexpectedly brought the problem to him. Now it had fallen to his duty to see Willoughby and examine him in the clearing-up of the affair. "One never knows," muttered Bannister to himself, "even one's next-door neighbour." Willoughby received them in his own room. He had stayed at the "Cassandra" so many times that he had come to regard one particular room as his own.

"Well, Inspector"—he greeted the two men with the utmost cordiality—"here we are again, then! What can I do for you this time?"

The pallor and anxiety that had marked his face a few mornings before were gone and Captain Willoughby looked at his best.

"Quite right," exclaimed Bannister. "You *can* do something for me. I am going to ask you an exceedingly delicate question. Think carefully before you answer it."

Willoughby's paleness returned. Bannister's remark had obviously rattled him. "What is it?" he asked anxiously.

"A few days ago you settled your bill here with a couple of five pound notes—is that so? Do you admit it?"

"Of course," muttered Willoughby; "what of it?"

"Only this. Those two five pound notes are very interesting indeed to us. Could you go a step further and tell us from where you got them?" Bannister prided himself upon what he considered was his ability to come straight to the point.

But Willoughby did not answer.

"I'll go a step further," continued the Inspector. "The cashier handed you change for a ten-pound note two days after you settled that particular account. Do you remember that? I should also like to know from where you obtained that one."

A look of annoyance flashed across Willoughby's face. "Look here, Inspector," he said with a well-defined note of asperity, "I'm well aware that you're conducting an investigation of a murder-case, and I've no doubt from all I hear about you that you're getting a rough passage. I am also equally aware that I should be prepared to assist you and all that"—he paused and gave Bannister the benefit of a straight look between the eyes—"but I'm damned if I can see why I should be expected to tell you where my own money comes from!"

Bannister smiled cynically. "Perhaps I shall be able to stimulate your imagination then. Give me those numbers, Godfrey, that I 'phoned to you from Westhampton."

The Sergeant passed the list over to his superior. Bannister held it judicially. "Those three notes I may tell you to which I have just made reference, the two 'fives' and the 'ten,' were handed to Sheila Delaney at the 'Mutual Bank,' Westhampton, by the cashier there on the morning that she was murdered. To the best of our knowledge, they were stolen from her in Branston's operating-room. That was why I put the question to you. Certainly we have no reason to suspect that they were taken from her before." He handed the list back to Sergeant Godfrey. "Perhaps you are now more likely—shall we say—to give me the information I am requesting? I think so, eh?" His tone was cold and hard.

Willoughby's face as the Inspector spoke became more and more an open register of astonishment and bewilderment. If he were not the victim of genuine surpass, concluded Bannister, then he was a most accomplished actor, for astonishment was written palpably upon every line of his face.

"What?" he exclaimed, "you're joking, surely."

"Don't be absurd. This is no time to quibble. And please come to the point."

Willoughby went white to the lips. He seemed about to make an angry retort when suddenly a definite sense of his own awkward position came home to him. The angry astonishment on his face gave place to a look of sullen determination. "Well," he said, "since you must know, those notes were paid to me by a well-known Seabourne gentleman. So you can rule me out of any connection with Miss Delaney."

"Name—if you please?" said Bannister curtly. He was eminently business-like now.

"Oh, I hate all this information-giving business. It seems to me always to border on the unspeakable. No decent man can ever—"

Bannister broke in again, even more curtly perhaps than on the previous occasion. "Cut out the sentiment. Can't you see it's to your own advantage to supply me with the information I want?"

"Of course I can," snapped Willoughby, "and can't *you* see that's just the reason why a decent chap doesn't want to do it? It's to my advantage and consequently to somebody else's detriment. That's just the point." He stopped again and bit his lip. "Well, I suppose there's no help for it that I can see. I'll tell you the whole story. My cousin is the well-known trainer of racehorses, Phipps-Holloway. He doesn't send out too many winners as he hasn't got a very big string now. But occasionally he pulls off a 'coup'—usually with a dark two-year-old. He pulled one off at the Newmarket First July Meeting. He had a colt engaged in the July Stakes—'Sherlock Holmes,' by 'Hurry On,' out of 'Popingaol.'" Bannister winced; he regarded it as a most unfortunate allusion. "He had won a good trial the week before and 'Lobster' gave me the tip. 'Lobster's' my cousin. The colt opened at 'tens' but somebody evidently had got wind of the good thing, for when 'The Blower' money got wafted back on to the course he came down 'with a rush' to 'fives' and actually started second favourite. I only got S.P. myself. I had a modest little tenner on, so I had fifty quid to draw. I drew it. Off my bookmaker, here in Seabourne. I've an arrangement that he pays all winnings in cash. That's all there is to it."

"Off your bookmaker?" yelled Bannister. "Who in thunder's he?"

Willoughby took out his pocket-book and handed Bannister the usual card of the ordinary "Turf Accountant." "Jacob Morley, 9, Macbeth Court Mansions, Seabourne."

Sergeant Godfrey was unable to restrain his excitement. "Jacob Morley," he cried, with a ring of triumph in his voice. "Jacob Morley! Don't you remember Branston's story the night we first investigated the murder?"

Bannister nodded complacently. "I do," he rejoined very quietly. "Jacob Morley was the name of the patient who had an appointment with Branston at the identical time that Sheila

Delaney was found murdered. He must have kept that appointment after all!"

Chapter XVIII
THAT LEADS ROUND THE MULBERRY-BUSH

"What do you mean, exactly?" queried Sergeant Godfrey.

"If you cast your mind back, Godfrey," enlarged Bannister, "Branston's evidence was pretty much as follows. When he was released from the workroom by his housekeeper after his unexpected imprisonment he rushed to the room where he found Miss Delaney lying dead. Then he described what happened afterwards as a 'schemozzle.' That was the actual word used. When I asked him if the gentleman arrived whom he was expecting at half-past two he stated that he never gave him another thought; he lost all sense of the impending appointment as it were. 'I clean forgot him,' he said. 'If he came he probably went away'—that was the gist of what Branston said, and it struck me as being perfectly natural." Godfrey nodded, affirmatively.

"Ay! That's so. I remember now—that's what Branston did say—quite right." Bannister turned to Willoughby. "Thank you for the information, Mr. Willoughby. But you quite understand by now that it was vitally necessary for me to obtain it? You will see also that I must now interview this Mr. Jacob Morley immediately. Good afternoon."

"Good afternoon, Inspector. I should be obliged if you would explain to Morley."

"Don't worry on that point," responded Bannister with grim earnestness, "I'll explain everything all right. You needn't lose any sleep." He made his exit, the Sergeant following upon his heels.

Macbeth Court Mansions were about half-a-mile distant from the "Cassandra." They were of an imposing appearance. It was obvious at the quickest and most cursory of glances that they were inhabited exclusively by the affluent. Speculating builders, bookmakers and master butchers almost monopolized the possession of them. Number nine looked as prosperous as any but neither Bannister nor Godfrey felt any surprise at that fact. They had been guardians of the country's law long enough to realize the Midas touch of a really successful and enterprising "Turf Accountant." Stable form has a habit of being so unstable. Bannister rang the bell. It was answered by a smart maid whose ancestors had undoubtedly seated themselves disconsolately and tearfully by the waters of Babylon. A few minutes later and they were conducted into the presence of the master of the house. Judging by the satisfied expression of his face more than one equine celebrity had recently rolled up "for the book."

"Good afternoon, gentlemen."

If the allusion to the maid's ancestry were anything like correct it was equally discernible to the careful onlooker that Mr. Jacob Morley's ancestors had lent assistance towards the hanging up of the harps.

"Good afternoon, Mr. Morley. Your maid told you who we were, I presume?"

"Yes," he smiled, benignly, "I am very delighted to see you, very delighted indeed. I shall be pleased to accommodate you. You will find that I shall always give you a square deal and my terms are very liberal—"

Bannister raised his hand in immediate protest. But Jacob was either blind or impervious to its meaning. He went on his way. "The Mayor of Seabourne, the Town Clerk, several of the magistrates—the Clerk to the Justices himself—they are all clients of mine. After they have fined the wicked people who back horses in the street with their paltry shillings, they send me their own little commissions—"

Bannister broke in sharply and this time was not to be denied. "You mistake the purpose of my visit, Mr. Morley. Kindly give me your closest attention. I am investigating the murder of a lady—a Miss Sheila Delaney—who was murdered here in Seabourne last week. You have no doubt heard of the affair? I am Chief-Inspector Bannister of New Scotland Yard."

Morley seemed thunderstruck and was profuse in his apologies. "I apologize, gentlemen. But business is business. You understand, I am sure. Yes, I read of the case. The local papers were full of it. Very dreadful. Very shocking. But why have you come to see me? I don't understand—?" He spread out his hands—a mute but expressive invitation for explanation.

For the moment Bannister was distinctly puzzled. He had met this kind of cleverness before during the course of his distinguished career—many times in fact—and he knew that it always demanded the craftiest of countering.

"I understand, Mr. Morley, that on the afternoon in question—to be precise on the fifth of July—that was the day of the murder—you had an appointment with your dentist, Mr. Branston of Coolwater Avenue at half-past two in the afternoon. You were supposed to call for a set of artificial teeth. A few minutes before that time Miss Delaney was murdered. Now, Mr. Morley, did you or did you not keep that appointment?"

Jacob Morley raised his hands eloquently. "I did not, Mr. Inspector. I did not! I was prevented by extreme pressure of business. Two of my clerks were away that afternoon, as a matter of fact. One was ill, the other was attending a wedding and I had given him permission to be absent. I did not go to Mr. Branston's. I had to postpone the appointment. I swear it. Ask Mr. Branston himself, if you doubt my word—he will confirm what I am telling you."

"Unfortunately Mr. Branston can't," replied Bannister rather coldly. "All he can say is that he didn't see you there, which you will admit isn't quite the same thing. There was so much confusion, consequent upon the discovery of the murder that he forgot all about the appointment that you had made with him and didn't remember it till late that same evening. Which hardly corroborates your story, Mr. Morley."

"It is in my favour," cried Morley. "It is on my side. It is not against me." He stopped to see the effect of his assertions. "Stop a minute," he cried, "I can prove what I say. I will show you. I went to him on the following Saturday afternoon—it was my Sabbath—I had the time—he fixed me up with my teeth then—

these same teeth that I am wearing now." He favoured Bannister with a tooth-paste smile, apparently as a guarantee of the truth of his statement. But the Inspector shook his head.

"The fact that you went on Saturday doesn't prove that you didn't go on the afternoon of the murder," he pronounced relentlessly. "You must see that."

Morley became crestfallen. "It is ridiculous to suppose that I had anything—" He stopped short and glanced furtively at Bannister.

"Shall I finish the sentence for you?" demanded the latter.

Morley wagged his head very slowly. Then he reacquired a touch of lost dignity. "I did *not* keep the appointment on the afternoon of the murder," he repeated slowly, and almost with resignation, "that is all I have to say."

"Very good," responded Bannister. "Then perhaps you can answer this!" He looked intently at Morley, who looked more startled and discomposed than ever. "Information has been given to the Police that certain bank-notes were stolen from the unfortunate girl—in fact for all we know that theft may have been the motive of the murder. I say—for all we know. The numbers of those stolen notes are also known to the Police. Does that interest you at all, Mr. Morley?"

Morley licked his lips and gazed at his questioner with something of the look that one associates with a rabbit fascinated by a snake. "No," he mumbled dryly. "Why in the name of goodness should it?"

Bannister's face grew sterner. "Then I will proceed, Mr. Morley. *Three of those stolen notes have been traced!* They were paid into the Seabourne branch of the Southern and Home Counties Bank. They came from the 'Cassandra' Hotel." He stopped here and watched Morley so closely that not the slightest movement of the latter's face could escape him. But only for a moment.

"The 'Cassandra' Hotel people took them from a gentleman who is staying there. Another of your clients, Mr. Morley, and one whom you didn't mention just now—a certain Captain

Willoughby." Morley went very white; his face seemed to be drained suddenly of every vestige of colour.

"Well?" he said thickly. "Well, and supposing I do know this gentleman, this Captain Willoughby, supposing he is a client of mine, what about it?"

"A very reasonable question, Mr. Morley," said Bannister, "and quite one that I expected." He became almost suave. "I shall be delighted to answer it. I have interviewed this Captain Willoughby in reference to his possession of these particular bank-notes and he in turn refers me to *you*."

"To *me*? To *me*? Tell me, Inspector, tell me more about these notes. What value were they?"

"Twenty pounds, Mr. Morley. Two 'fives' and a 'ten'."

Morley sprang to his feet and nodded excitedly. "I knew it," he cried, "I knew it! Everything is all right!"

"Knew what?" demanded Bannister.

"Wait a minute, Mr. Inspector. Have a little patience and I will show you something that will interest you very much. Yes—yes—very much indeed." He rubbed his palms appreciatively and went to his desk. What he had just heard had evidently made a big difference to his outlook. He pulled open a drawer on the left-hand side. He rummaged therein for a few seconds and then extracted an envelope. This done he came back to the Inspector and Godfrey.

"Look at that!" he exclaimed triumphantly. He held something towards them. It was a five-pound note. "The number, I mean," cried Morley. Bannister referred to his tell-tale list. "It is one of them," cried Morley again. "Yes? Am I then right? It is one of the missing numbers? For a certainty, eh?"

"It is, Mr. Morley," announced Bannister gravely, "and I shall be obliged with the explanation."

"You shall have it," replied Morley, all his confidence regained, "and I can assure you that I am more than pleased to remember so well to be able to give it to you. I paid those notes to Captain Willoughby—he had some successful and pleasant business with me last week. But another gentleman living in the district who does business with me was not so successful as

Captain Willoughby. As a matter of fact, for some months now he's been working a 'system.' A 'system' that has had a long run of failure, like most systems. I am sorry for him. He has lost a lot of money over it. But there—business is business. What can I do? I have to send my accounts in—" He paused and looked at Bannister slyly. "The gentleman that I've just mentioned—the gentleman who paid me the notes that I in turn paid to Captain Willoughby—is Mr. Ronald Branston—the dentist. He called here to see me—to settle his outstanding account. He usually pays by cheque, this last time he paid in notes. The note you are holding, Inspector, is one of them." Jacob Morley smiled complacently.

Chapter XIX
RONALD BRANSTON'S STORY

"Branston! Branston after all!" insinuated Sergeant Godfrey to the Inspector as they made their way back to the station.

"Before proceeding any further, Godfrey," said Bannister, turning to his companion, "tell me all you know about this Mr. Ronald Branston, the dentist. We can't get away from the hard fact that the only corroboration of Branston's story comes from one of his own staff—that Mrs. Bertenshaw of his—the housekeeper."

"Quite right, Inspector," said the Sergeant. "I've been thinking the same thing myself."

"Yet there's something else to remember, Godfrey, when you come to think of it. Something most important. In fact, in my opinion, it would be difficult to overestimate its importance. I've thought so all along. You know what I mean, don't you, Godfrey?"

"Not exactly, sir."

"I mean this. If it hadn't been for Branston's story—his account of his imprisonment and so on—it would have been at least ten to one on the affair being accepted as a plain case of suicide. If Branston wanted to murder the girl what on earth was to prevent him murdering her in exactly the same way as Doctor Renfrew considered she *was* murdered—walking quietly to his workroom as he states that he did—walking just as quietly back to the extraction room or whatever they call it and discovering upon his return, that 'Miss Delaney had committed suicide during his absence'? There was no need for any fantastic story such as he has told us, Godfrey." He continued in emphasis of his point. "Moreover, Godfrey, who would have doubted him? Would there have been anything to cause people to doubt him?"

Godfrey rubbed his chin critically. "How would he explain the missing notes? That fact was bound to come out sooner or later."

"That she had no money with her when she arrived at his surgery! She'd given it away! Thrown it away! Done anything with it!" He looked at Godfrey, then added, "Suicides don't need money, you know, Sergeant. It would have added colour to his story."

"I've got a good answer to that, Inspector," countered Godfrey.

"What's that?"

"Suicides don't want aching teeth pulled out. A man who has decided to cut his throat and spend the evening in the mortuary doesn't go out to get a haircut beforehand, or a shave," added the Sergeant.

Bannister nodded. "It's a damned good point, Godfrey— that—but I very much doubt whether Branston would consider it big enough to upset successfully his edifice of 'suicide.' If he did, he's a smarter chap than I've taken him for."

"Don't you think this criminal we're hunting for *is* a smart chap, Inspector?" queried Godfrey. "I do and that's a fact. I shouldn't like to meet many smarter."

"Not so bad," conceded Bannister, "not so bad, but I'll wager to prove myself his equal, don't worry."

They entered the Police Station, Bannister confident, Godfrey pessimistic. "Do as I told you when we started the discussion, Godfrey," said Bannister, "tell me all you know about Branston. It got side-tracked just now."

"Well, we've looked into him pretty thoroughly ever since the affair started, as you know. Nothing's been brought out to his discredit. He's been practising in Seabourne about three years, came down here from somewhere in the Midlands. His business has been very successful and continues to develop—he's certainly prosperous. He's unmarried and as far as we know, unattached. If there's a lady in his life Seabourne hasn't seen her. He's addicted to a flutter on the 'Turf' and is a magnificent dancer. I have been told he's the finest dancer in the whole of Seabourne. That's his history, Inspector, as far as we've been able to pick it up."

"H'm!" muttered Bannister, "not very much to help there. There's another thing that gets me, Godfrey. Those notes! Listen carefully to what I'm going to say now. Do you think any murderer who also stole those notes would circulate them? Do you think he'd run the risk of such a procedure?"

"Well," answered Godfrey, "come to that he might and he might not. On the whole, I don't think he would. But on the other hand he might think it a thousand to one against the numbers of the notes being known to anybody—that's the point, you see." He struck a match and lit his cigarette. "But I'll tell you what, Inspector," he supplemented, "since you've asked the question of me, I think if the murderer or murderess rather—I *should* say—were a *woman*—that *she* might have done. I've noticed from my own experience of our class of work that a woman often makes a mistake of that kind."

"Godfrey," said Bannister, "you know something or you suspect somebody! What are you hinting at?"

But Godfrey shook his head. "I know nothing, Inspector, that you don't know! But I'll admit that I'm hinting at something."

"Let's have it, Godfrey!"

"You said just now that we had only one person's corroboration of Branston's story of his temporary imprisonment in his workroom."

"That's so. Go on, I don't see—"

"Has it ever struck you that Mrs. Bertenshaw, the housekeeper who arrived so opportunely, shall we say, to release

Branston, might just as easily have shot the bolt that held him prisoner? She was the only person that you can swear was in the house with Branston and the murdered girl." He looked at Bannister anxiously, scanning the Inspector's impassive face to see how his theory was being received.

"By Jove," whispered Bannister, almost to himself. Then he shook his head in disagreement. "Where did she get the poison from, Godfrey, have you thought of that?"

Godfrey shrugged his shoulders. "Of course, I can't answer that for the moment, but it might be answered in several ways."

"Have you looked her up at all? I'm relying on you for spade work," asked Bannister.

Godfrey was ready with his facts. "She's a widow who lost her husband about nine years ago. She's got one son—believed to be abroad—in India, I think. She herself comes of a West Country family. Her maiden name was Warrimore."

"Nothing against her, then?"

"Nothing."

"How do you explain the stolen notes getting to Branston? You can't get away from Morley's story."

"Suppose we go to see him, Inspector," declared Godfrey.

"I don't think we can do better. We'll go up by car at once. Get one sent up here, will you?"

As they rounded the corner to Coolwater Avenue half an hour later, Bannister touched the Sergeant on the arm. "Something I've had on the tip of my tongue to ask you all day, Godfrey. Finger-prints! What results are there? I hear the report's through—I'm told it came through this morning."

"Scarcely any help at all. The brass bolt on the door of the room where Branston was imprisoned, gave us Mrs. Bertenshaw and Branston himself. The glass gave us Branston and Miss Delaney. Nothing there, you see, that you wouldn't naturally expect."

For the second time in a few days Bannister was admitted by Mrs. Bertenshaw and on this occasion he subjected her to a more careful scrutiny than on the occasion before. She piloted them into what was evidently Branston's library. The Inspector seized the occasion to have a good look round. Like the other parts of the establishment that he had previously seen, it was handsomely furnished. Moreover, the books on the shelves displayed the discriminating taste of the cultured reader. A cough heralded Ronald Branston's entry.

"Good afternoon, gentlemen, what can I do for you or is there news of importance?" His dark, good-looking face broke into a slight smile.

Bannister suddenly found himself unable to believe that Mr. Branston had managed to steer entirely clear of the feminine society of Seabourne. That story was a strain upon ordinary belief. At the same time he came to the point of his visit. "There *is* news, Mr. Branston," he said curtly, "you may as well know it at once. Miss Delaney was undoubtedly robbed as well as murdered."

"Robbed?" echoed Branston. "Robbed of what?"

"Something like a hundred pounds in notes—the numbers of which notes are known."

Godfrey could have sworn that Branston whitened a trifle as he heard this piece of news.

"Not only are they known, Mr. Branston, but what is more important still, some of them have already been traced. And traced to *you!*" A pause. "I shall be happy to hear your explanation, Mr. Branston." Bannister's voice held a relentless note.

The young dental surgeon winced. "Before I can do that," he said, "I must ask you to tell me more. I don't understand. How have the notes been traced to me?"

Bannister recounted the chain of events leading from Captain Willoughby down to Branston himself. The latter's face quivered emotionally when he heard the story of how Jacob Morley had stated the way in which he had come to possess the nomadic notes. He sprang from his chair and paced the room in obvious agitation. Then he swung round resolutely on to Bannister.

"I'll tell you the whole story of those notes as far as it affects me. Those notes were given to me by a lady. I advanced that lady fifty pounds a year ago at a time when she sorely needed it. I knew the reason for which it was needed and I fully approved of it. One day last week—Friday to be precise—the lady concerned paid me the fifty pounds back. Gentlemen, the lady in the case is Mrs. Bertenshaw, my housekeeper."

Bannister's eyes sought those of Sergeant Godfrey. They met.

Chapter XX
"FINDINGS—KEEPINGS"

THE INSPECTOR was the first man of the three to speak. Into his voice there had crept an added sternness. "Mr. Branston," he said, "I presume that you realize the gravity of your last statement, and also the extreme seriousness of your position generally?"

Branston went whiter than ever and his lips worked nervously. "W—what do you mean, exactly?" he murmured.

"Your story of the circumstances in which this young lady was cruelly murdered might very well be described as a fantastic one. That much surely, you would admit yourself? Moreover, its only corroboration comes from Mrs. Bertenshaw, from whom you now admit also receiving fifty pounds! In the very notes that had been originally in the dead girl's possession! You're in a nasty situation, Mr. Branston!"

Branston was quick to reply. "Whatever position I'm in, Inspector," he said, "I've told you the truth. I can't do more and I'm not going to do less. The story I have told you is a true account of what took place here on the afternoon of the murder—and *true in every particular*. I've put nothing in. Neither have I kept anything back." He paused with more than a hint of defiance. "You had better interview Mrs. Bertenshaw again," he added, "and see what she has to say. I should very much like you to."

"Send for her," said Bannister, with a curt movement of the head. Branston did so.

"Shall I remain here?" he demanded.

"For the moment," snapped Bannister.

Mrs. Bertenshaw advanced timidly—her timidity increasing perceptibly when she discovered the nature of the company.

"Yes, sir?" she opened, with a glance at her employer.

"These gentlemen desire to ask you one or two more questions with regard to what happened here last week, Mrs. Bertenshaw. Please tell them the truth." Branston turned away and lit a cigarette cavalierly.

But Bannister had already begun to congratulate himself upon the turn that affairs had taken. He had noticed a certain look in the eyes of this woman, a look he had seen so many times before in the eyes of people whom he had been forced to question that he was able to recognize it at once and which is more, apprehend its meaning. Mrs. Bertenshaw was frightened. There was no gainsaying that fact. The Inspector tried to tell himself that he was "warmer" than he had been before. The woman's thin anxious face met his.

"What is it you wish to know, sir?" she asked nervously.

Bannister appeared all urbanity—perhaps his most dangerous mood, if his opponents only knew it. "I merely want to ask you a question or two, Mrs. Bertenshaw," he said smilingly, "and I'm sure you'll find no difficulty whatever in answering them."

Mrs. Bertenshaw's eyes flickered in his direction, then dropped to the ground again. Bannister recognized the symptoms and went on. "A year ago—or at all events—*about* a year ago Mr. Branston here lent you the sum of fifty pounds. Is that so?"

The danger signals were now showing in Mrs. Bertenshaw's cheeks. "Yes, sir," she said in hardly more than a whisper. "That's perfectly true. He lent it to me to advance to my only boy who went to Calcutta. He had a good chance offered to him out there. Without that fifty pounds he couldn't have taken advantage of it. It was very kind of Mr. Branston."

"I see," said Bannister, "and I suppose the fact that you owed that fifty pounds to Mr. Branston has been a source of worry to you, ever since, eh?"

"What do you mean? I don't quite understand you." A mere whisper now.

Bannister continued inexorably. He was top-dog now.

"You were impatient to repay it shall, we say? A very commendable instinct." He smiled at her with a suggestion of beneficent approval. He almost beamed upon her. Then suddenly he struck—and struck home! "You repaid it yesterday, Mrs. Bertenshaw. *Where did you get it from?*"

Mrs. Bertenshaw's lips moved as though to reply to him but they failed, no sound passed through them, no answer was forthcoming. She was literally speechless. Branston looked at her sympathetically, Godfrey thought—no doubt he would have liked to come to her assistance—so pitiable an appearance did she present.

"I'm waiting to hear what you have to say," proceeded Bannister. "It shouldn't be difficult for you to answer after all. You must have got them from somewhere. Come now!"

"I found them," she whispered.

"Be very careful now—because there's a most vital reason why you should be very careful. Very careful indeed. *Those notes belonged to Sheila Delaney, the young girl that's been murdered!* That's been proved conclusively."

He stood and watched her. Mrs. Bertenshaw's eyes were fixed on him in a kind of frightened stare, but Sergeant Godfrey felt certain that the stare contained an element of surprise. Surprise that was not simulated.

"I don't know anything about that," she said agitatedly. "I found the notes, as I told you. I don't know anything about the murder. I never saw Miss Delaney in my life until I saw her dead in the master's chair. That's the solemn truth if I never speak another word."

"Found them?" exclaimed Branston in marked surprise.

"Found them?" echoed Bannister, incredulously. "Where, in the name of goodness?"

Mrs. Bertenshaw looked feebly across at Branston, seemingly to invite his assistance. But it was unavailing. If Branston knew anything he was not intending to divulge it. Mrs. Bertenshaw must tell her own story in her own way.

"I found those notes," she repeated, "and the money was a perfect God-send to me. No woman could ever speak truer words than those. I yielded to the temptation to keep silent about it. Please forgive me, Mr. Branston, if I've unwittingly brought any trouble to you. Nothing was farther from my intention. It makes me feel that I've repaid your kindness so badly. But I'll make a clean breast of the whole affair." She wiped her lips with her handkerchief. "In a way I'm glad it's all come out. I've been dreadfully worried and scared about it ever since it happened. I haven't been able to sleep properly. I found those notes on the very afternoon that Miss Delaney was murdered."

"Where?" rapped Bannister.

"I'll tell you. About five o'clock that afternoon—after the first excitement and everything had died down a bit—I had occasion to go along the passage towards the door where the master's patients usually come in. The door that's in Coolwater Avenue. In the hall there, we have a very handsome art-pot that stands on a pedestal in the corner—that high." She indicated the height with her right hand. "As I walked past it—on my way back that is from the door—I noticed something that I thought was tissue-paper lying inside the art-pot. I put my hand in to remove it—almost mechanically, you might say—it looked untidy, a thing I hate—when to my utter surprise I found that what I had thought was a bundle of tissue-paper was in reality a wad of bank-notes amounting to a hundred pounds. I was knocked all of a heap! My first inclination was to call Mr. Branston. But I hesitated. Then the temptation to say nothing came to me." Her voice broke and her self-control deserted her. She burst out sobbing. "I needed money badly. You people who never want for a few pounds don't realize what it is to be in debt year after year and to see little chance of ever getting out. To be forced to borrow for anything special because you have no margin. Self-denial and going without most of the things that make life worth living may mean the saving of a few shillings, month by month, but no more than that. It takes a lifetime to scrape fifty pounds together saving like that—and there was a hundred pounds here."

"How did you know it didn't belong to Mr. Branston?" Bannister flashed the question at her. She shook her head.

"I didn't know," she sobbed. "I had to take my chance. I listened, though, to hear any mention of him having lost any money—or if anybody else had. But I heard nothing. So I kept part of it myself and repaid the fifty pounds I owed to Mr. Branston."

"Didn't it occur to you to connect it with the murder?" exclaimed the Inspector.

"I didn't know what to think. I was terribly worried. What I said to myself was this. If the young lady had been murdered for her money, why was the money thrown into the art-pot? I puzzled my head over it at least fifty times, but I was never able to satisfy myself. There was no mention in any of the papers of the young lady having lost any money, so I couldn't be certain you see."

"She's right, Inspector," interposed Branston. "That's a poser to me. I frankly confess it. If the murderer took the money off Miss Delaney why in the name of all that's wonderful did he leave it behind—deliberately, at that?"

"He may have realized that to retain the notes spelt 'Danger' in capital letters. That is assuming this last story to be true. I'm damned if I know where I'm getting to. Show me this passage where you say you found these notes."

Mrs. Bertenshaw conducted them down. The art-pot stood upon the pedestal as she had described it—approximately four feet high. "That was where I found the money," she said simply. "It is easy to see into there as you pass by, especially on your way back from the door."

Bannister looked inside and then turned to Sergeant Godfrey. "Come on, Godfrey," he said, "this case is getting on my nerves. Good afternoon, everybody." He opened the door of the car and motioned to the Sergeant to precede him. "What do you make of it?" queried the latter. "Leaving those notes behind, I mean! After all—as the woman herself said—why take them to leave them behind?"

Bannister leaned over authoritatively and tapped him on the arm. "Supposing," he said, "supposing the murderer wanted something—very badly—and couldn't get that particular something without first taking the notes as well—what then?"

"I'm not good at riddles," said Sergeant Godfrey.

Chapter XXI
THE LORD LIEUTENANT GOES BACK A FEW YEARS

Mr. Bathurst strolled to the window of the smoke-room of the Grand Hotel, Westhampton, and looked at the red chimney pots of the town. It was certainly a very beautiful morning. The two miles along the Bedford road that he intended to travel within the next hour or so—the two miles that would bring him to Dovaston Court—would seem, he felt sure, more like two yards than two miles, under the exhilarating influence of that morning sun. Mr. Bathurst felt more light-hearted that morning than he had felt for many mornings since he had left London. The first part of his task was over—accomplished. His interview of the previous day with Alan Warburton had definitely cleared up the first part of the case. The task that had been entrusted to him by Alexis of Clorania had been successfully completed. "There now remains," he said to himself, half-humorously, "the Mystery of the Peacock's Eye! And how far is it connected with Warburton's blackmailing of the Crown Prince? Connected and yet not connected. A most interesting and intricate case," remarked Mr. Bathurst. "But nevertheless rapidly approaching a solution." At the same time Mr. Bathurst was beginning to realize that he would have to play his cards very carefully indeed to complete it as he wished. For he was beginning to form very clear-cut conclusions; conclusions that he confidently hoped would be even more firmly consolidated after the interview that he intended should take place this morning. For some appreciable time now—in fact, ever since the Bank manager's timely entry—he had been considering very carefully the testimony of Mr. E. Kingsley Stark. "And he has held the position of Manager since May of last year—a matter of fourteen months only," said Mr. Bathurst to himself. "Fourteen months," he repeated; "three months shall we say since the ominous Hunt Ball in this interesting old town of Westhampton."

Half an hour's brisk walking brought him to Dovaston Court and he quickly covered the length of the sweeping drive that took him to the front entrance.

"Sir Matthew Fullgarney is expecting you, sir," said the dignified personage whose duty it was to admit him, "if you will be good enough to step this way?"

Anthony followed his imposing guide down a hall with a beautifully polished floor into a sumptuously furnished room. A magnificent tiger-skin rug lay in a prominent position as he entered, while the walls were somewhat lavishly decorated perhaps, with many and varied trophies of the chase.

"I will tell Sir Matthew that you have arrived, sir. Please sit down." The personage departed. Anthony accepted the suggestion whimsically. He wondered if he looked as though he had been sufficiently impressed. Smiling to himself, he surveyed his immediate surroundings approvingly. Then he settled himself to await patiently the distinguished gentleman to whom he had written and whom he had come with express purpose to see. He was not kept waiting very long. The Lord Lieutenant of the County entered, caressing his white moustache in the grand manner. Anthony rose and bowed to him, and at the same time was conscious that two fierce blue eyes were regarding him unwaveringly.

"I have your letter, Mr.—er—"

"Bathurst," interjected Anthony hopefully.

"Ah, yes, that's it. Bathurst! I am Sir Matthew Fullgarney. I understand from the contents of the letter that you wish to see me personally. You go even further than that, I observe—you assert that it is important. Damn it, sir, for the life of me, I can't imagine *why* you want to see me. Have I ever met you before?"

"Never, Sir Matthew. And the loss has been mine—I fully realize that." Anthony smiled his reply.

Sir Matthew grunted. "Sit down then and say what you have to say. Please don't beat about the bush. I hate to have to listen to a farrago of words—two-thirds of which are usually entirely—er—redundant—er—tautological—er—er unnecessary." He blew his nose fiercely—intending it no doubt as an imposing battery of support.

"You will not find me wearisome, I hope," returned Anthony. "I will state my case in as few words as I possibly can. I have called to see you in reference to the 'Seabourne Mystery'—the murder of Sheila Delaney—a young lady with whom I believe you were not unacquainted?"

"A terrible affair, Mr. Bathurst," interposed Sir Matthew. "A truly shocking affair. It has disturbed me profoundly. It has upset me more than I can say. But you asked me a question, which I have not yet answered. I knew Sheila Delaney very well. Also, I was very much attached to her."

"Am I right in assuming that you also knew her father—the late Colonel Delaney?" Anthony's question came curt and crisp.

"You are quite right. I should think I did. None better. Dan Delaney and I were almost inseparables forty-odd years ago. He and I—and Desmond Carruthers—got into as many scrapes and damned well got out of 'em, too—as any three junior officers of the British Army ever did. By Gad! Mr. Bathurst, they were stirring times and no mistake. Times that we shall never see the like of again—worse luck. Now poor old Dan and all his family have gone—and the last in such a terrible way, too. A tragedy—there's no denying it." He paused and the fierceness of his expression softened a trifle as he meditated over the poor girl's untimely and tragic end.

"What you have just said brings me to another question," exclaimed Anthony.

"What may that be?"

"Have you ever heard during your association either with the late Colonel Delaney or with his daughter any mention of a very valuable jewel—rejoicing, I believe, under the somewhat fantastic *sobriquet* 'of the Peacock's Eye'?"

Sir Matthew Fullgarney sprang to his feet. Anthony Bathurst felt the two steel-blue eyes of his host glaring at him relentlessly. "'The Peacock's Eye'? What in hell do you know about the 'Peacock's Eye'?"

Anthony suffered this rather surprising outburst with complete equanimity. He had always possessed the tactful gift of making allowances.

"Not a lot, Sir Matthew. Very little, in fact. But enough to cause me to come to ask you for more. I have strong reason to believe that Miss Delaney was murdered for possession of the Peacock's Eye!"

Sir Matthew bordered upon the apoplectic. "God bless my soul, do you realize what you are saying? How could Sheila Delaney have had the 'Peacock's Eye' in her possession? It's too ridiculous for words, sir! What the—?" Sir Matthew fumed into aggressive speechlessness.

"Not so ridiculous as it may appear upon the surface, Sir Matthew. Please listen to what I have to say." He waved the Lord Lieutenant of Westhamptonshire to a seat again, for Mr. Bathurst had a way with him. Sir Matthew obeyed the gesture but glowered at Mr. Bathurst as though his suggestion had been completely unspeakable. Anthony took up his recital again. "According to the evidence of Mr. E. Kingsley Stark, the present manager of the Westhampton branch of the Mutual Bank, Miss Delaney took the stone known as the 'Peacock's Eye' out of the custody of the bank on the morning of the day upon which she met her death. There is therefore very good reason to believe that it travelled with her to Seabourne. And very certainly it was not in her possession when she was found dead in the dentist's chair at Seabourne. A remarkable chain of events, Sir Matthew, don't you think?" Anthony watched him warily. But Sir Matthew remained as he was—to all appearances bereft of the power of speech. "Having told you so much of what I know I want you to tell me more in return. Am I right in thinking that it lies in your power to give me the true history of the 'Peacock's Eye'?" His voice contained a note of quiet insistence.

The man addressed rose from his chair and paced the room it might be said belligerently. The situation as it had developed was novel for him. He came to a decision suddenly. Taking a letter from his pocket he referred to it in such a way that Anthony was irresistibly reminded of a huge bird of prey.

"You state here, Mr. Bathurst"—he tapped the letter aggressively with his bony forefinger—"that you are representing the Crown Prince Alexis of Clorania in a matter of paramount delicacy." Anthony bowed. "I don't quite see then how the devil that fact touches the 'Seabourne Mystery,' and the death of Sheila Delaney. What has the one to do with the other, tell me that?" He made his demand with all his old fierceness.

"Candidly, I can't, sir," replied Anthony, "at the moment, that is. But I hope to be able to do so when I get more data. That is why I asked you to tell me the history of the 'Peacock's Eye.' I have formed the opinion that to know that will help me materially."

Sir Matthew caressed the white moustache again in an endeavour to assume command. "You're asking me to go back a good many years, Mr. Bathurst. Forty-four to be exact. And forty-four years are not five-and-twenty minutes. But I'll tell you all I know." He chuckled at the savour of the reminiscence. "Dan Delaney, Desmond Carruthers and I were all Westhamptonshire born men and were junior officers together in the 8th Westhampton Regiment. We were sent to India. Eventually we found ourselves stationed in a wild territory of Baluchistan, near Quetta, and not far from the Bolan Pass. It's a mountainous, sandy desert of a place by no means thickly populated—the natives that do eke out an existence there live a nomadic, pastoral sort of life. Four years after we got out there a separate administration was constituted under the Governor-General's Agent in Baluchistan and things got a bit better. For which we were all devoutly thankful. But we fellows were a reckless, wild-harum-scarum set always ready for any desperate adventure that promised itself. The more perilous it was the better we welcomed it. The big bug in that region is the Khan of Kalat and there are all sorts of fancy religions knocking about round there, I can tell you."

"Pardon me interrupting a moment," interjected Anthony. "What was the name of the dialect spoken by the natives? Can you remember? I have a real reason for asking."

Sir Matthew wrinkled his brows. "There were many. Dozens of 'em in all probability. In the Central Provinces you get Hindi and Marathi chiefly, but up there, you find so many different tribal tongues. Where was I?"

"Ready for any desperate adventure," smiled back Anthony.

"Ah yes!" Sir Matthew rubbed his hands in evident enjoyment. The old man was back in the saddle again. "Well, as I said, we were a wild lot and although I say it myself, Delaney, Carruthers and I were perhaps the three most adventurous spirits of the whole crowd—as venturesome as we were high. I mentioned that there was plenty of religious fanaticism knocking about. When he *is* religious the tribesman takes his religion pretty seriously, I can tell you, Mr. Bathurst. We Europeans aren't made like it. Well, one day we got wind of a wonderful native temple, situated up by the Bolan Pass. It was supposed to be a most amazing affair and hundreds of their specially holy men were in the habit of making long pilgrimages to it. As a religious exercise, you know. Kind of Mecca! You know what I mean! Rumour had it also that no European had ever set foot inside it—or at all events if he had succeeded in doing so, he hadn't come out of it alive. Death was the penalty of entrance. All the young officers in our crowd were desperately keen to get inside it, when one day Dan Delaney discovered that he was in luck's way. He had a body servant attached to him who had been specially transferred for some reason or the other to the 8th Westhamptons from one of the native regiments."

"Lai Singh?" murmured Mr. Bathurst, with an almost affected nonchalance. Sir Matthew stared at him amazed and spellbound.

"Good God, sir," he declared, white as a sheet, when he pulled himself together, "how the devil did you know that?"

Anthony answered question with question. "You haven't seen Lai Singh then lately?"

"Haven't seen him for over thirty years—what on earth—?"

"I'll explain later," replied Anthony; "please proceed."

"Marvellous—marvellous—now let me see again—where was I?" He frowned in his attempts at recollection. "I know Lai Singh's father was in some way connected with the actual administration of this temple and as a result Lai Singh himself was able to put a lot of information in Delaney's way. To cut a long story short the three of us got away one night and got clean inside—penetrated in fact to the proper holy of holies— the inmost shrine. There we found what the natives called the 'Sacred Peacock.' Its body was of pure gold and the 'eyes' of its train feathers consisted of a number of blue-tinted emeralds. I can't tell you how marvellous it was. I regret to say that Delaney wrenched away the biggest of these and we were about to add to our spoils when Lai Singh rushed in with the news that in a few minutes we should be surrounded—the news of our entry had leaked out somehow. We got away by the skin of our teeth. Lai Singh was scared to death and warned us with all sorts of fantastic tales that the outraged gods would punish us though the punishment took years to materialize. Gad! What a lovely scrap it was, getting away that night."

Anthony broke in. "Delaney, I presume, regarded the 'Peacock's Eye' as his own personal spoils?"

"Not at all," replied Sir Matthew stiffly and with a distinct touch of frigidity. "We were brother-officers—it was a case of share and share alike—not only the 'spoils' as you call it, but the 'bright eyes of danger,' too. We drew lots for the stone. Strangely enough, Delaney was the winner. As far as I know he kept the stone till his death. It was a gorgeous gem exactly similar in shape to the 'eye' of a peacock's tail. Worth thousands, but Dan never realized on it. He kept it for its dazzling beauty—he was Irish—an idealist." He glared at Anthony. "That's all. Now it's your turn. Tell me what you know about Lai Singh! You staggered me just now. You knocked me all of a heap."

"I am quite prepared to believe that, Sir Matthew, but there is no magic about it. The explanation, like most explanations, is perfectly simple. Have you ever met Miss Kerr, Miss Delaney's old nurse?"

"Many a time," chuckled Sir Matthew; "you mean 'Pinkie'?"

"I believe that is the nickname by which she is, perhaps, even better known. I met her at 'Rest Harrow' the other day, when we were first investigating the circumstances of Miss Delaney's death. She told rather an extraordinary story. I should like your considered opinion on it. She states that about a month ago an Indian called upon Miss Delaney, at her home in Tranfield—calling himself Lai Singh. He asked for Colonel Delaney and informed her that he was the Colonel's old servant. He was unaware of the Colonel's death. Or said he was—that possibly is a more accurate version!"

"What?" roared Sir Matthew. "Lai Singh here in Westhamptonshire. That tale won't hold water. It's incredible—it's amazing—" He spluttered in his attempt to find suitable words to express his rejection.

"I can take it then," intervened Anthony, "that Lai Singh did not extend his visit to you?"

"To me? Good gracious, Mr. Bathurst, of course not! Lai Singh indeed! I haven't set eyes on Lai Singh for over thirty years, as I told you. What on earth gives you that extraordinary idea?"

"'Pinkie' Kerr is under the impression that he announced to Miss Delaney his intention of so doing," said Anthony, gravely.

"Good God, sir—you astound me—dear, dear—dear, dear!"

It was obvious that Sir Matthew was extremely perturbed.

"He certainly *enquired* after you," proceeded Anthony, "and also after the late Major Desmond Carruthers."

"Well—I'm damned—I suppose there's no possible doubt about this rigmarole, Mr. Bathurst? You're sure in your own mind that 'Pinkie' Kerr isn't giving way to a little romancing?"

"Her evidence is entirely uncorroborated—obviously—her mistress is dead—Lai Singh has disappeared. At the same time—" He paused.

"Well?" demanded Sir Matthew vehemently. "What?"

"It would be a remarkable story for her to *invent*," said Mr. Bathurst with a shrug of the shoulders. "Don't you think so?"

"Let me come to the point, then. What do you make of it?"

"That we are in very deep waters, Sir Matthew! Sheila Delaney has been the victim of one of the most cunning and cold-blooded crimes of the century and it's going to take me all my time to bring her assassin to justice. There's a big difference between suspecting a man and proving his guilt. There's a big difference, also, between *knowing* a man's guilt and *proving* it."

Sir Matthew glared at him, his cold blue eyes full of purpose. But Mr. Bathurst gave him back an equally unwavering stare.

"I quite appreciate what you say," said the old man eventually; "I appreciate it to the full."

"By the way, Sir Matthew, there is one more point before I go. Perhaps you would be good enough to enlighten me? Can you remember the Westhampton Hunt Ball—a year ago last February?"

"Certainly I can. I was present, naturally."

"Good. I was expecting you to say that. Now tell me this. Was the Crown Prince of Clorania present?" Mr. Bathurst watched him keenly and carefully. So much depended upon the exact terms of the answer. It came quickly.

"I have always understood so! His Royal Highness preserved his 'incognito,' it is true, but as far as I know he was most certainly there."

"Did you speak to him?"

"Of course. Most assuredly. I was introduced to him by Desmond Carruthers."

"I see. Please think carefully. For this question is most important. Did you at any time during the evening of the ball see the Crown Prince in conversation with or dancing with Sheila Delaney?"

The Lord Lieutenant knitted his brows. Then he began to shake his head negatively. "No—I can't remember that. Sheila at that time was flying round with young Alan Warburton. I can distinctly remember *him* being there. No! I can't remember her with the Crown Prince."

"Thank you. You mentioned Alan Warburton. I've had the pleasure of meeting him. I understand that there was a likelihood once, we will say, of an engagement between him and Miss Delaney?"

"That is so, most certainly!"

"Now, Sir Matthew, can you tell me this? Did the Westhampton Hunt Ball that we have been discussing coincide pretty closely with the 'Mutual Bank' scandal and the arrest and suicide of Sir Felix Warburton? Can you tell me that?"

"It did, Mr. Bathurst," replied Sir Matthew grimly. "Not merely 'pretty closely' but absolutely. Sir Felix committed suicide on the very day that the ball took place."

"Thank you," said Mr. Bathurst. "I rather fancy that my case is nearly complete."

Chapter XXII
GALLANT MR. BATHURST

He rose. Sir Matthew Fullgarney's face was a strange mixture of mystification and inclination towards asperity.

"Really," he volunteered with a stiff pomposity. "I don't quite understand—"

Mr. Bathurst smiled. "But I am inclined to linger with your permission, Sir Matthew, for a moment or two longer. I am sure you will do everything in your power to help me. That fact you have already demonstrated. I have heard much of Lady Fullgarney. I take it she accompanied you upon the occasion of the Hunt Ball?"

"Of course. I am not the kind of man to—but I don't quite see—"

"Ladies have proverbially brighter and keener eyes than we men, Sir Matthew. As we discover sometimes to our cost. It has just occurred to me that Lady Fullgarney might possibly be able to confirm or even supplement what you have just told me concerning the ball. It would strengthen my case considerably." He smiled sweetly.

"Very well," responded Sir Matthew sulkily. "To please you, I will send for her." He rang the bell. "Ask Lady Fullgarney to come to me, Warren, will you? Tell her that Mr. Anthony Bathurst has arrived and is now with me."

Anthony embarked upon an adventure of propitiation. "I don't imagine for a minute, sir, that Lady Fullgarney will really be able to add to the information that you have given me so clearly. I am deeply in your debt, Sir Matthew. But her mere corroboration will be important and most valuable."

Sir Matthew nodded. "Here she is," he said.

Anthony bowed to the lady. She in her turn favoured him with a charming smile. Sir Matthew performed the necessary introduction.

"Mr. Bathurst is a friend of the Crown Prince of Clorania," he added. "I expect you remember him." He evidently regarded this connection as an additional testimonial. "And he is also investigating the murder of poor Sheila Delaney. He wants to ask you something—he imagines—although he wouldn't admit as much—that you may be able to help him. He's an optimist, if he only knew it." He wheezed hilariously.

Lady Fullgarney smiled indulgently. Then she bowed to Anthony. "What a terrible affair, Mr. Bathurst. Of course we knew poor Sheila Delaney well. Close neighbours and closer friends. What help do you want from me?"

"I've been asking Sir Matthew a few facts with regard to the Hunt Ball of last year. You, in company with other beautiful women, were there, Lady Fullgarney, I take it?"

"I was, Mr. Bathurst. Are you Irish, by any chance?" Lady Fullgarney became roguish.

"'Tis my one claim to distinction, your Ladyship. That and perhaps a peculiarly-shaped nose."

"What about two very fascinating grey eyes?"

Sir Matthew snorted. This was too much!

"You and I apparently must be of the same country, I imagine," said Anthony. He bowed again. "What I wanted to ask you was this. You met the Crown Prince Alexis at the Hunt Ball?"

"I won't contradict you, Mr. Bathurst. His Royal Highness held the tips of my fingers for a much longer period than I considered necessary."

"His Royal Highness has a 'flair' for selection. Lady Fullgarney, and I'm certain it was never more happy than at that particular moment."

"And a 'flair' often develops a 'flame'!"

"Can it be wondered at?" murmured Mr. Bathurst with delicate suggestion. "Surely you will agree with me—you have a mirror—"

Sir Matthew's snort became a rumble of positive menace. Anthony recognized its significance.

"Can you tell me, then, Lady Fullgarney, if the Crown Prince of Clorania upon that evening of the Hunt Ball, to your knowledge, made the acquaintance of Sheila Delaney?"

"I don't remember ever seeing them together. But I'll tell you with whom I *do* remember seeing him—Daphne Carruthers—Desmond Carruthers' niece. She danced with him a lot. But she's a pretty girl, Mr. Bathurst. Matthew's noticed that, haven't you, Matthew?"

There was a dangerous coldness in her tone. Lady Fullgarney was turning the matrimonial tables.

"I can believe that," interjected Mr. Bathurst. "Sir Matthew has, of course, such a high standard of comparison." He gestured towards the lady. "Indeed I can't think of a higher."

"High enough to keep him quiet," she riposted.

"The quietness of supreme content," murmured Mr. Bathurst. He reached for his hat and stick. "I am loth to leave, Lady Fullgarney, but when I look at you discretion dictates my immediate departure."

"An Irishman with discretion?" queried the lady. "I find the two very difficult to reconcile."

Chapter XXIII
MR. BATHURST FORGETS HIS CHANGE

"Show His Royal Highness in!" said Anthony.

"Very well, sir," replied Falcon. "In one moment." He retired feeling very satisfied. He had had no idea that the Mr. Bathurst staying at his hotel was such a distinguished visitor. To number the Crown Prince of Clorania upon his visiting-list argued much, and eloquently, for his social standing. Chief-Inspector Bannister was something of a different proposition. Falcon was well aware of the Inspector's very high position at Scotland Yard and had His Royal Highness inquired for the Inspector, it would have occasioned him no surprise whatever. But for Mr. Bathurst—! It was surprising to say the least of it. Surprising but comfortably reassuring. He showed the Crown Prince into Mr. Bathurst's room and immediately telephoned the astounding news through to a friend of his—an occupant of a position on the Aldermanic Bench of Westhampton. This, he was fully conscious, was equivalent to getting the B.B.C. to broadcast the news, for the worthy Alderman in question was a prominent member of a Local Mutual Toleration Society. Alexis of Clorania advanced to Anthony, his hand outstretched in greeting. "I have been unable to compose myself, Mr. Bathurst," he said, "during your absence. I have been strangely worried and uneasy. I had to come. What success have you had?"

Anthony motioned him to be seated. "In what particular direction, Your Highness?"

The Crown Prince jerked back his head. "Either! Both! Have you progressed at all? Are you any nearer to a solution?"

Anthony stopped him with a quick movement of the hand. "I came to Westhampton, Your Highness, to kill, if possible, two birds with one stone."

"And you have had the success?"

"Not altogether, although I can say that I have strong hopes. Perhaps in the near future—"

The Crown Prince uttered an exclamation of impatient disappointment. "'Perhaps' is a word that does not make a very strong appeal to me, Mr. Bathurst. I do not wish to appear arbitrary or highhanded or even ungrateful for the work that you have done, but I am afraid I'm a man that judges merit only by actual results. No doubt the case was a difficult one, but your reputation was sufficient for me to rely upon you implicitly. Those letters that were sent to me—"

"Need trouble you no longer," contributed Anthony laconically; "that part of the case has been satisfactorily completed. It was very simple. I had almost forgotten it."

The Crown Prince sat bolt upright in his chair.

"Completed? What do you mean? Tell me, I beg of you. Do not keep me in suspense."

"I have interviewed the writer of the letters and Your Highness may rest assured that there will be no repetition of the offence. I took the liberty, however, of promising in Your Highness's name—if 'promising' be the right word to use in such circumstances—that there would be no prosecution."

"Was that wise, Mr. Bathurst? Is such a scoundrel to go?"

"Come, sir, look at the matter from your own point of view. Publicity is surely the last condition that you would court?"

Alexis appeared to be in doubt.

"Her Royal Highness, Imogena of Natalia," murmured Anthony.

Alexis' doubt vanished like snow under the sun. "Who was the blackmailer?" he demanded truculently.

Anthony hesitated a moment before answering. "Alan Warburton, an old lover of Sheila Delaney—the girl murdered in the dentist's chair at Seabourne. Can you in any way reconcile the two facts?"

Alexis sprang to his feet excitedly. "I told you, didn't I? I said find the blackmailer and you'll find the murderer."

"Not so fast, sir, if you please? Think in the first place where you are. What link was there between Sheila Delaney and yourself?"

"None," replied the Crown Prince. "None whatever—I swear it! That's the extraordinary part about it."

"Then why did Alan Warburton attempt to blackmail you?" broke in Anthony.

The Crown Prince spread out his hands. "How do I know? What can I say? It is all conjecture."

"Yet I think I know," replied Mr. Bathurst, "and time alone will prove whether I am right or wrong." Alexis gave a curious movement of the shoulders.

"It is a mystery and I fear it will remain a mystery."

"I am not so pessimistic as to think that. But I appreciate the fact that a difficult task lies in front of me. How is Miss Carruthers?"

His Royal Highness looked at him curiously. It struck him as strange that Anthony should have found time to inquire after Daphne Carruthers. What was his intention?

"All right. As far as I know. I haven't seen her since leaving Seabourne. I doubt if our paths will ever cross again. They probably lie far apart. But tell me—this man Warburton—how were you able to discover him? How did you run him to earth? You haven't told me."

"Oh, it wasn't too difficult a matter—that Bannister and I ran across this fellow Warburton's name while we were investigating the murder case. It kept cropping up, you see, in more than one connection. The connections were very significant. He was a man who was always breathing fire and slaughter against *you*. Against you in relation to Sheila Delaney. It didn't take me very long to put that particular two and two together. So I decided upon a bold move. I tackled him with your letters. He caved in—admitted the whole business, as I said just now. He'll trouble you no longer. For the future you can disregard his existence. But the more extraordinary features of the affair are yet to be explained. According to Alan Warburton's version of the facts, Sheila Delaney told him that she had been introduced to you at the Westhampton Hunt Ball that you attended in the February of last year. He seemed quite sure of his statement— which included also the fact that the introduction to you was effected by Major Desmond Carruthers—the Chief Constable of the county. Now I find those statements very hard to reconcile with what you have said throughout the entire case. You see my meaning, don't you?"

A dull red suffused the Crown Prince's cheeks. He was instant with his denials. "It is abominably untrue. I have never met this Miss Delaney in my life. There is some ghastly mistake somewhere—what you call a 'mixture-up.'" He gnawed at his loose lower lip. "This Mr. Alan Warburton is a liar!"

"Were you acquainted with Miss Carruthers' uncle—the Major that I just mentioned?"

"But of course! Daphne was a great favourite of his. All the same he never introduced me to Sheila Delaney. I've never met the girl. I would swear it on the Holy Relics."

"That's as far as we can get, then," smiled Anthony. "I'm coming up to town later on in the day. I have, however, two calls to make and one may take me some little time to see through. If convenient to you, sir, meet me on the Westhampton platform at four-fifty and we'll pick up the Wolverhampton express. It's a fast train to town."

The Crown Prince bowed and took his aggrieved departure.

The first of Mr. Bathurst's two advertised calls was at 21, Crossley Road. "Miss Kerr at home?" he inquired of the stout homely-looking woman who opened the door.

"Yes, she is. What name shall I say, sir?"

"Anthony Bathurst. Although I doubt if she'll remember it. Tell her somebody wants to see her in reference to the late Miss Delaney, one of the gentlemen whom she saw before at Miss Delaney's home."

"I'll tell her, sir." The woman speedily bustled back. "Come this way, sir, if you please. I'll take you into the front room. That's the best place for you to go. Miss Kerr will be with you in a moment or two."

When she arrived, Anthony saw that the time that had elapsed since their previous interview had only served to intensify the outward and visible signs of her profound grief. To-day she was showing him a face heavily lined with the marks of care and sorrow.

"Good morning, Miss Kerr."

"Good morning, Mr. Bathurst."

"I told you that I might want to communicate with you again, didn't I? Well, here I am. There wasn't time to write to you, I'm returning to town this afternoon. But before I go there's one more question I particularly wish to ask you." He smiled in the best Bathurst manner.

"What is that, sir?" inquired "Pinkie" listlessly.

"She's taking her trouble badly," thought Anthony to himself. "She needs to pull herself together."

"Just this point, Miss Kerr. I want you to cast your mind back to the occasion when Lai Singh—the Indian—called upon Miss Delaney—the incident of which you told us the other day. The point I want to emphasize is this. Did he speak in English the whole time he was here?"

"All that I heard him say was English," answered "Pinkie." "Yes," she proceeded, stressing her remarks with nods of the head, "I remember now. What you have just said has brought it back to me. Miss Sheila spoke to him in Hindustani, but it was in the wrong dialect or something. He couldn't get on with it. She said afterwards that he came from a different part of the country—belonged to a different tribe or something. That's why they couldn't make each other understand."

Anthony's reply held a trace of sternness. "Goodbye, Miss Kerr," he said. "You've been able to clear up something in my mind that's been troubling me—no doubt we shall meet again."

The second of Mr. Bathurst's morning calls to which he had made reference in his conversation with Alexis was of a somewhat extraordinary nature. The Editor of the "Westhampton and Chellingborough Independent" contemplated somewhat ungraciously the visiting-card that had been presented to him by a singularly dirty and ink-stained office-boy, but after a minute or two's thought decided that his time was not too fully occupied to see the gentleman described thereon.

"Tell Mr. Bathurst we can give him ten minutes, Fred," he remarked editorially. "But not a minute more."

Mr. Bathurst stated his business. As usual the introduction of the name of the Crown Prince of Clorania had a magical effect and worked wonders towards the establishment of a perfectly amicable atmosphere.

"I think I can manage that," said the Editor. "Let me see now—the affair took place in the early part of last year. I think that was the time, wasn't it?"

"It was," confirmed Mr. Bathurst, "February was the month to be exact. I can't give you any nearer than that."

"Ah, February! Now what is it—er—precisely that you want to do—to read all our reports and comments on the case, did you say?" He toyed with the paper-knife that lay on the desk in front of him.

Mr. Bathurst acquiesced. "If you would be so good that is what I should like to do."

"I may take it, I hope, that any news of interest—any special feature of the case that you are investigating—should it materialize—would be placed in the way of the 'Independent' before any of its—er—contemporaries?"

"You may rely on me," murmured Mr. Bathurst engagingly.

The Editor picked up his telephone receiver. "Bring me a complete file of the 'Independent' for the month of February of last year. Bring it up to my private room."

"Here we are," he declared five minutes later. "Here are our issues of February five, twelve, nineteen and twenty-six. I remember the affair made a big stir at the time. I remember the big London dailies gave it a rare lot of attention although news was by no means scarce at the time. Perhaps one of them might prove more useful to you."

"It's possible, of course," conceded Anthony. "But I thought the local paper would probably contain more detail in its report. A question of local interest and all that."

"I see. Will you run through them here? Or quietly elsewhere?"

"Let me have half an hour with them quietly, will you? I don't suppose I shall require them any longer than that. There are one or two features of the case with which I am not too familiar. I just want to have a closer look at them. Half an hour should be ample."

The Editor assented with a cordial smile and Mr. Bathurst thanked him appropriately.

The "Ram and Raven" proved to contain a quiet saloon and a table in the corner thereof served excellently for liquid refreshment and quiet reading. The issues of February five and February twelve each contained a column concerning the "Mutual Bank Frauds." The usual sensational headlines were well to the fore. "Astounding Disclosures." "Sensational Revelations." "Defalcations amounting to £250,000." "Prominent Directors Believed to be Involved," were among the many to be found at the head of the columns relative to the case. Sales must have been good during those weeks. In the issue of the nineteenth, Mr. Bathurst found something more pertinent to the subject of his inquiry. The paragraph that aroused his interest so acutely ran as follows: "Since our last issue we are able to announce authoritatively that important developments have taken place with regard to the amazing conditions prevailing at the Mutual Bank. These developments—the precise nature of which was being freely whispered in well-informed circles as long ago as last Monday—culminated on Wednesday afternoon in the sensational arrest of no less a person than Sir Felix Warburton, one of the Bank's most well-known and most influential directors. We are able to state that Sir Felix will be charged at Westhampton Police Court this morning (Friday) on charges of embezzlement and fraudulent conversion. The arrest was made at the residence of Sir Felix—'Wyvenhoe Towers,' Nillebrook." When he read the sentence which immediately followed, Mr. Bathurst rubbed his hands. He read on with as much excitement as Mr. Bathurst ever permitted himself to entertain. When he had finished, he astonished the barmaid who had ministered to his wants by putting down a ten shilling note in payment for a "Guinness" and departing without collecting his change. By the time he reached the offices of the "Independent" he was himself again.

"Well?" demanded the Editor, "got a scoop?"

Mr. Bathurst smiled and shook his head. "There's nothing here that I didn't know," he remarked, semi-truthfully.

Chapter XXIV
WHAT DID MR. BATHURST WHISPER?

Brigadier-General Sir Austin Mostyn Kemble, K.C.V.O., D.S.O., turned sharply in his revolving chair in his room at New Scotland Yard and spoke somewhat peremptorily. The post of Commissioner of Police is never a sinecure and very seldom a bed of roses. At the present moment he was being subjected to a good deal of Press pin-pricking and generally hostile criticism relative to the failure of his department in the matter of the Seabourne mystery. It can readily be imagined, therefore, that a temper habitually none too good was at this particular time showing certain but unmistakable signs of severe strain. Several of his subordinates needed no imagination to notice this fact. Three weeks had elapsed since Ronald Branston had so dramatically discovered Sheila Delaney's body in his surgery and despite the widely-circulated news in the columns of the Press that Scotland Yard were on the point of a solution and that an arrest was imminent, the murderer or murderers still remained at large. It had become apparent to the thoughtful that the Police Authorities were completely baffled. On the morning in question the "Daily Bugle," ready as usual to criticize destructively, had published a most scathing article by a novelist possessed of a most valuable copyright on the "Supine and Decadent Condition of New Scotland Yard. Its Causes and Remedy." The chief point of the article in question had been the oft-recurring statement that the "Seabourne Mystery" was the fifth unsolved murder since Sir Austin Kemble had assumed the cares of office. Incessant attention had been drawn to the fact that on three of these occasions Scotland Yard had been called in almost at once and that the old and threadbare excuse that the scent had been allowed to get cold prior to expert advice being taken could in no way be urged. In respect of the "Wokingham Wheel-barrow" murder, where the body of the murdered farm-labourer had been discovered lying across a wheel-barrow, in the instance of the crippled Polish moneylender, whose body had been found in a hedge upon the outskirts of Leighton Buzzard battered to death in horrible fashion by his own crutch, and now in this last murder at Seabourne, it was pointed out relentlessly that Scotland Yard had been there "when the tapes went up." But glaringly unavailingly. Its ineptitude was colossal! The article concluded with an impassioned appeal that the higher reaches of the Police and Detective professions should be radically reorganized and flung open as attractive propositions to the best brains of the country. Then and not until then could the country reasonably hope for better things!

"Well, Bannister?" snapped Sir Austin. "I presume you have had the pleasure of reading this clotted tripe served up by the 'Bugle' for its readers' daily mastication? What about it? I'd like to blow their damned offices up." He crumpled the offending newspaper in his muscular hands and flung it savagely into the waste-paper basket under his table.

"Those articles don't worry me, sir," replied Bannister. "That's only paper talk."

"That's all very well, talk's cheap, I know full well—"

"When I say to you that they don't worry me, sir, I have no wish to seem or to sound offensive. I'm not, as it were, throwing the responsibility of failure upon you. I'm quite prepared to shoulder my share. What I meant was this. I've tackled a few hundred cases during my time here, sir, and I can honestly say that my failures have been few. And some of those I'm including in the category of failures were only comparative failures. I'm due for retirement, as you know, in a month or so, and I shall leave no stone unturned to hang this Seabourne murderer—take it from me. I wouldn't have my last case a failure for a fortune. And I am not entirely without a ray of hope at the moment."

Bannister spoke quietly, confidently and determinedly. He was a man whom it was difficult to rattle.

Sir Austin moved uneasily in his chair but at the same time appeared to be a little mollified. "I'm well aware of that, Bannister, and I'm not disposed to blame you overmuch. That's why I decided to run this little conference now. I spoke to Chief-Inspector Macmorran yesterday and told him that I intended to have a chat with you about it. I asked Mr. Bathurst to come along too, because I knew he had been interested on behalf of the Crown Prince of Clorania and was in close touch with the case. Also, I have heard something of his reputation. I remember the Hanover Galleries murder very well and I have had the pleasure of meeting Sir Charles Considine." He smiled at Anthony and if the smile contained a tinge of condescension and just a hint of patronage, Anthony consoled himself with the comforting thought that a Brigadier-General is usually no respecter of persons.

"Now, Bannister," said Sir Austin, "where exactly do you stand? What do you know? Let me hear it."

Bannister took some sheets of notepaper from his coat pocket. "It's a most mysterious and baffling case," he began. "That's not said in any sense of self-defence. I don't suppose for one moment that the omniscient fiction-weaver whose effort illuminates the columns of the 'Daily Bugle' realizes one-tenth of the difficulties that the Police have encountered. You know the main outline of the case, sir, so I won't waste your time or my own with any unnecessary detail. Rather will I condense my report and give you the salient points as they impress me." He looked at the Commissioner for approval. A quick nod from Sir Austin gave it to him. "First of all," he continued, "we were faced with that remarkable attempt on the part of the murderer to confuse the identity of the murdered girl with that of another lady—Miss Daphne Carruthers. Why? Was it deliberate? You might venture half a dozen reasons and yet be wrong. For there is the undoubted fact that both Miss Delaney and Miss Carruthers had a Westhampton connection—please note that! Then, taking events in what I will term logical sequence, we have:

one, the association—the *admitted* association, mind you—of the Crown Prince of Clorania with Miss Carruthers, and, two, the association of the Crown Prince with Miss Delaney by Alan Warburton, who was—we have good reason to suppose—Sheila Delaney's discarded lover. Not a bad mixture for a detective to commence with, eh?" Sir Austin Kemble grunted non-committally. "Don't forget also," proceeded Bannister—a suggestion of resentful vehemence creeping into his tone—"that Sheila Delaney had the Carruthers girl's suit-case in her possession and that a room was actually booked for her at the 'Lauderdale Hotel' in Miss Carruthers' name. Booked by telephone—two people in the 'Lauderdale' vouch for it."

Sir Austin broke in rather dictatorially.

"Tried tracing that call?" he said brusquely.

"I have that," replied Bannister instantly, "unsuccessfully." He jerked his head with impatience. "What I've told you so far, I'll call, for the sake of clarity, the first section of the case. I'll now embark upon what I will term the second. Miss Delaney, at some time or other, was robbed—you know that, don't you? She was robbed of one hundred pounds in notes and also—what is much more to the point—of a supposedly wonderful precious stone worth a very large sum, I believe. The figure 'twenty thousand pounds' has been mentioned to me in connection with it."

"That's the stone to which you refer in your notes as 'The Peacock's Eye'?"

"Exactly—a blue-tinted emerald, I believe—stated to be unique as far as *individual* possession goes. If there are others floating around nobody has seen them. Now we come to a most extraordinary chain of events. Extraordinary and yet ultimately with quite a simple explanation. According to my investigations the stolen notes—or some of them—were first traced to a Captain Willoughby—a guest at the 'Cassandra' Hotel, Seabourne. This Captain Willoughby, I may say, has a connection—through his fiancée—with no less a person than Miss Daphne Carruthers. Mark that! When I got here I felt I was nearly home. Not so likely! Willoughby got the notes from a bookmaker! Who is a patient of Branston, the very dentist concerned with the murder! Still on the track, say I. Morley, the bookmaker—the dentist's patient—got them from Branston himself! There I am again—going in a circle. Would you believe it? Branston turns up—he got them from his housekeeper, who released him—so they say, the pair of them—from his surprising imprisonment when Miss Delaney was being murdered! And the housekeeper found the notes on Branston's premises after the murder! Or says she did. Some little kettle of fish, don't you think, sir? Some little mayonnaise, eh?" He wiped his lips with his handkerchief. It was easy to see that Bannister was amazed. "Let the 'Bugle' have a blow at that. Nevertheless, I've got a stray theory—I'm very hopeful, as I told you earlier. I've almost decided to arrest Branston and the house keeper—Mrs. Bertenshaw—I can make out a strong 'prima-facie' case against them." He paused, waiting for his Chief's comment upon this last statement.

Sir Austin drummed upon the table with the fingertips of his left hand, apparently uncertain. "Can't see it myself," he interjected. "Not on what you have given me so far. What about this 'Peacock's Eye'? Where's that?"

Bannister shrugged his shoulders rather impatiently. "I can't trace any attempt to dispose of that so far. All the notorious 'fences' have been and are still being very carefully watched by some of our best men. In my opinion not more than four of the known 'fences' would look at the proposition."

"And they are?" put in Sir Austin.

Bannister thought for a moment. "Levigne and Kharkoff in Paris—Stefanopoulos in Amsterdam—and Schneitzer here in London. Personally—of course, I may be wrong, I know—but I wouldn't consider anybody else."

To Anthony, of course, the four names were entirely unfamiliar. He docketed them in the pigeon-hole of his memory and was just in the midst of the requisite mental process when Sir Austin Kemble turned to him and addressed him. He noticed that the Commissioner was smiling again. "And you, Mr. Bathurst—what have you got to tell me? Is your story on a par with Bannister's? Are you in agreement with him? Or have you formed a different opinion?"

Anthony returned smile for smile. "Frankly, sir," he said, "Chief-Inspector Bannister has given you more information than I could possibly have done. I was with him at Westhampton when the first news of the stolen notes came through to us and I left him to follow that particular trail on his lonesome. I haven't investigated it at all. So he's got ahead of me, you see. I can only cry *'Peccavi.'* Perhaps I should have attached more importance to it."

Sir Austin Kemble looked at him long and hard.

"Perhaps?" he queried.

"Perhaps!" insisted Anthony.

"You mean—"

Anthony shrugged his shoulders. "Well, I shouldn't arrest either Branston or Mrs. Bertenshaw on the evidence submitted if I were the Inspector. Still, don't mind me, I'm only an amateur."

Bannister frowned into space.

But Sir Austin Kemble stuck to his guns. "You have something in your mind, Mr. Bathurst," he said very deliberately; "I am sure of it. I should be pleased to hear what you have to say—that was my purpose in asking you to be present at this interview. Three heads are better than two. I am all attention."

Anthony bowed. "I'm complimented, sir—many thanks. At the moment though, I'm afraid you'll find me something of a disappointment. I am like the Chief-Inspector here. I feel that I am still confronted with very grave difficulties. Until those difficulties are removed my hands are of necessity tied. It would be worse than useless for me to bring a charge against any person unless I were fully prepared to prove that charge to the hilt. That is my position now in a nutshell. I have formed certain ideas. I am willing to admit that much. Beyond that, however, I cannot go. All I can do is to wait, very patiently and very hopefully. Perhaps one day my chance to prove the truth of my theory will come." He spoke very quietly, but both Sir Austin and Bannister were able to detect the wealth of infinite purpose in his voice.

"I don't know that I altogether follow you, Mr. Bathurst," said Sir Austin. "What do you mean exactly when you say that you must wait? For what must you wait?"

Anthony's eyes regarded him with unswerving steadiness. "For the murderer to make a mistake, Sir Austin. When that happens I hope to be aware of it. *When* I'm aware of it I shall draw the net round—*tight*. I shall want your help, sir, of course, and Bannister's, too. I don't mean for a moment that I'm big enough to carry it through single-handed. But that's my intention—to bide my time." There was no element of braggadocio in what he said, merely the coldness of quiet determination.

Sir Austin started his finger-drumming again. He was dissatisfied. "Permit me to remark, Mr. Bathurst, that the time for you to move may *never* come. The murderer—or murderers possibly—may never make the mistake for which you are suggesting that we should wait. How do we go on then?" Anthony was unmoved by the Commissioner's suggestion.

"How then?" He thought the question over for a moment or two and then quickly discarded it as a real possibility. "Take it from me, sir, the move *will* be made. It *must* be. You need have no qualms upon that point whatever. The move for which I am waiting will be the natural sequence—perhaps corollary is the better word—of Miss Delaney's murder. It will be tedious and irksome—this waiting period, I agree—but at all events when I move I shall be *sure*. It is a comfortable thought—to be *sure*—"

Sir Austin rose from his chair. "Very well, then, Mr. Bathurst, since neither Bannister nor you can advise any immediate course of action I must bow to your joint decision and wait. Even though it imposes a strain upon my patience. I will inform the Crown Prince of Clorania of what has passed between us. Good-day." He held out his hand to Bannister and then to Anthony. As he left them at the door of his room the Inspector turned to Bathurst.

"What's your point, Mr. Bathurst?" he said.

"What's this move you say you're waiting for? I couldn't follow your argument at all. You amateurs amuse me."

"I expect we do," returned Anthony good humouredly. "But you're asking me too much to tell you what the precise nature of the move will be. I'm not a clairvoyant. At the same time, though, I am quite willing to tell you something of at least equal importance—that is, of course, if you would care to hear it?"

"What's that?"

"The name of the person who murdered Sheila Delaney."

Bannister regarded him with a look of amazement mingled with incredulity. "What?" he exclaimed; "are you serious?"

"Perfectly," replied Anthony. He bent his head a little and whispered a name in the Inspector's ear.

Bannister gasped. "Never!" he declared. "You can't mean it!"

Anthony nodded gravely.

"Good God!" exclaimed Bannister again; "you can't mean it, Mr. Bathurst."

"I do—but it'll be a very difficult matter to drive the charge home. Nobody realizes that fact more than I. Think of the issues involved."

"I'm thinking," said Bannister; "it certainly will be some job! Well I'm damned!" He shook his head, still pondering over the amazing nature of Mr. Bathurst's confidence.

Chapter XXV
MR. BATHURST'S PATIENCE IS REWARDED

The golden sunshine of July passed into the mellower maturity of August. August in its turn yielded place to the quieter beauty of September and russet-brown October reigned at due season in the latter's stead. The mystery of the murder of Sheila Delaney—in the words of the cheaper Press—the "Dentist's-Chair Murder" yet remained unsolved. The "Daily Bugle" continued its bugling. Sir Austin Kemble allowed himself at various odd times to dwell somewhat bitterly upon the vaticination of Mr. Bathurst and at other times was sorely taxed to restrain his growing impatience. Chief-Inspector Bannister was doomed to suffer the biggest disappointment of his hitherto distinguished career. The day for his retirement from his high position in the Criminal Investigation Department arrived after the manner of Time and Tide, and he was no nearer to arresting Sheila Delaney's slayer when that eventful day came than he had been on the fateful July evening when Sergeant Godfrey had dragged him into the case. Sir Austin shook hands with him in farewell and shrugged his aristocratic shoulders in rather cynical commiseration. "I know how keen you were, Bannister, to complete your Seabourne case and I also know the many difficulties against which you have been forced to contend. The fact that you have failed is merely to be deplored—that is all. To err is human. You take with you my very best wishes. Good-bye."

Thus the mantle of Bannister fell upon Macmorran, and after the manner of mantles apparently made an excellent fit. Bannister however had not relinquished the trail altogether. Mr. Bathurst read his letter with undisguised interest. He also replied to it immediately.

> "My dear Bannister," he wrote, "Hearty congratulations upon your well-earned retirement. Which is it to be? The Sussex Downs or the entrancing West Country? I am perfectly certain that either would be graced by your presence. In relation to the question that you raise with regard to the somewhat baffling case that exercised our joint intelligences a few months ago, please don't worry, you may rely on me. Rest assured that I should never attempt to conclude my case without acquainting you and inviting your valuable cooperation. I have too much admiration for Scotland Yard in general and incidentally yourself in particular. Also it might prove too big for me to adopt any other methods single-handed. I told you whom I suspected upon the occasion of our last meeting. You alone know of that suspicion. I am still waiting now, as I was at the time that I gave you my confidence. Hold yourself in readiness to move at a moment's notice. When that time comes I will communicate with you. Then my dear Bannister—we will taste success! And till then—
> "Faithfully yours,
> "ANTHONY L. BATHURST."

This letter afforded the Ex-Inspector both consolation and satisfaction. At any rate, he would share in the triumph when the hands of Justice closed upon the criminal. He decided therefore to postpone his departure to the selected spot for his retirement at any rate, for a month or two—say till after Christmas. But Fate decreed that he was in action again before then. Anthony Bathurst's expectations were realized. On a misty morning in mid-November that promised a better day the *S.S. Nicholas Maes* steamed out of Hull and began to plough her way through icy-cold green waves towards the rising morning sun and the City of Amsterdam. She was an undistinguished unit of the Holland S.S. Company but on this particular occasion perhaps, stood nearer to a place in the maritime sun than ever before. For "among those sailing" were two plain-clothes men from New Scotland Yard—ostensibly ordinary tourists—and a handsome, stalwart and venerable Indian. The passenger-list recorded the Indian as "Ram Das" and the two plain-clothes men as "Hobbs" and "Sutcliffe." All these names, it is needless to say, had been assumed for the occasion. Similarly also Ex-Chief-Inspector Bannister, in at the death, true to Mr. Bathurst's written promise, had thought it safer and better to register in a name other than his own. You never know how the sight of a name, observed quite by accident, will strike a person's remoter memory and awaken an undesired interest. The two plain-clothes men were under explicit instructions to hold no communication whatever with anybody. Ram Das, or Lai Singh as we will call him from now henceforward was to be shadowed to every step and watched to every action without his suspicions being in any way aroused and New Scotland Yard is not in the habit of sending one man—eminent though he might be—to do two men's work.

Five hours' voyage out of the port of Hull the passengers of the *Nicholas Maes* who had summoned sufficient courage and hardihood to brave the wind and weather on the top deck had their attention diverted for a few moments by an aeroplane that flew joyously over them and rapidly left them far behind. It was apparently making for the coast of Holland. Lai Singh, keeping as much in the background as possible, regarded it with the stoical calm of his race and the pseudo-tourists (never very far away from him) were quick to detect this. It may be observed that the aeroplane in question carried a trio of eminent passengers—Sir Austin Kemble, the Chief Commissioner, the Crown Prince Alexis of Clorania—whom Mr. Bathurst had insisted upon being present, and no less a person than Mr. Bathurst himself. They made Amsterdam—the spider-web city of the "Land of Water"—in excellent time and made their way, piloted by the Chief Commissioner, to the Kalverstraat.

"A little light refreshment," explained Sir Austin to His Royal Highness, "will prove most acceptable to every one of us. Also I have arranged to meet Cuypers in the *Café Suisse*. Cuypers is the head of the Dutch police," he explained. "And an excellent fellow, I assure you."

The gentleman mentioned was already there when they arrived. He spoke English fluently and greeted Sir Austin as an old friend and comrade.

"I received your message, Sir Austin," he announced after the necessary introductions had been made, "and I have arranged that what you asked me will be attended to in every detail. The *Nicholas Maes* will be in to-night and will dock in the De Ruyter Kade. Your special gentleman will be carefully watched ashore by two of my most reliable men and if he doesn't go direct to where you are expecting him to go—no matter—my men will never lose sight of him. If he does go straight on as you anticipate that he will—they will follow—to lend a hand—should a hand be wanted." His fat face wreathed in smiles. It was a great honour to meet and work with the illustrious Sir Austin Kemble of the English police. He always welcomed the opportunity.

The Chief Commissioner nodded in acquiescence. "Good," he commented. "Just what I want."

Cuypers went on, flattered at Sir Austin's commendation. "Your own people who are watching on the *Nicholas Maes* will join forces with my two men if they deem it necessary. I have arranged all the particulars with regard to that. A signal will be given to prevent any confusion arising. Is there anything else you would desire to know?" He disposed of his Lager with extreme satisfaction and gave an order for four more.

"Only this," replied Sir Austin, a trifle defensively perhaps. He turned to Anthony. "I am relying on you implicitly, Mr. Bathurst. You have no *doubt* you say?"

Anthony smiled. "None at all, Sir. Austin. Tell Mr. Cuypers what I imagine is going to happen when Lai Singh arrives."

Sir Austin caressed his upper lip. "Stefanopoulos—Cuypers. Has he been pretty quiet lately? Can you tell me? Because we're confident that he's going to be in this job."

Cuypers' white teeth flashed into an appreciative smile. "But so! Well, I am not surprised. If it's precious stones—there is always that possibility. But he is slippery! I cannot tell you how slippery, gentlemen." He leaned forward to them impressively over the marble-topped table. "Stefanopoulos is one of the three biggest 'fences' in Europe. Possibly the biggest of all—excepting perhaps the notorious Adolf Schneitzer. It is only the really big stuff that he touches. The stuff that's too big for the smaller men. Do you know his—his—?" He paused to collect the word he wanted. "What do you say—his pre—I know—antecedents?" His audience expressed their ignorance. Cuypers continued. "His father was a Greek who was employed for many years in the diamond-cutting industry of this city down in the Zwanenburger Straat. He got into trouble after he married one of our women and took to crime very thoroughly. In time he became an expert. His son—our man—is one of the craftiest devils you could meet. We've had him three times and wanted him many more times. But he's like an eel. He's cleared some of the biggest diamond robberies of recent years both in Europe and the States. And you think he's going to occupy your present attention—eh?"

"Let me tell you this," rejoined Anthony. "We have been waiting for a certain movement to be made by somebody in our country concerning the disposal of a very valuable, precious stone. A very big thing indeed. The bird we are trailing has flown to Amsterdam. Do you think I am very far out if I deduce the probable presence in the affair of M. Stefanopoulos?"

Cuypers shook his head. "Rather would I say, without hesitation, that you have hit the right nail on the head. At any rate," he shrugged his shoulders expressively, "if your man is here and you are here to watch him wherever he goes—you cannot go very far wrong. Even if the trail as you call it doesn't lead to Stefanopoulos."

Sir Austin, who had been talking quietly to the Crown Prince for a moment or two broke in. "Where does this Stefanopoulos live?"

"In the Jewish Quarter," replied the Dutchman.

"Far from here?" queried Anthony.

"Take a tram along the Geldersche Kade past the Fish Market into the New Market. Get off by St. Anthony's Weigh House. You can't miss that—it's a rather quaint red-brick affair carrying round towers and spires. It was the old East Gate of Amsterdam. Go down a side turning just before Joden Bree Straat—the first turning on the left before the canal. Stefanopoulos lives in the second establishment on the right. But I shall be coming along with you when the fun starts—so you need have no worry about finding your way."

"It is most essential that we should be able to interview Stefanopoulos before he receives his visitor," remarked Anthony.

"That also shall be arranged," said Cuypers. "I will see to it."

He was as good as his word and early that afternoon the notorious Greek "fence" of International reputation was privileged and surprised to receive four visitors. The establishment in the Jewish quarter to which Cuypers escorted them was externally unpretentious and to all appearances in no way significant of its proprietor's world-wide notoriety. It was situated on the fringe of that part of the City of Amsterdam devoted for many years to the fascinating industry of diamond-cutting. To Anthony Bathurst, the quarter with its stalls and booths was as much reminiscent of London's "Middlesex Street" as of anything he knew and the domicile of Stefanopoulos might have been removed *en bloc* from the Whitechapel Road. Cuypers beckoned to them.

"Come right in with me," he said, "and let me do the talking."

"What is the gentleman's ostensible business?" asked Anthony.

"He's a registered moneylender," replied Cuypers, "and I for one, should be sorry to get in his clutches. He's reputed to be the fourth richest man in Amsterdam." He put his forefinger to his lips. "Leave it to me."

As they entered a bell jingled noisily. Anthony noticed that they stood behind a high counter that ran all round the shop, for shop perhaps described the place most closely. From the apartment in the rear a curious figure shuffled towards them. Half Greek and half Dutch—as he had been described—but facially and physically he might have passed for "the Jew that Shakespeare drew." Cupidity and cunning were the twin lights of his eyes. And with that strange tactfulness of the habitual criminal—that sixth sense that also seems to be the life as it were of the other five—he divined that his four visitors carried for him an element of danger. This too—before he perceived the identity of Cuypers. But he betrayed no outward sign of his temporary discomfort. The school in which he had been trained was a hard one. He bowed with the servility of the race whose worst qualities he had usurped and whose best qualities he had discarded. Cuypers addressed him in English. He knew that Stefanopoulos was a cosmopolitan. To the astonishment of the Crown Prince he replied in the same tongue.

"Good morning, gentlemen. Vy am I thus honoured? Mynheer Cuypers is pleased—"

The Dutchman cut him short summarily. He bent forward over the counter and spoke for a few moments to Stefanopoulos in a low tone—so low that the others were unable to catch his words. The Levantine started back eventually in spluttering denial but again Cuypers checked him. "We know," Anthony heard him say—"we *know*—so save your breath—Demetri. You'll make nothing out of this deal, take it from me, and if you don't arrange to do what I've just asked you, I'll have you arrested within half an hour from now."

Stefanopoulos snarled and showed a row of dirty yellow teeth. His lip curled back in menace. "You talk big! Pah! You can't! What for am I to be arrested? I'm an honest trader—mind that, Mister."

Cuypers administered the *"coup de grâce."* "Ever heard of the Contessa D'Amaldi? And her nine pigeon-blood rubies? If I couldn't prove it, my friend—I'd hold you twelve months on a charge of 'fencing' them while I sought round for evidence. Got that, Demetri? Very well, then—we shall be here at five o'clock. Understand! Have everything ready—you know what to do."

"I had to frighten the old vulture," he explained jocularly as they passed out, "but in this particular instance, I really think he knows nothing. Lai Singh as you call him knows what you English call 'the ropes.'"

Sir Austin Kemble laughed. "Better than he knows what lies ahead of him," he murmured, looking at his watch. "In about six hours time, shall we say?"

Chapter XXVI
RENDEZVOUS

Cuypers tapped his Smith-Wesson significantly. "Understand, friend Demetri," he announced decisively, "no tricks! The first hint that you are playing us false—and—" He fingered the revolver with a wealth of meaning. The Greek made no reply. Evidently he did understand. Cuypers went on. "I shall be here at your side all the time. Never more than a few inches away from you. Your assistant, do you see? I shall have a pen and ink and write—when your visitor comes—understand? I shall also have *this*." More business with the revolver. "My three friends here will take up their position behind that door which will be left ajar." He pointed to the door of the shop-parlour that communicated with the passage leading to the back of the house. "Lai Singh, when he arrives, will walk into a trap. For your place will be covered from the outside as well, my good Stefanopoulos. A famous English detective is here as well as my three friends—no less a person than Chief-Inspector Bannister of New Scotland Yard. I expect you have heard of him—I've no doubt he has of you. He will work from the outside in case of an attempted get-away on the part of your visitor—do you understand, little rabbit?"

The old "fence" nodded sullenly—he wasted no words.

"To your places then, gentlemen. Remember we may have to wait some time. But it's dark by five. I shall expect our man to come straight on here from the quay-side." Anthony squeezed himself into the musty-smelling passage with his two eminent companions and arranged his own position so that he commanded the view through the crack of the door. "A chink of vantage," he remarked to the Crown Prince.

"A seat on the stairs will do for me for a time," remarked Sir Austin sadly.

"And for me," supplemented Alexis, "this place has a most infernal smell. I doubt whether I can endure it for long."

Cuypers took a black velvet skull cap from the pocket of his jacket and put it on his round head. He patted it dramatically. "Pen and ink, Demetri—please! Quickly, too! And don't forget, if the occasion demands to address me as 'Pieter—Pieter Steen'. I am—for the next hour or so. Your very good clerk."

Stefanopoulos, maintaining his sullen demeanour, put the writing materials in front of him. Cuypers grinned at him almost benevolently. "And one of your very best cigars, Demetri. You make an ungracious host! And a drop of real Schnapps. That's right—and have a drop yourself, old boy. Show this poor native who's coming to see you this evening a touching picture of the master hob-nobbing with his trusty old confidential clerk. Your very good health." He smacked his lips in gratified appreciation as Stefanopoulos grunted an unintelligible rejoinder. The two hours that followed reminded Anthony as he stood upright in the passage of that weary vigil in the garden of Considine Manor when he awaited with others the coming of the "Spider." Neither the Crown Prince nor Sir Austin Kemble seemed particularly inclined to conversation. Remarks between them were few and far. A large old fashioned clock that hung on the side wall of the evil-smelling passage announced the winging of the minutes with jaunty loudness. At times its ticking was the only sound that disturbed the ominous silence. In Anthony's heart there was a feeling of quiet triumph—but there was also a dangerous coldness. He was on the point of avenging a particularly cruel and callous crime and he was inclined to regard the case as perhaps—the door of the outer shop jangled discordantly! Through the crack of the door he saw the muscles of Cuypers' face set rigidly as Stefanopoulos rose to his unsteady feet and shuffled once again into the shop. He heard a deep voice cut into the noise of the Greek's shuffling slippers. Words passed that he was unable to hear. Then the two people came nearer.

"Salaam, sahib! You speak the Angleesh—yes?" Anthony could not catch the reply but he saw Stefanopoulos usher his caller into the private apartment where Cuypers was seated. Sir Austin and the Crown Prince crowded noiselessly behind him in the passage. Anthony could now see the visitor quite plainly. He could see an Indian, clad in the white costume affected by his race, with turban on his head. He was a man of splendid physique. A flowing beard gave him the appearance of age and wisdom and his dark eyes glowed with excitement.

"What can I do for you?" mumbled the old Greek.

Lai Singh glanced meaningly at Cuypers busy with pen and paper. "My business is with you alone."

"Be easy on that point. It is my clerk—you need not fear."

Lai Singh hesitated for a moment and glanced round the room suspiciously. Then his fingers played delicately round his white turban for a palpitating second or two, and there flashed across the drabness of the squalid room the emerald-sapphire brilliance of the "Peacock's Eye." Its rendezvous was reached at last!

Stefanopoulos eyed the dazzling gem with greedy lust.

"So!" he permitted himself to mutter.

"I have come to trade," declared Lai Singh. His tone held the silkiness of malevolent menace. "If you will deal justly with me. If not I will kill you as I killed for—"

Demetri broke in. "This, eh?" His cunning eyes gleaming with cupidity caught those of Lai Singh and held them for a brief period.

The Indian laughed cruelly. "You have said. 'Twas but Justice if you only knew."

Stefanopoulos was silent. He held out his hand for this stone of liquid beauty that had come to him so unexpectedly, yet was not for him. His fingers itched to hold it; to feel some of its flaming fire. "Let me look at the stone," he growled.

Lai Singh pushed it over very slowly, watching the old man as a hungry cat regards a mouse. Stefanopoulos held it to the light watching its flashing points of scintillating brilliance play round the room. The eyes of Lai Singh wandered upward, fascinated at what the Greek was doing. As they did so Cuypers rose like lightning and covered the Indian with his revolver. Simultaneously, Mr. Bathurst, similarly armed slipped through the door behind which he had been standing and covered Lai Singh from the rear.

"Don't move," he said, "or I'll put a bullet through you. You are arrested for the murder of Sheila Delaney at Seabourne in England on July fifth. See to him, Cuypers!"

As the little Dutchman advanced and snapped the handcuffs upon the prisoner, Anthony was acutely aware of a flow of concentrated hatred and deviltry that flooded him from the dark vindictive eyes of the arrested man. They flicked from Stefanopoulos and Cuypers to the Crown Prince and Sir Austin Kemble, embracing them all, but they always returned to dwell banefully upon Mr. Bathurst. Unmoved, the last-named walked quietly to the prisoner. "Gentlemen," he said, "I don't think any of you quite realize yet the real truth of what has happened." His hand went to Lai Singh's face and he jerked suddenly and strongly at the Indian's beard. The spirit-gum failed to withstand the challenge. The beard came away in his hand. "Don't you find the costume rather chilly, Bannister," he said lightly, "for this particular season of the year?"

Chapter XXVII
SIR AUSTIN KEMBLE REMOVES HIS HAT

"Dinner is served," said the butler.

"Will you escort Lady Fullgarney, Mr. Bathurst? And you, Sir Austin, might be good enough to take Lady Brantwood? Thank you. If Lady Kemble will honour me?" Sir Matthew Fullgarney led his guests into the brilliantly-lighted dining-room of Dovaston Court. "I should have been delighted," he said, "to have had the Crown Prince of Clorania with us for Christmas but, of course, he has a very much more important engagement"—he chuckled—"the wedding, I believe, is fixed for the last day of the old year. I suppose you are going, Mr. Bathurst? Surely, you should be the guest of honour?"

Anthony laughed. "I was invited, Sir Matthew, it's true—but like the Crown Prince—I had an important engagement myself, last week. I wasn't sure how long it would last—so in the circumstances, I placed myself at Lady Fullgarney's disposal instead." He bowed, "I am sure that excellent judges would agree that I chose the better part."

Lady Fullgarney bent over to him eagerly interested. "Was there ever any doubt?" she asked. "Did any of you important people on the inside of the case wonder what the verdict was going to be?"

Anthony regarded her quizzically and Sir Austin Kemble cut in with a reply. "The jury were only absent five-and-twenty minutes," he said gravely, "that fact will demonstrate to you very clearly that they didn't entertain very much doubt about it."

"There was none," boomed Sir Matthew from the head of the table, "the evidence was conclusive. In a short time, thank God, the world will be well rid of a thorough-paced scoundrel. Three Sundays for him are three too many. Grant, bring me another half-dozen oysters, will you?"

"Besides thanking the Almighty, Matthew, don't you think you might also thank Mr. Bathurst?" put in Lady Fullgarney.

Her lord and master glared. "Don't you think so, Sir Austin?" she continued, turning to the Chief Commissioner, "won't you support me?"

Sir Austin smiled at her gallantly. "Always, Lady Fullgarney! And in this particular instance, without a second's hesitation. There is no doubt about it. None knows better than I that Mr. Bathurst achieved a personal triumph. I shall never forget it. The memory of the arrest in that room at Amsterdam that I told you about when you came to London will remain with me always. To say that I was amazed is beside the point. I was stupefied." He sipped his wine.

"I am going to ask you a great favour, Mr. Bathurst," said Lady Fullgarney.

"Command me," replied Anthony.

"After dinner, I am going to ask you to tell us all about everything. Just how you came to think it all out. You know, like Sherlock Holmes used to explain to Doctor Watson. My guests are simply dying to hear."

"Really," said Anthony, "I can't believe that you will find me as interesting—"

"It's perfectly true, Mr. Bathurst," supplemented Lady Brantwood. "I find the investigation of crime positively enthralling."

"I am in your hands, then," murmured Anthony. "I will commence," he said, when the gentlemen joined the ladies about an hour later, "by asking you all to regard my account of the tragedy as a strict confidence. It will be obvious to you that this *must* be so—thank you! My introduction to the Seabourne murder actually occurred about a week before the murder took place." There were interested murmurs of incredulity. "That may sound strange," proceeded Mr. Bathurst, "nevertheless it is true. The Crown Prince of Clorania was being blackmailed. He engaged me on the case. Needless to say there was a lady in it. He kept her name secret. It did not take an overwhelming supply of intelligence to see that the trouble was coming from the Westhamptonshire neighbourhood. Now—inasmuch as His Royal Highness had only been in Westhampton *once*—when he attended last year's Hunt Ball—I made the evening of that

Ball my starting-point. At this stage—just as I had reached that conclusion—I received an urgent call from the Crown Prince at Seabourne to the effect that the lady in question had been found murdered. You know where and you know how. He then told me her name—Daphne Carruthers. Mark you—a Westhampton girl."

"One of the best," ejaculated Sir Matthew, "I remember—" A look from his wife silenced him.

Anthony went on. "He also told me that in answer to a suggestion from her, he had come to Seabourne and arranged certain matters very satisfactorily. In short there would be no more chance for successful blackmailing. But Miss Carruthers almost immediately upon leaving him had been most unaccountably murdered! He was badly frightened. Terribly afraid that he would be suspected and that all the story that he had been so zealous to keep secret would be revealed. Then Miss Daphne resurrected herself and telephoned to him—and I began to get interested. Who was the dead girl and why had she been confused with Daphne Carruthers? There I reached my second point of investigation. I couldn't honestly blame Bannister for the error of identification. Suit-case—the booking of the room—both tallied. I began to ask myself the meaning of this piece of substitution. Why was the dead girl's identity hidden? Was it *to shroud Sheila* or was it *to call attention to Daphne*? Remember all Sheila's personal belongings had been taken! I hesitated for some time between the two possible theories. Then I came to a decision. There was little doubt that the suit-case had been stolen from the 'Cassandra' Hotel—the question was *when*? I was able to find out from the luggage porter at the hotel that although the case had gone on to the luggage-wagon on Wednesday evening—on Thursday morning it was not there. Now consider this. I learned that the telephone-message booking a room at the 'Lauderdale' for Miss Carruthers had come through at ten-fifty on Wednesday night. Doesn't that strike you as being very late? Wouldn't you expect a person booking up a room for the following mid-day either to book earlier or leave it till the morning of the day itself? What was the urgency? There are plenty of hotels in Seabourne. No—I formed my first main conclusion although I didn't give it away and considered it carefully more than once afterwards. *The idea was to hide the identity of Sheila and inasmuch as the stolen suit-case belonged to Daphne Carruthers—the dead girl would be supposed to be Daphne Carruthers for a time at least—therefore at ten-fifty the room was booked in that particular name.* Do you follow me?"

"Excellent, Mr. Bathurst," contributed Sir Austin, "sound reasoning."

"And yet Daphne was the very girl about whom *the blackmailing process had been*. Strange, wasn't it? The Crown Prince had no knowledge of Sheila! Why was Sheila dead? Why did the murderer want *time*? But there was this point. I began to think very seriously about the group of people staying at the 'Cassandra'—*the hotel from which the suit-case had been stolen*. Consider who they were! The Crown Prince, Daphne herself, a Captain Willoughby who knew most of them—*and Chief-Inspector Bannister*. He was there—you see—right in the circle of suspicion. The next stage was at Tranfield. Bannister went up—I went with him—Tranfield interested me—from more than one point of view. We discovered that the car that took Sheila to Seabourne had been driven back to her home at Tranfield. There was actually a Seabourne newspaper in it. Why had it been driven back? The answer was easy. The house had been searched for something—what it was I will tell you later. It was here that Sheila Delaney's old lover—Alan Warburton came into my calculations. Here, at any rate, was a motive. The jilted lover—jealousy—ample motive, if you think it over. But a new aspect of the case struck me and just as I was considering it—I made a find. In Sheila's bedroom I found a postcard. Just an ordinary postcard perhaps—the message I may describe as horticultural and amatory—it was signed 'X.' But it contained the word 'irides'—the true Greek plural of 'iris.' Now ninety-nine people out of a hundred say 'irises' when they speak of more than one 'iris.' Our unknown correspondent however was meticulous concerning his plurals. *So had been Bannister!* More than once he had used 'maxima' to me in conversation and I had been particularly struck with the fact that he used the word 'data' as a plural—with a plural verb—quite correctly. But nearly everybody uses 'data' as a singular noun and with a singular verb. People say 'data helps' not 'data help.' I rubbed my hands—I'm afraid it's a habit of mine when I begin to 'get hold.' Yes—Bannister was particularly precise about his plurals."

"Wonderful, Bathurst," intervened Sir Austin, "a touch of genius—that. He was a Dulwich boy—you know."

Anthony smiled. "Thank you, Sir Austin. Well, after a time the theory I had formed concerning Alan Warburton developed as I expected it would and I was able to dispose of my blackmailing case quite smoothly You will understand what I mean very shortly. Meanwhile, Bannister delivered himself into my hands! Miss Delaney as all of you here know had a nurse-companion—she was first mentioned to Bannister and me by Daphne Carruthers—down at Seabourne. She spoke of her surname as 'Kerr'—but she pronounced it 'car' as in motor-car. Now I submit that anybody hearing that surname and having no knowledge of the spelling would ordinarily assume it to be 'Carr'—by far the commoner form of the two. Certainly I did. But when she came in answer to his telegram I happened to get hold of it and noticed that Bannister had actually telegraphed to her as 'Kerr'—so I got her to write her name down on an envelope for me. She wrote it 'Kerr.' *He had addressed her in that form because he knew her name, and didn't think of the pitfall it carried for him.* Still—I said to myself—'what was the motive?' The answer soon came—or rather part of the answer—we got news of 'The Peacock's Eye'—the great blue emerald. I heard of the mysterious Indian who had come miles to see you, Sir Matthew, but who nevertheless failed to turn up. He called on Sheila—it was *safe* doing that—she couldn't detect his lack of knowledge of Hindustani—you could. *He left you alone.* He was *counterfeit*. I only wanted one link now—how had the criminal met Miss Delaney? I got it. The 'Bank Frauds' scandal gave it to me. Now listen—I will at this point reconstruct the entire case. In the February of last year, Chief-Inspector Bannister visited Westhampton in connection with the 'Mutual Bank' Frauds and was actually the officer who arrested Sir Felix Warburton. For confirmation of that see the 'Westhampton and Chellingborough Independent.' He accompanied the Chief Constable, Major Desmond Carruthers, to the Hunt Ball. Carruthers kept his identity a secret."

Lady Fullgarney leaned across excitedly. "We saw them together. I remember him well. We couldn't place him, could we, Matthew?"

Anthony nodded and proceeded. "There he saw Sheila Delaney. They were introduced. His 'incognito' was maintained. They fell in love with each other. He was a fine man, you know. Fine physique—and so on. But Fate played a strange trick. The Crown Prince was there—also 'incognito'—known only to the few. He was with Daphne Carruthers. Alan Warburton was there—with Sheila—he had the mortification of seeing her sudden infatuation for Bannister *and he mistook him for the Crown Prince of Clorania*. I am inclined to think that Sheila purposely allowed him to do so, or perhaps even told him that it was so. He says that she did. In fact, I question if she ever knew his real identity—he was a married man with two children, you know. I doubt if she even knew his real name. But this is all conjecture. God alone knows what story he told her. But Warburton knew he had a rival and a successful rival. He began to blackmail him eventually, knowing of the approaching Royal marriage. Now things began to get a bit too hot for Bannister. It may have been his wife, it may have been his impending retirement urged him to finish the intrigue."

"He was young to retire, wasn't he, Mr. Bathurst?" queried Lady Brantwood.

"The police retire young," replied Sir Austin Kemble, "it depends upon their term of service. Bannister was forty-seven when his retirement fell due."

Anthony took a cigar from the box Sir Matthew offered him. "Then Sheila signed her death-warrant. She told him of her unique legacy 'The Peacock's Eye.' He coveted it—he would possess it and rid himself of her at the same time. He laid his plans accordingly. He arranged his holiday at Seabourne and adopted horn-rimmed glasses in case he should be recognized afterwards."

"How do you mean?" asked Lady Fullgarney; "that isn't clear to me. Why afterwards?"

"In case he should touch the case at all officially—he was in Seabourne remember—and get to Westhampton again—as he eventually did. He wanted the Bannister of the Hunt Ball forgotten as much as possible."

"I see," said Lady Fullgarney.

"Then he got Sheila to obtain the jewel from the bank and come to meet him at Seabourne. He poisoned her with prussic acid administered from a syringe. At least that's my opinion. Her visit to the dentist's gave him his chance. He followed her in at the side-entrance, waited for Branston to leave her as he guessed he might—pushed the bolt to imprison him—and strolled into the surgery. It was easy—a matter of seconds. If anything had gone wrong it wouldn't have mattered much—he had just called in to see how she was. He would have poisoned her somewhere else. But he wanted to make certain of getting time *to visit the bungalow at Tranfield*. Therefore she must not be identified immediately. To that end he had stolen Daphne Carruthers' suit-case from the 'Cassandra' Hotel the night before, and booked the room at the 'Lauderdale' in her name. The suit-case was substituted for Sheila's own in her car and Sheila's pushed under the seat at the back. She never knew."

Sir Austin broke in. "Where was he when Sheila went to the 'Lauderdale'?"

Anthony considered for a moment. "After he met her outside Seabourne—he left her—he took care not to be seen with her in Seabourne. But he knew of her intention to visit Branston. When he had murdered her, he took all Sheila's belongings—there must be nothing to connect her with herself *or with him*, and all the keys she carried. Any communication in his handwriting mustn't be found on her—for instance. The notes were dangerous—they might be traced—he left them behind as he went out. They would confuse the issue. *He went straight back to Tranfield in Sheila's car.* There must be nothing at 'Rest Harrow' to connect him with her—no scrap of writing. He *had* to go to make sure! There were probably photographs, etc., to be destroyed. The evidence of the waitress in the teashop at Calstock—four miles from Tranfield—that he was there at five-forty on the evening of the murder told heavily against him at the trial. Sheila had told him, in all probability, that she kept all his correspondence in a private drawer in her bedroom. No doubt he sounded her as to that on one of their numerous assignations. *But he left the one postcard behind*—it was caught in the folds of a scarf. It eluded his search. I was a little bit puzzled at first as to whether he had time to do all this and be back in Seabourne by the late evening as I knew he had been. It *was* possible—I proved it so. He left Seabourne in the car for Tranfield about two-ten—and could make it soon after six o'clock. He caught the seven-four fast train from Westhampton to Euston—arriving at eight-eight. A quick dash across to Victoria—and he landed in Seabourne again at half-past nine. Willoughby gave evidence that he remembered him being there as the band performance was finishing. He was unable, if you remember, to put forward anything of an alibi for the day of the murder except that. He couldn't produce anybody else who had seen him. He couldn't shake the case for the Crown."

"When did he take the 'Peacock's Eye,' Mr. Bathurst?" asked Lady Fullgarney.

"I imagine Miss Delaney gave it to him to keep temporarily. He had infatuated her. I attempt to explain it like this. When he masqueraded as the Indian and called at 'Rest Harrow,' it was with a very definite purpose. Sheila had told him all about the stone's history—so he made up his mind to frighten her. She had told him about Lai Singh and her father. I suggest he frightened her with the notion that this Indian was not really her father's old servant but a servant of some frightful native vendetta—you know the kind of thing I mean. Priest's vengeance extending over generations. Against which banks and strong-rooms would be useless. Sheila got a bit nervous. He prevailed upon her to let him take charge of the 'Peacock's Eye'—presumably for greater safety. When his hands closed upon it—Sheila faced death!"

"How did he get the prussic acid?" queried Lady Fullgarney.

"That was never conclusively proved. Very likely in an obscure town, months ago. A man in his position could wield many influences, you know." Anthony stopped, as though awaiting further questions.

"Go on, Mr. Bathurst," interjected Sir Matthew; "let's hear the end of the story."

"There isn't a lot more, Sir Matthew. I called upon you, as you remember, and confirmed my suspicions about the mix-up of identity at the Hunt Ball. Alan Warburton *must* have been wrong! Both you and Lady Fullgarney who had been present at the ball were positive that the Crown Prince and Miss Delaney had *never* met, and were not seen together. It only remained for me to prove my case. My suspicions—unsupported—were valueless. I knew it might mean a long wait. But I felt certain that the time would come for 'realizing' the 'Peacock's Eye.' I succeeded in allaying any possible suspicions the murderer might have had very completely. In fact I bamboozled him beautifully. I told him a lot of the truth and one or two lovely lies. *I even whispered the name of the assassin in his ear.* Only it happened to be the wrong name! Still—it sufficed for him. I promised he should help me to capture him. He did—but not in the manner he anticipated." Anthony chuckled reminiscently. Lady Fullgarney's eyes danced and sparkled in excited interest. "How did you know when to move, Mr. Bathurst—when the Amsterdam trip was coming off?"

"He was watched night and day, Lady Fullgarney. Sir Austin Kemble here helped me tremendously in that. He put four of his best men under my orders but he didn't know himself how I was using them. I swore them to secrecy. I had *'carte blanche'*! When the man we were watching entered his house one morning and 'Lai Singh' emerged, I knew we were nearly home. I was right. The time for action had come. We followed him to Hull and from there across to Holland. I hope you enjoyed our little trip, Sir Austin?"

"I raise my hat to you, Mr. Bathurst," declared Sir Austin. "A most able piece of investigation. I am proud to have worked with you."

"I love you more than ever, Mr. Bathurst," said Lady Fullgarney. "I am perfectly shameless over it."

"Pauline!" exclaimed Sir Matthew, "you go a little too far. By the way, Mr. Bathurst. It's a small point, but I'm curious. When you told Bannister who the murderer was—whom did you accuse? What was the name you whispered to him?"

Anthony knocked the long piece of ash from the end of his cigar very deliberately. He bowed to his host. "Yours, Sir Matthew! I'm sure you won't—"

Mr. Bathurst has always maintained that Lady Fullgarney's laugh is the most musical of his acquaintance.

THE END

Made in the USA
Monee, IL
26 December 2019